BUTTERMILK BOTTOMS

A Novel by Kenn Robbins

Ψ

University of Iowa Press

Iowa City

University of Iowa Press, Iowa City 52242

Printed in the United States of America

First edition, 1987

Book and jacket design by Richard Hendel

Typesetting by G & S Typesetters, Inc., Austin, Texas

Printing and binding by Edwards Brothers, Ann Arbor, Michigan

Library of Congress Cataloging-in-Publication Data

Robbins, Kenn.

Buttermilk bottoms.

I. Title.

PS3568.02333B8   1987   813'.54   87-4997

ISBN 0-87745-169-9

For my mother

PART ONE

Ollie Gus pouted. Her new cot didn't sleep right, she said. The food tastes funny up here, she said. The air stinks, she said. The folks ain't friendly, the houses ain't friendly, the air, the streets, and nights ain't friendly, she said. She wanted to go back home, she said so loud that half the neighborhood heard her. After all that, she pouted and kept mostly to herself.

Vaughn Brodie took to the streets like he had always lived in the Bottoms. Nothing to it, he said. Easy as shucking corn, he said. He made his mark on the streets after a time.

It was Cora New who didn't know about their new home. The floors wouldn't clean the way she wanted them. The windows, what few there were, needed replacing. And a good coat of whitewash would have done wonders for everybody's spirits, meaning her own. It was Vaughn Brodie's easiness on the streets that bothered her, too, and Ollie Gus' insistence on pouting.

"Go to school," Cora New ordered her on the fourth morning of their coming to the Bottoms. Killie Willie listened from the other side of his bowl of hot oatmeal. He listened, knowing his daughter, Ollie Gus, well enough to be sure that nothing his wife could say could succeed in getting the gal off her rump and out of the house.

"You go to school," Ollie Gus said back.

"I'm gonna bust you upside the head," Cora New promised, and she meant it too, Killie Willie knew. He smiled from his chair on the other side of the room. He hadn't heard his woman of twenty-odd years use such strong terms with their daughter, not when they had lived back home in Frog Level.

So Ollie Gus pulled out of her pout long enough to get herself dressed and all prettied up. Only she didn't go to school. She hid under the stairwell all morning and into the afternoon.

"Well?" Cora New asked when Ollie Gus came into the tenement that afternoon. "Well, how was it?"

"Hate damn school," Ollie Gus told her and retired to her room and pouted the rest of that day.

Ollie Gus couldn't explain it. She hadn't understood half of what was going on around her when she was back home. And now that all of them were up here in this godforsaken hole of a world, she didn't understand a thing. And she couldn't get anybody to listen to her. She yelled as loud as she could. She even went so far as to beat her head against the iron radiator in her room. Nobody paid her any mind. She beat it so hard the first day she got to the Bottoms that a small speck of blood appeared between her eyes. But her mama, Cora New, wiped it off and told her to behave herself. Why was it nobody would listen to her? The Bottoms wasn't meant to be lived in. She knew that, she could always rely on her smelling to tell her what she needed to know. And this place with all its dirt and scum and fear and dread was BAD! She hated herself when she did something bad. But in Buttermilk Bottoms, a place where she found herself living because of her trust in her old man, Killie Willie Matt, she was so full of hating that she could hardly stand herself. She had to scream out or die. And she had screamed until her lungs were black and blue. It did no good. It hadn't made her feel any better. It hadn't made her hating go away. It hadn't made the Bottoms any better either. So she hid herself in her room and refused to do anything but eat (she always ate regardless), curse her papa for trucking her off so far from her real home, and obey her mama.

Ollie Gus didn't have a window in her room. All that was in there with the exception of herself, a cot, and a wardrobe that it was shameful to call anything like a wardrobe was four bare walls, once upon a time painted pale green—or was it supposed to be yellow? She couldn't tell. She couldn't stand a windowless room. That's why she asked her mama for a dollar or two. She never asked anybody for anything, much less money. So Cora New couldn't help herself when she asked, "What you need a dollar or two for, sugar?"

"Needs me some damn crayons," Ollie Gus admitted, though she wasn't sure that it was crayons she really needed.

"Crayons?" Cora New questioned. Ollie Gus nodded. "What for?"

"Just needs me some damn crayons, Mama, just needs them." And Ollie Gus got her dollar or two. "For school," she lied.

She didn't know where to start looking for crayons in the Bottoms. The only person outside her own folks she had spoken to since getting off the bus was the kid everybody called Billo. She sought him out that day.

"What you want with crayons?" he asked.

"Just needs them!!!" Billo was fearful that she was going to hit him, and he wasn't in much of a mood to be hit by a female her size.

"Okay, okay, you needs em. I can appreciate that." He thought for a bit. "How much you needs crayons?"

"Two dollar worth," she said, holding out the money.

Billo snatched the bills away and stuffed them in his pocket. "I get you the best crayons there is in the Bottoms," he said. And off he went. Ollie Gus didn't think about the fact that she probably wouldn't see her money again, or Billo, or any crayons—at least not from him.

But that night after Killie Willie had come home from the deli and everybody had eaten the leftover sandwiches he brought with him, there was a light tap on the hall door. Vaughn Brodie cracked the door just a little. Nobody was there. Lying on the floor just outside the doorway was a small box of brand-new crayons, sixteen colors in all. Vaughn Brodie brought the things back to the kitchen with him, a silly little smile on his face.

"Mine!" Ollie Gus screamed, snatching the crayons from her brother and scatting into her room where she locked herself away.

"Musta been hers," Vaughn Brodie said with a little shrug.

Nobody heard a peep out of Ollie Gus the rest of that night. And they thanked the Lord for his blessing.

The next morning Cora New roused everyone in her usual way, turning everybody out of bed and shaking them awake. Only she didn't have to wake Ollie Gus. She was already dressed for school and ready to head out.

"What's the matter with you?" Cora New asked as Ollie Gus ate her breakfast without complaining for the first time.

"Nothing."

"You seem so . . ." She couldn't think of the right word. "So quiet."

"You complaining, Mama? Hate damn complainers." And Cora New was content.

Killie Willie set off to work, Vaughn Brodie set off to wherever it was he went to, and Ollie Gus headed out for school. Only this time she actually went. She didn't hide under the stairwell, she didn't loiter outside the building, she didn't look for something to divert her from where she was supposed to go. She actually went to the school and sat for the full day on the front steps, studying the strange sort of life that surrounded her there in the Bottoms.

Cora New scrubbed the floors. It had become a daily chore for her to scrub the floors. No matter how many times she scrubbed them and no matter what tool she used to do the job, they still felt slimy to her. But she was bound and determined to get her floors clean even if she died doing it. She opened up Ollie Gus' room to air it some. Without a window the room grew stuffy without much trouble. She hated the room because of that. For Cora New a room without a window was too much like a coffin, and she hated the idea that her only daughter had to spend so much of her time in a room like that.

She stopped. Maybe her eyes were deceiving her. But she stood in the doorway of Ollie Gus' room looking out of a large picture window and seeing the sky and fields, the woods and streams of their place back home in Carolina. It was so real that she grasped her chest lest her heart decide to jump clear of it. Then she sat on the edge of Ollie Gus' cot, shook her head, and said, "My, my, ain't that something . . ."

Cora New set out to discover Buttermilk Bottoms in her own way and in her own time. She obeyed only one of the principles of living in a place like the Bottoms: she didn't go out after dark. But other than that she was on her own, exploring the Bottoms for all the place had to offer.

And no one ever bothered her. She had heard the horror tales about how folks treated one another in the Bottoms, but for some reason no one even spoke to her. Maybe it was the way she carried herself: straight, eyes front, all business. Maybe it was the shape of her chin: firm and determined. Or maybe it was that she looked like the kind who would take no trash off anybody, which was exactly the kind she was.

"Why don't you carry fresh vegetables?" she asked Michael Pogo after trying to buy her family's food from him. "No decent human being can live without fresh vegetables," she said.

"We got cans," Michael Pogo said.

"Ain't the same, Mr. Pogo. A human being needs and I mean NEEDS fresh vegetables."

After that Michael Pogo stocked at least one fresh vegetable once a week. And usually it was already sold before Cora New came in.

Before long Michael Pogo had an entire row of fresh vegetables all the time. If he had been the happy kind it would have made him smile. But Michael Pogo never smiled.

Cora New became a speaking acquaintance of at least one of her neighbors. Her name was Martha Bird Blotchley, probably the biggest female she'd ever laid eyes on. Martha Bird Blotchley lived in the place just above the Matts, and she could be heard every night walking her dog round and round the room. Some folks said she had an alligator too, only Cora New had never seen it. Even Ollie Gus seemed to like Martha Bird: Martha Bird was probably the only female around who was larger than she.

Cora New had Martha Bird down during the day for coffee and tea cakes. Martha Bird would eat all the cakes and drink most of the coffee while she filled Cora New's head with all that was bad about the Bottoms, her life, and especially Michael Pogo. Martha Bird loved Michael Pogo. For some reason Cora New had a matchmaker complex, a hangover from her days back in Frog Level when many of the womenfolks relied on her to help them win their men.

"Maybe if you tried hanging around Mr. Pogo's store," Cora New suggested.

"Done that," said Martha Bird.

"Well?"

"He told me I was blocking traffic."

"How about if you wanted to buy something that he didn't stock—you know, like I did?"

"What don't he stock?"

"He don't lay in much in the way of meats."

"He'd never stock meats."

"Why not?"

"'Cause he's a vegetarian. He can't abide anybody who eats red meat." Martha Bird devoured a tea cake in two bites.

"Well, maybe you better not tell him you like meat."

"Already have. Big mistake."

"Oh." Cora New looked her neighbor over. Martha

Bird wasn't a bad-looking woman for her overwhelming size. She had a very cute face. "You could try a new hairdo," she said.

"This is a new hairdo. You don't like it?"

"Oh, yes, lovely. But does Michael Pogo know it's new?"

"Course. I told him. He didn't even notice. Just went on washing his carrots."

"Well," said Cora New, "you've got to get him to notice you somehow. Where does he go after he closes his shop?"

"To bed."

"Good. Be there when he closes up."

"Have been. He lives upstairs and hardly never comes out of his store for anything, not even for a breath of fresh air."

Cora New was growing weary of Martha Bird's love for a man like Michael Pogo who obviously didn't want her. She watched as another half-dozen tea cakes disappeared. Maybe if you didn't eat so much, she wanted to say. But didn't.

"I'm too fat," Martha Bird said. "But somebody tole me that Michael Pogo likes his women with plenty of flesh on their bones. So I eat to please Michael Pogo. I don't like being so fat. But if it pleases Michael Pogo . . ." She sniffled just a little. "Only he don't know that I exist." She got up to leave. "Better run," she said, "got a couple of pies baking upstairs. Bye."

Helping Martha Bird get the attention of Michael Pogo became an occupation for Cora New. It helped pass the days while she waited for her man to come home from work. She remembered how she hooked Killie Willie. It was when they were both young and spry and filled with a love for being alive. They had gone to a barn raising, not together of course, but they were both there. Killie Willie had been too shy to ask Cora New for a dance. So she had asked him. And they danced the rest of the night together. From that time on they did everything with one another. So she thought, maybe if Martha Bird put her cards on the table and asked Michael Pogo out. They could do something together, it didn't matter what. If it had worked for Cora New, there was no reason why it wouldn't work for Martha Bird too.

She suggested the idea to Martha Bird.

"Hate it," Martha Bird said. "He'd never go out with me. Mainly because there ain't no place to go. Where would we go? What would we talk about? What would we do? He won't want to do anything. He'd never go anyplace with me. You really think I should ask him?"

So Martha Bird did. With Cora New's help and support, Martha Bird showed up at Michael Pogo's store right at closing time one night, dressed in her very best outfit and with the best perfume her money could buy gracing her neck. She stood in the doorway, waiting for Michael Pogo to come lock up. "Wanta take me for a little walk, cutie?" she said to him as he stood there waiting for her to leave.

Michael Pogo said nothing. He gave Martha Bird a little shove, clearing her from his door and back into the street. He slammed the door shut, bolted it, and disappeared inside. Martha Bird stood there for the longest time, slowly growing angry with Cora New and her meddling.

Cora New decided then that there was no good way to matchmake in the Bottoms. She turned her attention back to her floors and her scrubbing.

She needed something to do, though. The money that Killie Willie was bringing home was enough for them. The food that he brought from the deli was good and filling. There wasn't any need for her to seek work. She just needed something to do with her time. Back home in Frog Level she had spent time in the employ of some of the finest families in town, cleaning, ironing, making clothes, and so on. If she only knew how to go about it, she could do the same kind of work up here in the city.

She started looking.

It didn't take her long, not the way that Cora New went about it. She learned in her walkings that the Bottoms ended just two blocks away. There was a park down that way that was full of little ponds and sidewalks and trees and statues. And a dozen or so blocks on from there, she discovered that there were all sorts of better places to live. It was there that she started her search for work.

Her approach was simple enough. She stood on street corners at three in the afternoon, watching where small children came home from school. When she found a place that had more than two smaller kids, that was where she went calling. In fact, she would follow the children into their houses, chatting with them and making them laugh at her way of talking. Then she would meet their mothers and tell them how good a worker she was and what she was capable of doing. She knew that all she needed was one house, that as many others as she wanted would come from that one. That's the way it had worked back home. And it worked in the city too. She was hired to do cleaning once a week for the Gilworthys, who had three children—aged eight, six, and three, all girls. Their place was a penthouse in a fancy building that overlooked the park. And they had plenty of money, Cora New could tell, judging from the fancy furniture, paintings, and silverware in their place. Of course before they put Cora New on, they had had to call Frog Level and ask for references from the McBees, the Bedenbaughs, and the Shealys. But once she was on and once she showed what she could do, it was all downhill after that. The Mathiases hired her on as did the Bleechers, the Canterburys, the Masons, and the Levys. And the money just poured in.

"Darn good place to live," Cora New said to Killie Willie one night when things seemed to be going almost too well for them.

Killie Willie just gave her a look. He knew better. He

knew that there wasn't much of a life living in a sorry neighborhood like they did, working in a deli cooking food for others to eat, cleaning their houses, and tending to their kids. He knew that the only way of life for him was tilling the fields back home, slopping the hogs, milking the cows, and taking care of his own by loving the land. No, Killie Willie didn't care much for what they were about, but at least for the moment it seemed that things couldn't be much better.

Josef Daniello Wiscovich ran a good clean deli even though his apron was dirty. He grinned a lot because business was good. He had an honest face that had a difficult time hiding the fact that Joe Wiscovich enjoyed his life.

Joe didn't change either. Always the same, day in and out. He was a likable fellow, Killie Willie had noticed that about him right away. Even that first day when Killie Willie was setting about, trying to find his way around the city, that day he'd come off the bus inside the biggest building he had ever seen and set off looking for his cousin, Johnny Mack Lindsay.

Killie Willie stood at the end of the counter nearest the glass door. He rested from the push and racket of the street by leaning on the counter with half his weight. He watched others come and go. Still others sat at the counter or ordered their food and carried it to one of the small booths along the wall, and when finished they would leave messes and pay at the register near Killie Willie's elbow.

"Want something?" Joe Wiscovich asked him. "You want to see a menu or what?" And he pointed to the chalkboard hanging behind the counter.

Killie Willie looked at the board and nodded. He watched all the eating. He was puzzled over the way that folks ate there in the city. Where in the world did it all come from? He watched Joe dish the stuff out: tomatoes and lettuce and onions and potatoes and beef and ham and cheese and milk and beer and on and on. There was no room for gardens, he could see that for himself. Just concrete and an occasional scrub tree—not even fruit trees at that but plain old dwarfed oaks and maples. Just buildings and tons of people. Every one of them had to eat. And Killie Willie was sure enough hungry himself. The meat smelled as good as any they had grilled back home. Smelled better, in fact, because it was here and he could hear it sizzling on the grill back of the counter. He longed to sit down and find out just how good the meat tasted.

"Listen. Either order or get the hell out of the way," Joe Wiscovich said, smiling as he said it.

"How do I do it?" Killie Willie asked.

"It? What's it?"

"Get me something to eat."

"Well, hell, try sitting down, why don't you?"

Killie Willie sat. He didn't feel comfortable. He had never taken a meal in any place but his kitchen back home, a meal put down before him by his mother and then by Cora New. But he was too tired and too hungry to worry much about it.

"Okay," Joe said, beaming his friendly smile. "What'll you have?"

"How much for the least expensive thing you cook?" he asked.

"Grilled cheese. A buck ten plus tax. A buck seventy-five if you want pop."

"Pop?"

"Yeah, you know, a Coke. Where the hell you from, hayseed?"

"Frog Level."

Life stopped in the deli.

Everyone looked at Killie Willie as if he came from another planet, as if he was some sort of strange creature with hair in the wrong places.

"You said . . . ?" Joe's eyes conveyed the disbelief of all in earshot.

"Frog Level." Killie Willie pointed toward the street as he said, "It's down yonder a piece."

"Down yonder a piece!"

The deli was filled with laughter. It was as if all the voices laughed in unison and all the mirth was aimed not at Killie Willie but at Frog Level, which after all was only down yonder a piece.

Killie Willie couldn't help but smile. It made him feel right proud that others—and so many of them too—could share in his joy over the memory of his hometown.

"On the house," Joe Wiscovich said as he placed a hamburger all the way, an order of fries, and a huge Coke on the counter in front of Killie Willie.

"Let me pay for it," one of the customers said.

"No, me, Joe. Let this one be mine."

At any rate, Killie Willie ate free that day. And he ate with relish. His stomach welcomed the long-overdue meal. And it was GOOD! The best burger Killie Willie had ever put in his mouth. In fact, it was so far better than anything he had ever expected that Killie Willie didn't want to stop eating.

Life was back to normal in Joe's deli. The image of that special place down yonder a piece danced out of everybody's heads just as quickly as it had danced in.

Killie Willie pushed his empty plate back and settled at the counter as if he belonged. He took Johnny Mack's letter and looked at the outside of the envelope. Maybe someday, he promised himself, maybe someday soon . . .

"You know where I might find this place?" he asked Joe, showing him the letter.

"This you?" Joe said, pointing to the name on the envelope.

"It's from my first cousin, Johnny Mack. He was supposed to meet me down at the bus depot, but something
must of happened, I guess."

"Forgot you, did he? Well, it's a tough town in some
ways, Killie Willie Matt." He looked at the man in front
of him. "What sort of name is that—Killie Willie."

"Mine," Killie Willie said.

"You're joking with me, right? Nobody could be named
Killie Willie."

"Maybe not, but I am."

"Josef Daniello Wiscovich. That's me. There's a name
for you. Nothing queer about a name like that. My
friends call me Joe. You—you can call me Joe." He turned
the letter over in his hands. "What was it you wanted
to know?"

Killie Willie told him about Johnny Mack, about how he
lived in Buttermilk Bottoms but didn't have a telephone
and he, Killie Willie, didn't know how to get in touch with
anybody, not even home in Frog Level.

"The Bottoms, huh?" Joe said. "Too bad."

"Why's that?"

"This city is among the worst in the world, about as
bad a place as any there is. And the worst area of this
city, the baddest place on earth—well, it's the Bottoms.
So I am told. I have lived here nearly twenty years and I
have not made it up to the Bottoms. And I don't plan on it
either, not in this life."

"How can it be as bad as that?"

"I don't know, friend. It is what I hear. It is what they
print in the dailies. If I was you, I would be free like
water and run home." Joe wiped his counter with force.
"Nobody needs what they tell me is in the Bottoms."

"Well," Killie Willie said, "I got no place else to go."

"God bless you, friend. May he go with you." And he
took the orders of several new customers.

Killie Willie picked at his teeth. He stared out the

plate glass window. There was so much human life outside. Where there were so many people, Killie Willie rea-
soned, there had to be work for him to do. His problem
was finding it. He didn't know how to begin.

"I'm not in the habit of renting counter space," Joe said
as he grilled meat at his broiler.

"What say?" Killie Willie asked.

"I'm telling you—you're taking up my business space,
friend. Move it, okay?"

"Do you need help here?"

"Why do you ask?"

"Well, seems like you here alone, you need some help
maybe. I'm a good worker. Hard worker."

"I had me a boy up to the middle of the week." Joe
thought about his help and scratched his pate. "He
stopped out on me. I heard he was sent up for shoplifting
or something like that. You ever stole anything down in
Frog Level, friend?"

"Don't take to stealing, ain't right to steal."

"You ever cooked?"

Killie Willie hesitated. The lie raced through his head,
but to him lying was as bad as stealing if not worse. "No,
sir," he said but nodded all the same, hoping to imply
that he had what it took to learn the trade.

"How about a broom? You think you could learn to do
the proper thing with a broom?"

"Guess I could."

"And dishes—without breaking them? You have anything against rubbing grease off dirty plates?"

"Nothing I know of."

"Well," Joe pondered, "let me think about it. Why don't
you come back by sometime next week? We'll talk."

That was how Killie Willie found his work. It was work
he dearly loved too. That plus he got to take the leavings
home with him afterward. Cora New took to that just as
quickly as everybody else did. It was nice, she said,

having somebody else do the cooking in the house. Fact was, and everybody seemed to know it, just about everything about their living in the Bottoms was downright everloving nice.

Except for Vaughn Brodie. He had been the one who most wanted to make the move to Buttermilk Bottoms. He had dreamed of how things would be and how he would find everything exactly the way he wanted. It wasn't that he was disappointed in the Bottoms. It was sort of the way he expected it to be. But he wasn't accepted into the place as easily as he had dreamed. He was too much the loner, too much the outsider to find his rightful place. And like his papa, he just didn't understand the way folks did things in the Bottoms.

He sat on the fire escape landing, studying things out. What little of the city he had seen didn't please him much. It was like another planet, and he was the alien. He had explored around. He had ridden the subway into all parts of the city. But still he knew he hadn't seen much of it at all. Farther up in the Bottoms he found places that looked like some dude had stuck dynamite under and set it off half a dozen times. And then this place that his mama insisted wasn't near so bad as it seemed was to his way of thinking worse than anything he could imagine. It was going to take some getting used to, no doubt about that. He puffed on a cigarette and blew the smoke out his nose. The taste of the smoke in his mouth was much more pleasant than the taste of the air in the Bottoms.

Maybe his papa knew more than he did. Maybe Killie Willie had something on the side that made his breathing such air more acceptable. He didn't know. And he was in no mood to ask, just let things ride the way they were. Maybe it would be like Killie Willie said: "It sort of grows on you. After a while you'll see it ain't so bad." Killie

Willie had been right that time when Vaughn Brodie had come home angry at his schooling and said that he wouldn't take it anymore and was going to drop out of school as soon as he turned sixteen. Killie Willie had said then that he, Vaughn Brodie, could get used to anything, school included, if he'd stick with it long enough. Vaughn Brodie had stuck with it and actually came to like his schooling well enough, but when he turned sixteen he dropped out anyway.

Vaughn Brodie seemed content to sit alone on the back landing. So Cora New and Ollie Gus left him there.

One day something happened that Vaughn Brodie didn't tell anybody about. He was sitting on the front steps of the building, watching things going down—his words for it—when a dark-looking creature that once upon a time must have been a human being came up to him.

"Hey, kid," he said, "got a dollar?"

"Got nothing."

"Got fifty cents?"

"Got nothing."

"Got a quarter?"

Vaughn Brodie just sat there.

"Got a dime?"

Vaughn Brodie was silent. The thing moved in very close. Vaughn Brodie could smell the insides of the man's belly as he breathed. Before Vaughn Brodie could move, there was a shiv under his nose, the point blunted but still deadly.

"What you got for me now, huh?"

Vaughn Brodie didn't breathe. He had two quarters left over from his visit to Michael Pogo's store, but he wasn't in the mood to be parted from his money. He didn't care what it cost. So he said, "Got some blood in me if you're obliged to do some cutting."

"Just might be."

"Then do it."

The blade inched closer to his nose. It touched skin. The cold steel was pressing forward when Vaughn Brodie said calm and easy, "You cut me, man, and I swear to Jesus I'll find you and slice you in such little pieces that the rats'll fight over the giblets."

"I kill you right here," the voice said.

"Man, you ain't good enough to kill nobody. You closer to dying right now than I'll ever be."

"Shee-it."

Vaughn Brodie's hand had found a loose brick in the crumbling wall of the tenement building. The hand came around, brick in it, just as the blade drew first blood from the edge of his nose. The brick landed on the thing's temple, thudding like it would if it hit an overripe watermelon. The thing crumbled down the steps in a heap of rags and stench. The shiv fell helpless at Vaughn Brodie's feet. And the thing scampered like a whipped puppy down the street and fell in a pothole as deep as a grave.

Vaughn Brodie tasted his blood. It flowed over his lip like a spring. He gathered in the knife. It wasn't much of a blade. Dull. Very little point left. The spring for the switch was broken. But it had good balance and felt warm to his touch. He slipped the shiv inside his shirt. He would put it to good use, that was certain.

"Good Lord Jesus," Cora New said when she saw the blood dripping from his nose. "What happened to you, child?"

"Nothing," he said as he washed the blood from his face. It was strange, Vaughn Brodie knew, but he felt more at home just then than he had felt since coming to the Bottoms. It was as if he had initiated himself into a special club. He felt strong, he felt a burning in him, he felt free. And he couldn't explain it to his mama because she wouldn't understand.

"I want to know how you got cut like that, Vaughn Brodie." She seemed determined.

Vaughn Brodie just smiled. He was feeling good.

Ollie Gus saw the blood and screamed. But Vaughn Brodie was used to that.

Vaughn Brodie spent the rest of that afternoon sharpening his knife, giving it a point, repairing the spring, and remaking the blade into something more his style. A genuine Carolina pigsticker, made to order.

And with it in hand, he felt right smart wandering through the streets of the Bottoms after that.

Nobody heard the crash in the kitchen when he worked his way through the window from the fire escape landing. All slept soundly as he stumbled over Cora New's special purchase kitchen chairs or when he fell to the floor with a thud. All snored on.

What woke them, what brought Killie Willie and Cora New and Vaughn Brodie and the rest of the building and probably all of the Bottoms out of a deep sleep, was Ollie Gus' terrified scream. Later when Killie Willie focused on it, he didn't see how it was possible for a human being to scream the way that Ollie Gus had screamed. But then he'd never had happen to him what had happened to her that night, and who knows? He'd probably scream that way too.

When Killie Willie forced his way into Ollie Gus' room with Vaughn Brodie just behind him, pigsticker ready for anything, what he found was something he should have expected. There was Ollie Gus pressed out of her cot up against the wall that she had colored. And in her cot where she should have been, sound asleep though nobody understood how he could have been with all the commotion, was Nate the Wino, stinking drunk.

"Jesus H. Christ," Vaughn Brodie said.

"Vaughn Brodie, watch your mouth," said Cora New.

"It's okay, honey!" Killie Willie yelled to Ollie Gus, trying to stop her ear-shattering scream. "It's just Nate, Ollie Gus. It's just Nate."

It took some doing, but Killie Willie finally calmed his

daughter. He and Cora New took her into their room and put her to bed while Vaughn Brodie tried to rouse the wino.

Killie Willie should have known. That first night he had spent in their new place should have told him to beware of just such things from that fellow, Nate the Wino.

Killie Willie had found the place—Johnny Mack's place—but no Johnny Mack. He'd been shot by the pigs, folks tried to tell him, shot while standing on a street corner doing nothing, just standing. Killie Willie didn't want to believe that, especially since he was bringing his family into such a place. And then, when he found Johnny Mack's things all over the place in the flat, he knew that something had happened, he wasn't sure what.

"You stay here two, three months before they kick you out," his friend Junktown Buck from somewhere up the street in the Bottoms told him that first day. "You tend to Johnny Mack's things, then skedaddle out of here back where you belong. Don't get caught up here in the Bottoms. That's damn good advice, mister."

What he found in the place surprised him some. He looked out the kitchen window at the massed remains of a building that once had looked like the one he was standing in. There was a landing to his flat and a fire escape outside the window, and he could see that his first cousin had used that landing a lot because there, leaning up against the brick wall, was Johnny Mack's homemade fishing stool. Killie Willie had watched him make it.

"Beware the Bottoms," Junktown Buck said as he took his leave. "Even for a lifer like me, this place ain't healthy at all."

Alone on the landing, Killie Willie unfolded the fishing stool, sat on it, and leaned back against the brick wall . . . He dreamed of Cora New, of his pigpen, and of his cousin Johnny Mack Lindsay having his head blown off by a bunch of gawking police . . .

His eyes popped open. Something rustled in the room

behind him. He didn't want to turn and look through the window. The noise was as of something sniffing around in the junk that splattered the room. And Killie Willie smelled the faint odor of sewers. As far as he knew, no self-respecting haunt would hang around in the sewers, so whatever it was nosing around in his new home was living. Killie Willie turned. He stopped breathing for a moment. There on the table in the kitchen eating from an open can of rotting corn was a beagle hound. He looked closer. No, it was a black cat. Even closer. Damn if it wasn't the biggest sewer rat he had ever seen. It ate its fill as Killie Willie watched, then hopped to the floor and scampered off in search of other morsels. Killie Willie couldn't keep his body from shuddering. Lord knows the one thing he could not abide was rats. And he had just seen the king of them all, filling its gut in what he hoped would be his place now and in the future. But he was too tired that night to concern himself over a sewer rat. He was soon sleeping soundly again, this time with dreams of rats eating at his earlobes.

Sometime that night Killie Willie was stirred awake again. Something bigger than a rat had moved inside his place. It was dark as a coffin inside and out, and Killie Willie didn't dare move this time.

Whatever it was moved again. It crashed into something hard. That was followed by a muffled "damn" followed by a stumbling, a crash, and silence. Maybe it was a spirit, but Killie Willie couldn't fathom a haunt that could feel enough pain to give a damn about it.

He rubbed his eyes, trying to remove the sleep. He peeped through the window into the dark room. Nothing. He climbed into the kitchen. Still nothing. The light switch on the wall—no bulbs in the sockets. He struck a match. The junk in the room was the same. But the door into the back room was ajar.

For some reason that night, standing as he was in the dark with a door staring at him agape, Killie Willie thought of Cora New and how she looked the first time he saw her. He thought of the time he took her out back in the middle of the haying season: it was then he knew that he and she had made Vaughn Brodie. He remembered how it felt to touch her fingertips with his own. And he didn't know why it was he remembered such things here in the Bottoms in a strange flat looking at a door that swung open. Maybe it would be the last time he would have a chance to remember her and the kids. Maybe in the morning he would be found with his head split open and nobody around to know who he was and he'd be dumped out back for God knows what to find . . . And Vaughn Brodie. What would he do in this world without a papa to give him the leading that a growing boy needs? He remembered how his own papa had looked the morning he dropped dead in the cotton fields back home, pale as a man of his coloring could be, his eyes too wide, his mouth draining strains of life. And Killie Willie stood there, staring at the open door. He wished with all his heart that he had handled the raising of his own son differently.

He crossed to the door and shook the match out. He opened the door just enough to allow him to slip quietly into the room. He stood, listening. Whatever it was in the room *snored.*

Killie Willie's first instinct was to get the hell out of that damn building, out of the Bottoms, out of everything. In all his life he'd never felt so completely alone and so completely helpless as he felt that split moment when he stood there listening to somebody or something snore.

He struck another match. He saw a body prone on Johnny Mack's cot! He doused the flame more from reflex than from intent. His reaction to the human being there in his room caused him to ram into a side table, creating enough clamor to raise the dead. He froze. But the snoring continued.

He lit another match. The man—whoever he was— still slept. He lay with his feet dangling from the cot, his head close to toppling off the back edge, his mouth gaping open. The snore became similar to the bullhorn that the sheriff back home used to use during festival days. From the look of the man's clothes and the dreadful smell that came from his shoes, Killie Willie knew that there was little to be afraid of from the figure asleep on the cot.

He gave the body a hefty shake and yelled into its ear. The man snored. Killie Willie sniffed. He could have sworn that he was standing next door to old man Abercrombie's homemade still out in the back woods. And Killie Willie knew there was no stirring the fellow that night.

He pulled a filthy blanket off the cot, shook it firmly, and crawled under it in the middle of the room. He was unaware of anything else that happened that night in that place so far from his home.

The sun shone in Killie Willie's face.

"Howdy," somebody said when he opened his eyes.

Killie Willie rolled over. He couldn't make anything out because of the sun.

"You snore something pitiful," the voice said. "Woke me up half a dozen times, your snoring. Have some breakfast?" And he offered the contents of the can of corn. "All I could find. Don't mind eating corn, do you? What's a sweet roll but crushed-up corn and some sugar and sugar gives you heart attacks. Besides eating corn you can drink it. Yeah? Ain't seen you here before. You can call me Nate. Everybody calls me Nate. Real name's Nathaniel, but nobody calls me Nathaniel. Nate the Wino! Yeah? This corn's fair to good. Could stand a little heating but they turned the electricity off about a week ago. Course you can't eat much of this stuff. Give you botulism. You ever had botulism? Damn stuff'll kill you if you ain't careful. I've had it ten dozen times, probably more. Beans're just as bad, though. Don't care much for beans. Give me gas."

Killie Willie was as stiff as the floor he lay on. He tried to rise, but his legs cramped. He beat on them, urging the circulation back.

"You want to do some ankle stretches, get the blood down to the heels. Me, I get all stiff in the shoulders and neck. Gonna have me some case of arthritis sometime soon. I can feel it coming. Sure you don't want some corn?"

"Sure."

"Well . . . I done told you who I was."

"You ain't tole me why you're here."

"And you ain't the same. Seems that we're both what you call it in the dark. Besides, why not be here? Better than sleeping in culverts. A shame to let such as this go untended, what with Johnny Mack's passing, God rest his soul. I'll just have your share of this corn then. Yeah, a pity to let things go a-wasting, that's what I say. I see enough waste in my line of work to do anybody else twenty lifetimes. Waste not, want not. That's what I live by. You knew Johnny Mack?"

"Guess so."

"Never met the man myself. Shame, too. Heard all sorts of good things about him. Honest fella, they told me. You gonna be round here long?"

"This be my place now," said Killie Willie Matt.

"How come's that?" Nate asked after a time.

"Well, seeing as how I'm Johnny Mack's kin, I moved in last night. You can finish your breakfast, though, before you leave."

Nate gulped down the rest of the corn, wiped his mouth with the tail of his coat, and stood up. "Still don't know who you are, mister."

"Call me Killie Willie."

"Sure will. Sure will do such a thing." And he left, staggering a little but holding his head as high as his shoulders would let him.

So it seemed to Killie Willie, now that he thought of it, that it was only a matter of time before old Nate the Wino would return. And he'd done just that, to the total dismay of his overgrown daughter. She screamed, Lord have mercy how she screamed.

"Gimme a hand," Killie Willie said to his son as he tried to raise Nate from the cot.

"Pathetic, ain't it?" Vaughn Brodie ventured as they lugged Nate the Wino through the kitchen. They dropped him on the floor while Killie Willie unbolted and opened the door. Nate slept on. They carried him into the hall and dumped him on the steps, leaving him there to finish out his night's rest.

Vaughn Brodie smelled his hands. He washed them, but the stink wouldn't come off. Killie Willie took all the bedclothes off Ollie Gus' cot—he didn't want his baby getting crabs.

"How long we gonna stay here, Mama?" Vaughn Brodie asked.

"Don't rightly know, boy," was her reply.

Cora New got Ollie Gus quieted down somehow. "Who was that?" Ollie Gus wanted to know.

"Just a harmless old sot," Killie Willie told her. "He ain't gonna hurt nobody. Let's get back to bed, baby."

The next morning, Nate woke up as stiff and bent as the steps he had been sleeping on. He wandered away to wherever it was that he spent his time. Nobody knew and nobody wanted to know anything about Nate the Wino's daily life. It was best left alone.

Ollie Gus woke with a vague memory of what had happened. She seemed to remember things like something warm being pushed up against her, like something hot breathing on her neck, something wet and clammy folding across her breast. And in the light of day the sensations she had felt weren't all that bad. In fact, she had a strange sort of fond memory for what she had felt. She didn't understand it at all, but for some reason she sort of wanted those sensations again.

"What's it like, Mama," Ollie Gus asked, "being touched—you know—that way, by a man?"

"What way, honey?"

"You know—THAT way."

"Well, it's nice enough—for a while. But like most things it loses its charm after a time."

"Yeah?" said Ollie Gus. "Hmmmm."

She hadn't had a chance to see much of Nate the Wino. And now she wanted to know what the man looked like. After all, he was the first to touch her. In one sense of the word she had lost her virginity. The man owed her something, even if only a glimpse of him in daylight. So that day, instead of going off to school, she traipsed around the Bottoms trying to find her man, Nate the Wino.

Everybody she asked knew Nate, but none of them knew where to find him. She searched all that day and the next and the next. But no Nate the Wino. Some people tried to help her out by giving her reasonable suggestions about where to look, but most couldn't be bothered by any female who wanted a man like Nate. After a week or so, she gave up her search and returned to her spot on the steps of the schoolhouse. Nobody bothered her there. Nobody seemed to mind that she never entered the building. She sat and dreamed.

The subject of most of her dreams, mainly because she couldn't find him, became Nate. She had seen enough movies to know what a true romance was supposed to be like. She saw herself as slim and graceful, soft-spoken, and butterflylike. She saw Nate the Wino as the perfect specimen of human flesh, strolling along a beach with a perfect stride, touching his woman (namely herself) with tenderness while manfully fighting off all villains. Oh, in her dreams both she and Nate the Wino were something else. And each day that she dreamed her dreams, the romance became wilder and more aggressive until one day, though only in her dreams, Ollie Gus gave up the other part of her virginity.

"You been looking for me?"

The voice shook Ollie Gus out of her most delicious daydream.

"Who you?" she asked.

"That fella you been looking for. Name's Nate. Really it's Nathaniel but all my friends calls me Nate. You can call me Nate. You that newcomer's daughter, ain't you? I seen you around. I heard you asking where you might find this here fella name of Nate. Figured it was me. You real cute, you know that?"

"Don't touch me!" she yelled as he reached out for her hand. "Hate damn folks what touch me!!" He stank in ways she never dreamed that a person could stink. There was nothing at all graceful about the man, nothing even manly. He was just another living organism like the rats she had seen scampering about in the back lot or the cockroaches she had squished in her room.

"You like ol Nate?" he said. "You a good-looking chick and ol Nate knows how to do with good-looking little chicks. You want to come to my place? I got me a place. You'd like it there. We could have us a time there. You wanta come?"

"Where?"

"Oh, not so far from here. Come on. I show you. Real nice place I found me. I show you."

He led her off down the street.

Nate the Wino's place was down under a bridge. Nobody used the bridge anymore. Once it had carried all sorts of traffic, but now it was just there, no coming, no going, just there. Under the bridge and between the two support studs Nate had put himself up a little lean-to, just large enough for him, his bed, and the little things he picked up along his way. The hole into the lean-to was so small that Ollie Gus couldn't make it in. So Nate had to set about enlarging the opening—which didn't take long at all.

Inside it was damp and musty and had the same odors that Nate carried with him everywhere. His bed was nothing more than a worn mattress with the ticking falling out. Next to that was a broken lamp that couldn't work—there was no electricity. Against the opposite wall was a dart board with no darts. And finally there was Nate himself, taking up much of the room, drinking from a foul-smelling bottle that was so soiled with smudges that you couldn't see the liquid on the inside.

"Want some?" He offered her the bottle.

"What's in it?" she asked.

"Oh, little of this, little of that. I find a beer can with a drop or two in it or a whiskey bottle with a tad left, I empty them all into here. Makes smooth drinking sometimes. This one's got a bit too much beer in it for my taste, but I can't complain. Never cared much for beer. You?"

"Never tasted it."

"Then give it a whirl. Then I'll give you a whirl."

She put the bottle to her mouth. The stuff inside was more like spit than anything else. It touched her tongue and she thought for sure she was going to puke. But she soon forgot about the rancid taste in her mouth as Nate made his move on her. At first she didn't understand. She had seen the movies where the man put his mouth against the woman's and they sort of hung there, stuck for a little time, not moving, not breathing. But it wasn't her mouth that Nate went for. It was something they never showed in the movies—at least not the movies Ollie Gus had seen. His head disappeared underneath her skirt.

Ollie Gus stood straight up. Her head and shoulders ripped open the makeshift roof of the lean-to, sending splintered wood and shingles in all directions. When her head came up, so did her knee, catching Nate squarely on the end of his nose and flipping him backward, through the dart board, through the wall, and down the embankment. Ollie Gus didn't look for the opening into the shack. She charged through the lean-to, destroying what was left of it, screaming and cursing all men as she did so.

Nate was on his feet, blood squirting from his nose. He squittered like a squirrel away from the woman who was treating him so sourly. "You whore!" he yelled at her, though he knew full well that that wasn't her problem. "You damn whore!! What you doing to me?! I'm your friend! You whore!!!"

She didn't hang around to argue the point with him. With the toss of a shingle and an epithet that would have shriveled a more significant man, she stormed away, leaving her movie love beneath Nate's bridge.

Killie Willie became something of a cook. He could grill the best burgers and the best double-cheese fried sandwiches and even the best deep-fried cucumber sticks in that part of town. Folks who came in once always came back a second time and a third because they knew Killie Willie was master of the grill. And Joe Wiscovich loved the business.

"Doing damn good these days," he'd say. And to keep his worker well content, he upped his pay to seven dollars an hour and let him keep eighty percent of the tips he took in for himself. Killie Willie had never had so much money in his life. And he was feeling good about things.

Since he could trust Killie Willie not only with the cooking but with the register as well, Joe took to leaving him alone in the deli during slow hours. There wasn't much to do anyway. He'd walk over to the park or down to the garment district and visit with friends, leaving Killie Willie on his own to do with the deli as he saw fit. It honored Killie Willie that his boss would trust him so. He determined that nothing would happen to lessen the way he was thought of or change the way he was treated.

It was during one of Joe's minivacations from the deli that Junktown Buck showed up. He sat at the counter, eyed the place, told Killie Willie how lucky he was to be working at such a joint, and finally ordered a ham and cheese with onions, a side order of onion rings, and a beer. Lord, how the man enjoyed his food.

After eating, Junktown sat around jawing with Killie Willie for fifteen minutes or more. Then he got up from his stool and started for the door.

"Hey, Junktown," Killie Willie stopped him. "You ain't paid yet."

"I ain't?" said Junktown Buck. "How much I owe you?"

"Three twenty-eight."

"Well, tell you what. Why don't you just put it on my bill?" And he was out the door.

"But we don't—" Killie Willie didn't get a chance to finish. As far as he knew, Joe Wiscovich didn't allow credit. So what did Killie Willie do? He did what he had to do: he pulled three dollars and twenty-eight cents from his pocket and rang it into the register.

The next day Junktown Buck showed up again, only this time he had two of his friends with him: Toadface and Hungry Sam. The three of them sat at the counter talking in hushed tones. Killie Willie didn't want to wait on them; he had an idea that they were up to the same trick Junktown had pulled the day before. But they didn't leave, so he had to ask them what they wanted.

"You got money in that register?" Hungry Sam said more than asked. He had a mean look in his eyes, the kind of look that Killie Willie had seen a couple of times down home in Frog Level. Each time he'd seen it, the person had been up to no good.

"Ain't much there," Killie Willie said. "Been slow today."

"Nuff, though, I betcha," said Toadface. Killie Willie could see how he had gotten his name. The man had warts all over the place, even at the corner of one eye. It made him look almost Chinese on first glance.

"What you fellas have?" Killie Willie asked.

"Why don't you give us the cash there in that drawer?" Hungry Sam said.

"Well, I don't rightly think I ought to do that."

"How come?" Junktown Buck said. "Ain't we your friends?"

"Well, guess so."

"Then seems like you'd want to do your friends a favor—like I needs me some money and you got money so you ought to give me some. You'd never miss it."

"Well, you see, it ain't mine. Belongs to my boss, and he ain't here to give it to you."

"But you here." Toadface had turned so that he was looking through the plate glass window into the street. "Give us the money."

"You want something to eat," Killie Willie said, "I'll give you something to eat. But I can't give you money. That wouldn't be right."

"Who cares bout right?" Hungry Sam was eyeing a sweet roll under a glass cover. Killie Willie pulled the roll from its place and put it in front of him.

"On the house," he said, assuming the same kind of attitude he'd seen Joe Wiscovich use time and time again.

"You one hell of a friend," Sam said, gulping the roll.

"How come you ain't gonna help us out, Killie Willie?" Junktown said.

"Cause I can't. You know I can't. You want something to eat, I'll fix you up something to eat, but it'll cost you. Nothing like yesterday, Junktown Buck, I ain't in no mood to get took again like you done me yesterday. You want something to eat, you pay me up front and I'll fix it for you. That's all I can do for you."

"You hard, man," Junktown said. "We could bust this place apart, you know that?"

"Sure you could," said Killie Willie, "and you could probably cut my hands off if you were of a mind to, but that don't change nothing. I can't give you no money from the till. Just ain't right."

Junktown Buck rose from the stool. "Come on, no good sitting around here." And he led the way out of the deli. At the door he turned back to Killie Willie, winked at him, and said, "No hard feelings, right? I mean, you understand, right?"

"Guess so," Killie Willie said.

And they were gone. Killie Willie relaxed as best he could, opened the register drawer, and counted the money. Over two thousand dollars. He felt rotten, like he had cheated somebody. He had told his friend Junktown Buck a bald-faced lie. And his conscience wasn't about to let him forget it.

Vaughn Brodie couldn't find work, mainly because he didn't look for any. He wandered the streets like a stray dog looking for somebody he could call master.

Then he saw her.

It was late one afternoon, right around nightfall. She was coming out of a dingy-looking hotel, fixing her mini-skirt. She was a tall thing, very skinny, very leggy, very at ease. Her face was highlighted with rainbow colors. Her hair was bright blue. Her skirt was red vinyl, her blouse (loosely buttoned) clung to her near bosomless frame like silk, and a lizard skin purse hung down to mid-hip. To Vaughn Brodie, Fay Leigh was a walking vision, the most beautiful, the most magnificent female he had ever seen. And he determined to tell her so if it took a lifetime.

Fay Leigh finished with her skirt and began her casual stroll away from the hotel toward Junkie's Corner. Vaughn Brodie followed along behind her at a distance, wondering how he was going to go about the task of meeting her and making her his own. She was in no hurry. In fact, it appeared to Vaughn Brodie that she was waiting for somebody, though not somebody special. And it didn't take her long to find that somebody.

A guy with a beer gut hanging three inches over his belt buckle called to Fay Leigh from across the street. He called to her: You got anything you can give me? and she answered: Yes, I certainly do; and he said back: Anything special? and she said: How special do you want it? and he said: Oh, bout twenty dollars' worth; and she said: You got fifty then follow me, if not, get lost. And the man followed her back to the dingy hotel.

They disappeared upstairs.

Vaughn Brodie waited. He counted his wad of money. Ten dollars, all in ones. If only he had a job, if only he could earn himself some quick dough, if only he dared ask a loan of his papa, if only . . .

Fay Leigh didn't give him much time to contemplate his lack of funds. She emerged from the hotel in something of a huff. Behind her came the guy with the beer gut. She said: Next time know your potential, mister; and he said: Couldn't help it, Jesus!

Fay Leigh started her stroll once again as Vaughn Brodie watched. A young fellow in a white dress suit with a red bandanna about his neck walked over to her, took her purse, emptied its contents into a Saks Fifth Avenue shopping bag, and was off. Fay Leigh hardly stopped. She kept her eyes working the streets while her pimp took her earnings. She didn't want to miss any possible business. Besides, keeping books wasn't her job.

She leaned against a lamp post, took a yo-yo from her purse, and put the string on her middle finger. She leaned against the post while doing some of the fanciest tricks with the yo-yo that Vaughn Brodie had ever seen. He was more impressed than ever. Any female who could work a yo-yo that well deserved to meet a man like Vaughn Brodie, no doubt about it.

"You damn good with that thing," Vaughn Brodie said as he eased up behind her.

"I'm damn good with lots of things," she said. She must have seen it in his eyes, that look of complete devotion and desire to worship, because she stopped her yo-yo in the middle of a lady's walk and said, "Hey, mack, don't crowd me, okay? I'm working, so get lost."

Vaughn Brodie loved the sound of her voice. He even loved the way her eyes flashed when she chastised him for hanging around. There wasn't a thing about her that he didn't like. He even thought that her bright blue hair sticking out in all directions was attractive in its own way. It sort of accented her deep blue eyes.

"My name's Vaughn Brodie," he said soft and sexy.

"Big fucking deal," she said and returned to her yo-yo.

He didn't have anything else to say. He stood around for a while longer, looking mostly at the tops of his shoes. Just then he realized how out of place those shoes looked. He wanted to hide them somehow. Even his pants had "Carolina" and "Frog Level" stamped all over them. He was going to have to do something, that was certain. And do it quick.

A midget was talking quietly to Fay Leigh. They whispered back and forth, he took out his wallet and gave her three twenty-dollar bills, and she led the way up the street to the hotel.

Vaughn Brodie wandered off. He hated the city. He hated himself inside the city. He knew that for him to make his way in that part of town, he was going to need the kind of money it took. New shoes, new shirt, new pants, new everything—that was what it took. So he started out to get it, the easiest way he knew how.

Killie Willie, as was his habit of late, stopped in at Michael Pogo's store on his way home one afternoon. He would buy one thing or another. But it wasn't the buying that caused him to stop over. It was the gossip about what had been going on in the Bottoms on that particular day. There were always some folks hanging around the store, and they all loved to talk about what all bad had gone down during the nights and days of Buttermilk Bottoms. But on this particular day, nobody was hanging around. It was just Michael Pogo alone.

Killie Willie bought himself a pack of gum and had started on his way home when Michael Pogo stopped him. Now, that was something of an unusual event since Michael Pogo hardly ever said a word to anybody, and that usually in response to a direct question. He never initiated a conversation—that is, until this particular day.

"Scuse me, Mr. Matt," he said in a low southern drawl, "but that boy of yours . . ."

"Vaughn Brodie?"

"That be the one, Vaughn Brodie. He come by here early today. You best have you a heart-to-heart with that boy, Mr. Matt, else you ain't gonna have no boy to heart-to-heart with."

"How you mean, Mr. Pogo?"

"You ask him. He know what I mean. Yes, sir, he know what I mean." And that was all. Michael Pogo crawled back into his shell of silence as he shined his apples.

Killie Willie thanked him kindly and continued on his way home.

Cora New met him at the door. She looked bothered in a way that Killie Willie didn't care for. She didn't let him get inside the place before she started in on him.

"You gonna have to have a talk with that son of yours, Killie Willie," she said, her eyes spitting fireballs at him. "I swear, I don't understand it, but if you don't tend to it I don't know who will."

"What's he done? Broke a law or something?"

"You talk to him."

"I can't talk to him if I don't know what I'm to talk about."

"Just talk to him. He's in his room," said Cora New.

"Now look here, Cora—"

"Don't talk to me, Killie Willie, I ain't the one what needs talking to. It's your son, Vaughn Brodie. Now, do it!" And she pushed him toward Vaughn Brodie's room.

He found Vaughn Brodie where Cora New had said he would. And the sight of his son dressed in snow white pants, snow white shoes, a hot pink silk shirt, and a blue bandanna round his neck stopped Killie Willie in his tracks. "Goodness gracious, boy, what's happened to you?!"

"Just thought I'd dress up a mite," he said. Vaughn Brodie sat at a new desk-type table lit by a new brass lamp. He was fiddling with small plastic bags and other stuff that Killie Willie didn't recognize.

"What's that?" Killie Willie asked, pointing to a soft white powder piled on the desk.

"Coke," Vaughn Brodie said.

"And that?"

"That's pot, Papa."

"And those tablets?"

"Quaaludes."

"What's a Quaalude, Vaughn Brodie?"

"Just vitamin C, Papa, you know, to keep a body healthy."

"What you doing with all this stuff here?"

"Getting it ready to sell."

"Who you sell this stuff to?"

"Anybody what wants it."

"You want it?"

"Sometimes."

"Who you working for?"

"Friend."

"This friend got himself a name?"

"Dopey."

"Where'd you get them clothes?"

"Bought them."

"You must sell lots of this stuff to afford them kinds of clothes," Killie Willie said.

"Yeah, some."

"This stuff legal?" Killie Willie moved so he could see his son's eyes when he answered, but Vaughn Brodie avoided him. "Look me in the eye, boy, and answer me."

"That depends on what you mean by legal."

"I mean, you gonna get yourself in trouble dealing in this kind of truck?" Killie Willie felt like blistering his son's backside for lying to him.

"Yeah, guess so, if I get caught."

"Get that stuff out of my house," Killie Willie said.

"Ah, come on, Papa—"

"You ever knowed me to do anything illegal, Vaughn Brodie?"

"No, sir, guess not."

"You ever want to know of me doing anything illegal?"

"No, don't guess so."

"Then don't ask me to do something illegal now."

"I ain't. This stuff belongs to me."

"And till you turn twenty-one, *you* belong to me. Get that truck out of my house. And don't bring any of it back." Killie Willie's hair was bristling. How could his own flesh and blood disrespect him so? "And take them clothes off, Vaughn Brodie. You look like you're one of them pimps we see on the streets. Take them off and let your mama burn them out back."

"The clothes are mine," Vaughn Brodie said. "I wear whatever clothes I want, Papa. Just like you wear whatever it is you want."

Killie Willie thought for a bit and then nodded. "No more pot in my house. You understand that?"

"I understand."

Vaughn Brodie bagged all his stuff and put it inside the hatband of his new white fedora and the zippered part of his newfangled belt. "My Lord," Killie Willie said to Cora

New as he watched his son leave the place. He wondered where he would go, but he didn't dare ask.

Within two weeks, Vaughn Brodie was back trailing after Fay Leigh. She could always be found either coming or going at the dingy hotel over near Junkie's Corner. Vaughn Brodie admired her even more, and the distance between them had been lessened somewhat by his new-found wealth and sophistication.

He waited for her at the Corner. He had bought himself a beautiful wooden yo-yo with a jewel in the middle. He wasn't too good with it, but he felt certain that the toy would draw her to him.

He was right.

"That's real nice," Fay Leigh said to him as she admired the yo-yo. "Let me try it." In her hands the jewel flashed like a cat's-eye. The yo-yo rocked in the cradle, walked the dog, and came in through the back door in Fay Leigh's hand. It was like magic watching her do trick after trick with a toy that baffled most others.

"You're real good," Vaughn Brodie whispered in her ear.

"You should try me sometime," she answered, giving him back his yo-yo.

"I got fifty dollars. How's that for a start?"

"Up front?"

He pulled the money from his pocket and put it in her hand. She counted it, smiled, and gestured with her shoulder for him to follow her. And he did, gladly.

The inside of the hotel was dingier than the outside. The room had a washbasin and a dirty mattress and nothing else. And that little bit had cost him an extra ten dollars for an hour's stay.

Fay Leigh leaned against the basin and slipped off her high heel shoes. "I'm your first, right?"

"Lord, no," said Vaughn Brodie.

She laughed out loud and mocked him, "Lord, no? Where the hell are you from, boy?"

He almost told her Frog Level, but he stopped himself in time. "Upstate," he said, hoping she didn't pick up the lie look that he couldn't hide from his mama.

"Yeah, sure, upstate. Well, that's good enough for me." And off came her blouse. She folded it neatly over the edge of the basin and was unzipping her skirt when she stopped. Vaughn Brodie had become a statue, frozen in a stare. He had never seen naked breasts for real before. Oh, sure, he had drooled over naked pictures and talked big to all his buddies back home about his scores and so on. But this was real. There, standing as big as a moving picture, were two gorgeous tits, small, round, and firm.

"Anything the matter?" she asked.

"Oh, Lord, no," he said.

"Well, don't just stand there. You ain't paying me enough to gawk," said Fay Leigh. Even with that, she had to help him undress. Otherwise they would have been there all night long, which wasn't too bad an idea as far as Vaughn Brodie Matt was concerned.

Killie Willie's conscience was something he neither understood nor controlled. If he did something that he knew was wrong, he had to correct that thing in the best way possible. Otherwise his conscience wouldn't let him sleep nights. And he had done two conscience-ridden things. For one, he had let Vaughn Brodie get by with something that he knew deep down inside him to be totally wrong. Worse than that, totally illegal. He should have punished Vaughn Brodie in the proper way and then laid down the righteousness that was his and his father's before him. But he'd done nothing. He had let Vaughn Brodie do what he pleased without even a significant lecture to set him straight. Killie Willie had failed Vaughn Brodie as a father. And he didn't know how to go about putting things right with his boy.

The second wrong plaguing Killie Willie was the lie he had told Junktown Buck, Toadface, and Hungry Sam.

It ran through his head over and over how he had told them there wasn't much money in the deli's cash register when there had been over two thousand dollars in it. He even told Joe Wiscovich about it. That got Joe into the habit of removing the cash once a day. He said he didn't like the idea of folks he didn't know coming into his place and asking about his hard-earned money when he wasn't there. Telling Joe had only made things worse in Killie Willie's head.

If he couldn't right the wrong done Vaughn Brodie, at least he could take care of the lie he'd told. On his day off he decided to seek out Junktown Buck. It was Sunday, and he knew that most of the men in the neighborhood gathered at the bar down near Junkie's Corner and watched the afternoon sporting events on television. It was the weekly gathering place for most and everybody always had a grand old time.

"Yo, Junktown!" Killie Willie called across the crowded bar.

Junktown waved to him and then returned to the boxing match on the TV screen.

Killie Willie pushed his way through the crowd. "Gotta talk to you, Junktown."

"Yeah? Bout what?"

"How you been?"

Junktown turned. "That what you want to talk to me about? How I been? This your first time in this joint, ain't it, Mr. Uptown Big Shot Short Order Cook?"

"Guess so," Killie Willie said.

"Well, what is it that the Big Time Uptown Short Order Cook wants with us lowly nit-picking Bottoms folks?"

"I sort of lied to you the other day," Killie Willie explained, "and I wanted to apologize to you for it." Then he proceeded to tell his friend everything, how he hadn't known there was over two thousand dollars in the register down at the deli, and how he hoped Junktown wouldn't hold his lying against him.

Junktown Buck wasn't about to hold such a thing against a friend like Killie Willie Matt. He even called Toadface and Hungry Sam over and told them about the confession too. They were so pleased with what Killie Willie told them that they bought him a couple of rounds of beer and treated him to a bowl of fresh popcorn.

Killie Willie left the bar feeling so good about himself that he decided then and there to find Vaughn Brodie and take care of that matter as well.

He found his son out back, sitting in the rubble pile busting up old cinder blocks with a pointed stick. It looked to Killie Willie as if Vaughn Brodie was trying to work something out, and the thought passed through his head that maybe he shouldn't interfere with the boy right then, that maybe the time wasn't right for confessions. But he was feeling too good to turn back.

"You look sort of peaked, boy. Anything the matter?" he said from a distance.

"No," Vaughn Brodie said, and he smashed another cinder block into a dozen pieces.

"Yo, Vaughn Brodie, you can talk to me, you know."

"Bout what?"

"Bout whatever's pesking at you."

"Ain't nothing . . ." And he wandered off a little ways. Then he turned back. "Papa—how'd you know when you loved Mama?"

"How'd I know? Well, I don't rightly recall. Seems to me that I've always loved her, I guess. Never really thought about it much. Cept when I was up here alone and all y'all were back home. Then I thought about it some. Yeah, thought about it a lot then."

"You remember how you felt about her—you know, your first time?"

"Well, I felt sort of . . ." Killie Willie nodded his head several times. "Yeah, I remember that. Shoot, I ain't thought about that for so long I'd forgot it. We was just kids then, didn't know what we was up to. And then pow, all of a sudden, we was in love, and married, and then Ollie Gus come along, and you, and well, here we are. Ain't much else to it cept that we're still here, still struggling along together. Twenty-four years, Vaughn Brodie, that's how long me and your mama have been hitched and I pray to the good Lord that we have twenty-four more good years. How come you interested in all this?"

"No reason," Vaughn Brodie said. He smashed another cinder block.

"You got something you want to tell me about, son?"

"Don't reckon so."

"You ain't in trouble, are you?"

"I hate the way I talk, Papa. I hate it. Folks up here look at me like I'm the stupidest dumb-ass hick they ever laid eyes on."

"Don't use that kind of language with me, boy."

"And you just as bad. Both of us and Mama and Ollie Gus. Nothing but stupid dumb-ass hicks."

"Vaughn Brodie?"

"Huh."

"You talk that way around your mama and I'll whip you so fast I make your head spin."

"I ain't talking this way round nobody. Shouldn't be talking this way round you."

"Why not? I'm your papa, ain't I?" Killie Willie could see that his son's eyes were clear, but he felt that he had to ask him anyway. "You ain't on one of those Quaaludes, are you, boy?"

"No, I ain't on nothing."

"Then something else must be messing with you. You ain't in love, are you?"

Vaughn Brodie didn't say anything to that. He looked his papa in the eye—and shrugged, casuallike.

"She a nice girl?"

"I like her."

"She like you back?"

"Oh, Fay Leigh likes everybody."

"That right? What is she, a missionary?"

Vaughn Brodie laughed. "Yeah," he said, "in a manner of speaking, yeah, Fay Leigh's sort of a missionary."

"When you gonna bring the girl home to meet your family?"

"Christ," he whispered, "she don't even know I exist." And he started off across the rubble pile.

"Yo, Vaughn Brodie!" Killie Willie called after him. "You bring the young lady on home with you some night. Your mama and me want to meet your friends, son." But he was already out of hearing.

Killie Willie felt more like a papa than he had felt in a coon's age. It had been a good day off from work. He had straightened things out with Junktown Buck and now he even felt good about his one and only son. Yep, not a bad day at all.

He looked around at the rubble pile. He had seen it

lots of times from a distance. But now that he was standing in the middle of it, he noticed that from where he was
he couldn't see anything but piles of concrete, bricks,
broken furniture, metal and wood beams, and so on. He
climbed one of the mounds for a better look-see. The
rubble pile was gigantic. It seemed to go on and on.
There wouldn't have been this much junk if the tallest
building in the world had been blasted to pieces and
dumped in the middle of the vacant lot. It was a shame,
Killie Willie thought, to let such good land go to waste.
He imagined clearing away the rubble down to the good
clean earth, tilling the soil, and planting a garden come
springtime. The idea seemed to him to hold real possibili-
ties. Only he didn't know who owned the land or the
rubble. And he didn't have the desire to find out. So he
put the idea of gardening out of his head—at least for the
time being.

One day Ollie Gus got up the nerve to enter the schoolhouse. It was after classes in the late afternoon and most
of the kids were gone. The building itself had always
looked oppressive to her from the outside, nothing at all
like the schoolhouse they had back home in Frog Level.
There it was nice and clean and looked like a place where
a body could learn things that were good. But the schoolhouse in the Bottoms wasn't like that at all. It was all
cinder block, brick, and wire mesh. And writing on the
walls and scum on the floors and dirt and trash and paper
and cans and everything else that goes with human waste
strewn about the halls. There wasn't anything good about
the school at all, and Ollie Gus believed that if any learning took place inside that building, it had to be something
bad. And Lord knows, Ollie Gus hated anything bad.

She wandered into the main hall. There were a couple
of neighborhood kids hanging about who stopped their
talk when Ollie Gus came into sight and moved away

from her as if she had some sort of social disease. There was a dank smell in the place, a mixture of dirt and body odor and lack of good circulation.

A frail-looking man with spectacles half an inch thick stopped her in the middle of the hall. "Can I help you, miss?" he said.

"Just looking," said Ollie Gus.

"Oh? Well, what might you be looking for?"

She couldn't think fast enough, so she lied. "Books," she said.

"Well, come right this way then. Have we got books for you!"

The man led her down the hall, around a corner, around another corner, through a breezeway, and into another building that didn't look at all like the main one. It looked brand-new, it looked like it had never been used. It looked like someplace special.

Inside the walls were clean. The floors sparkled. And the people, what few there were, seemed to like being where they were. And there were rows and rows of books, magazines, newspapers, and catalogs. Ollie Gus couldn't help but smile to herself. So much learning stored away from everything, hidden like something to be shunned so nobody could possibly find it. Actually she laughed right out loud.

"Is there any book in particular, miss?" the man asked.

"No," she said, "just books. You really got books, ain't you?"

"Why don't you look around," said the man, "and if you find anything, please let me know." And he left her alone.

"Oh, wow," she said, and off she went.

At closing time they had to push Ollie Gus out the door of the school library. She had found a section that was stocked with some of the prettiest picture books she had ever seen. She had wanted to take some of the books home with her, but they wouldn't let her. She wasn't a student, so she had to leave them behind. But she knew she'd be back the next day and the next and the next. To her that library place was really something else.

That night she tried to tell her mama about her discovery. She tried to describe some of the beautiful pictures she had found all stored away in this one giant building. She gestured with her hands and she tried to put things into words, but she didn't know how to get her mama to understand.

"Why don't you take me to see this place?" Cora New said.

"Cause you can't go there," said Ollie Gus. "You a mama, you ain't no student. They ain't gonna let nobody in what ain't a student. Don't you know nothing?"

"You're not a student, so how come they let you in?"

That stopped Ollie Gus. She tried to reason her way out of the hole she had made for herself, but all she could think to say was, "Hate damn mamas what think they know so much!" And she strayed to her room where she slammed the door shut.

The next morning, Ollie Gus called her mama into her room. Cora New did what her daughter wanted. "There," Ollie Gus said, pointing to a two-foot-square segment of the wall in her room. "That's what I was telling you about being in one of those books. You see how pretty that place is?"

On the wall was a color crayon drawing of one of the most beautiful mountain landscapes Cora New had ever seen. She sat on the edge of Ollie Gus' cot and folded her hands in her lap as she stared at her child's handiwork.

"That's really something," Cora New said. She couldn't take her eyes off the incredible picture.

"I tole you it was pretty, didn't I? And that's just one of them, Mama. They got thousands and thousands of places and things in that book building. I tell you, Mama, it's really something else."

"How'd you do that, Ollie Gus?" asked Cora New.

"I don't know. Just did it, I guess."

"That is really . . . really . . ." But she couldn't find the word to express herself. "I'm proud of you, honey."

"For what?" Ollie Gus wanted to know. "I didn't do nothing. Somebody else done that. I just copied it."

"Out of your head?"

"Uh-huh."

"Lord, I sure couldn't do a thing like that. That is really . . . something."

Ollie Gus excused herself. It was time to beat it back to the school building and hope they would let her back into the library now that she knew she wasn't a student. There were a whole lot of pictures she hadn't seen yet and a whole lot of things she wanted to share with her mama.

Cora New took time off from her job in midtown to go shopping for her daughter. In a small art shop, she found a large pad of paper, some colored pencils, a box of watercolors, a palette, and a whole bunch of paintbrushes. She also bought a small box of charcoal sticks and drawing pencils. The man behind the counter tried to sell her some oil paints, but Cora New didn't figure that Ollie Gus would know how to use them.

When she got home with her gifts, Ollie Gus was already busy in her room drawing on another section of her wall. When she saw all the things that her mama had bought her, Ollie Gus didn't know what to do or what to say. So she burst into tears and wept like a little baby as she hugged her mama so tight that Cora New figured she was a goner for sure.

It got to where Vaughn Brodie came home from wherever it was he spent his days later and later until one night he didn't come home at all.

Cora New didn't want to go to sleep but Killie Willie forced her to, saying that he would sit up until Vaughn Brodie dragged himself home.

It was well past midnight when Cora New shook Killie

Willie awake. He had fallen asleep with his head on the kitchen table.

"He home yet?" she asked.

"Don't guess so," said Killie Willie.

"You think we ought to call the police?"

Killie Willie thought about it. He remembered the stuff that his boy had had hidden inside his hatband and belt. Even if he wasn't already in trouble, calling the police in on him would probably cause him a heap. So he couldn't report Vaughn Brodie's not coming home to anybody. It was a problem and Killie Willie didn't know what to do about it.

"I'm gonna have a good heart-to-heart with that boy when he gets home," he said with as much firmness as he could call up.

"*If* he gets home, you mean," said Cora New.

"Well, there ain't no reason to sit up for him. He comes home if he comes home and that's that. Let's go to bed."

Vaughn Brodie didn't come home.

Another day passed and still no Vaughn Brodie. Cora New hurried home from work to find his bed still not slept in. And she wanted to cry. It was all she could do to hold her tears inside her head. What if something bad had happened to him? She had heard tales of folks simply disappearing there in the Bottoms. They were never heard of again. Some folks believed that there were hundreds of dead bodies buried in basements and in rubble piles and in secret closets all over Buttermilk Bottoms, and if there should ever be a tornado, all those skeletons would come popping out. Cora New didn't want to think of Vaughn Brodie's body being dumped in the river or covered over by a pile of rubble. She didn't want to think it, but she couldn't help it. And there was his cot, still made from the day before. She knelt beside it and prayed that the good Lord in all his wisdom would bring her boy back home.

Ollie Gus shocked her from her prayer. "Look what they let me bring home, Mama!" she shouted as she came in from the hall and held up a large picture book from the library.

"Real nice, honey," said Cora New and pushed past her to her kitchen to start the evening meal.

"You sick, Mama? Hate damn mamas what get sick," said Ollie Gus and slammed the door to her room.

Where was he, she wondered. He had told Killie Willie about a girl named Fay Leigh. Who was she? Where did she live? Could she be found? What was Cora New supposed to do?

Vaughn Brodie had been such a pretty baby, the prettiest little boy Cora New had ever seen. He had had the thickest head of hair and the brightest, whitest teeth and the clearest and blackest eyes in all the world. He took up walking at six months, talking at eight, and fighting at ten. As a babe he knew no fear, while most his age feared him. He had been such a sweet child—until he got grown.

That boy was the beginning and ending of Cora New's life, only she'd never let him know it. She had visions of Vaughn Brodie lying in a ditch somewhere with his skull cracked open. Or worse—she had visions of Vaughn Brodie leaving somebody else lying in a ditch . . .

She tried to shake such thoughts from her head, but as usual they refused to go. Because if they did, they would be replaced by visions far more gruesome, visions of Vaughn Brodie not coming home ever again, simply not being heard from. Never, to Cora New, was unbearable.

There was something inside her boy that Cora New couldn't understand. How it got there she didn't know. It was as if he wanted to defy everybody, not just his mama and papa but the good Lord himself. It was as if there was a creed that he and he alone followed. There were already things in Vaughn Brodie's life that made Cora

New shudder when she thought about them—which wasn't often—and him only just turned eighteen.

Oh, back home in Frog Level Cora New had waited on the porch of their house a hundred times, so there was nothing new in this waiting of hers in the Bottoms. Only this time it was different. This time there was a strange world out there waiting to gobble Vaughn Brodie up and spew him out in a trillion pieces. Lord love us, she thought as Killie Willie began the deep breathing of sleep. Lord dearly love us.

There had been that time when Killie Willie had left them to find himself this place in the Bottoms, leaving all of them back home in Frog Level to fend for themselves until he could find his way in the big city. That night Vaughn Brodie hadn't come home either, not for a long, long time.

It had been past midnight when Vaughn Brodie had pulled himself through the screen door back home and collapsed fully clothed into his bed. Cora New hadn't spoken to him. She knew it would do no good. She stood over her son, her baby, that tiny little thing that had nearly killed her in his birthing. She wanted to take him into her arms and hold him tight and sing to him or coo or at least kiss him lightly on the forehead. She had felt alone that night too. She had felt weak, like she wasn't good enough for this life. She had felt deserted. Then when he came home in a state, he crawled into his bed and snored.

"Vaughn Brodie?" she whispered to him.

"Huh?"

That startled her. She had thought him to be asleep. "You awake?"

"Uh-huh."

"Vaughn Brodie?"

"What is it?"

"We gonna need you, Vaughn Brodie."

"Know it."

"We gonna have to lean on you. You gonna have to be a man in this house."

"I'm tired, Mama," he whispered.

"Vaughn Brodie?"

"Huh?"

"You drunk, Vaughn Brodie?"

"Wish to God I was," he said. He turned over. He stared blankly into the dark wall of that house way back then and knew that no, he wasn't drunk, he wasn't on anything, he just hadn't wanted to bear the responsibility of talking to anybody. But he had come home.

That was then. Now, this. She sat on the beat-up sofa in their flat, wondering where her boy was now. It was her greatest fear, that the Bottoms would do her family in.

The hall door creaked open. Junktown Buck poked his head into the room. "Miz Matt? Seems I got me a kind of package out here," he said and left the door standing open behind him.

Somebody was half-yelling, half-sobbing out in the hall. Cora New's heart skipped a couple of beats. It was unfair that Killie Willie wasn't awake. She knew deep inside her belly that she needed him then and there as the panic rose into her throat. Dear Lord Jesus, she prayed, don't let it be my baby!

Junktown had him by one arm, Toadface by the other. They half-dragged, half-carried Vaughn Brodie in from the hall. And Cora New sat down with a thud in one of her kitchen chairs. "Oh, sweet Lord," she said aloud. And that was followed by a beam-shaking scream from Ollie Gus.

"It ain't bad," Vaughn Brodie said from inside his mask of blood. "It's okay, Mama, it's okay." And they lugged his body into his room and laid him down on his cot as gently as they could.

Cora New regained control of herself. The sight of her

only boy dripping blood had almost done her in. But the instinct to tend to her own returned. She was by his side before he was stretched out good, and Ollie Gus stood in the door screaming like a treed wildcat.

"Tell me what happened," said Cora New as she removed Vaughn Brodie's bloodstained shirt and as Toadface tried to comfort Ollie Gus, who flew back to her room and locked herself away.

"Guess he'll have to tell you that ma'am. I don't know a thing," Junktown said.

"You think he looks bad? You should see the other guy," said Toadface with a huge smile spread across his warts.

Cora New turned a killing glare on Toadface. He wasn't up to her brand of wrath. He excused himself and returned to the hall to wait for Junktown Buck.

"He in any trouble?" Cora New asked.

"Not with the pigs."

"Who with then?"

"Oh, some folks what lives here in the Bottoms. Ain't nothing serious, though, ma'am. You might call this an initiation fee. Your son's been adopted, so to speak."

"By who?"

"The Bottoms."

"You a friend of my husband's, that right?"

"Yes, ma'am, Killie Willie and me make right good friends."

"Then you'd do me the favor of leaving now."

"I'll wait till Killie Willie wakes up if you want me to."

"I prefer that you leave, sir. Now."

Junktown excused himself. Such a woman, he thought as he left. Killie Willie Matt ought to thank his lucky star for giving him such a woman as that.

Cora New washed Vaughn Brodie and found that he had ten or so thin razor slices on his chest and back, a couple of loose teeth, a broken nose, and a cut above the left eye that needed stitching. She had learned to stitch a man when just a girl. Her own papa would come home most Saturday nights battered much like Vaughn Brodie, and it was her duty to patch him up for work the following Monday morning. It had been years, but she remembered how to go about repairing a man.

Vaughn Brodie winced with pain each time the needle entered his skin. Fortunate for him, she thought, that he wasn't in charge of all his senses; otherwise he'd be climbing the walls from the pain. He would feel it soon enough, how well she knew, just as soon as whatever it was he was on wore off.

She cried that night. It was the first time she had cried since moving to the Bottoms. She had been determined not to let this move get to her. But there are limits, she told herself, there are limits. And this was one of them. She wept silently, alone, and gave comfort to herself.

It was the only comfort that she really knew.

Vaughn Brodie woke with more aches and pains than he knew his body could manage. His head felt like it was filled with tinfoil. His left eye was bandaged, as was his nose. And smaller bandages covered most of his chest and back. He tried to rise from his cot, but his legs didn't seem to work exactly right. So he lay there, wondering what he could do to make his body throb in more places.

"Hey," Ollie Gus said. She had been sitting by his cot all morning.

"Not so loud," Vaughn Brodie said, closing his eyes.

"I ain't done nothing."

"Where's Mama?" he asked.

"Work. So's Papa. I told them I'd hang around and tend to you when you came to. You look stupid, Vaughn Brodie."

"Thanks."

"Why'd you do this, Vaughn Brodie? I hate you for doing this."

"I just got . . . caught up," he said. And more than anything he wanted to be left alone to suffer his pain.

"It's a girl, ain't it?"

"What's it to you, huh?"

"It's something. You the only brother I got, you know that? I don't know what I'd do . . ." But she didn't finish the thought. "Want something to eat?"

"Sure." She gave him a piece of toast covered with grape jelly and a glass of milk. He made a face at the milk but drank it anyway.

"Was Mama bothered?" Vaughn Brodie asked.

"What you think?"

"How about Papa?"

"Lord, Vaughn Brodie, you should have seen how you looked when those men brought you in here."

"Pretty bad, huh?"

"You want to see?"

"How do you mean?"

"You stay here." And she left the room. He could hear her rummaging and tossing things. Then she came back with her new drawing pad. "You sure you want to see?"

"What have you got there?"

She opened her pad and put it in his lap. What he saw made his throbbing body twist up inside. He caught a gasp in the upper part of his throat. And he felt like he would burst—he wanted to cry out with an anguish no one else could share. There on the sheet of paper, drawn in charcoal and colored with watercolors and what he could have sworn was real blood, was his own face as Ollie Gus had seen it the night before, broken and twisted and dripping life fluids onto his breast. The drawing was so real, so lifelike that Vaughn Brodie at first thought he was looking at a photograph, but there was more on the sheet of paper than the portrait of himself. There was also the feeling that Ollie Gus held for her brother and the fear she had felt that he might die. There was love and hate and confusion all caught in the line and color of the painting. He couldn't look at it any longer. He would have wept if he had.

"I didn't see it coming, Ollie Gus," he said. "I should of seen it coming."

"Tell me," she said.

"I paid for the hour. Fay Leigh and me were there together. Oh, Ollie Gus, she is so . . . so . . . Jesus, I can't think of words to tell you about her. We were there, and I gave her some of my very best stuff. I took some too. I ain't in the habit of eating my own shit, but I did. And we sort of lost track of what time it was. And before I knew it, there was her pimp, beating up on Fay Leigh and me. Yelling and swinging his knife. He cut her bad, baby, he cut her real bad. I should of seen it coming, though. It ain't that hard to see things coming."

"This Fay Leigh—what's she like?"

"Oh, she's really . . . really . . ." He couldn't put his love into words.

"You love her, huh?"

Vaughn Brodie felt his bandages. He touched his mouth and thought for a bit. "Yeah," he said. "I guess I do."

"Gee," said Ollie Gus.

Vaughn Brodie closed his eyes, his arms folded across the drawing pad. "Can I keep this?" he said.

"You mean you want it?"

"Yeah."

"Guess so."

"Thanks, Ollie Gus. You something special."

"You shut your damn mouth!" Ollie Gus yelled. "Hate damn brothers what don't know nothing!" And she stormed out of the place, heading for the school and the library and the pictures and her dreams.

Vaughn Brodie crawled out of bed. His back and legs felt like somebody had been walking on them with spikes. His store-bought clothes were ruined, so he had to pull his Frog Level duds out of storage. They smelled like mothballs. His new shoes were still fine, so he wore them. He checked his soiled pants for his roll. It was still there. At least the damn pimp hadn't robbed him too. He

had a score to settle. But first he had to see if Fay Leigh
was okay.

The only place he knew to look for her was the dingy
hotel. The white bandages on his head made him feel
conspicuous. But worse than that, he felt like a hick once
again, wearing his old clothes. He vowed to get him a
complete wardrobe just as soon as he could, and the
way things were going for him that wouldn't be too terribly long.

He asked the man behind the counter at the hotel
about Fay Leigh. The man shrugged, which Vaughn
Brodie knew meant that she was upstairs alone. So he
went up.

Fay Leigh was asleep. Her neck and shoulders were
bruised. She had a couple of knife cuts on her arms. But
other than that she seemed fine. He sat on the floor beside her. He wanted to touch her breast, to kiss her neck
and hands. She woke more from instinct than from any
knowledge of his presence in the room.

"What the hell do you want?" she hissed.

"Come to see how you are," he said.

"I'll live."

"I'm gonna kill that son of a bitch."

"Why? Bobby didn't do you no dirt. Man, he done you a
favor! And you too much the hick to know it."

"Ain't no hick."

"Just get the hell out of here and leave me alone."

"You don't want me to kill him for you?"

"All I want from you is for you to leave me alone!"

"But you my baby, Fay Leigh."

"Out. Get out! You don't get out, I swear I'll tell Bobby
to kill you next time, and he will!! So get the hell out of
my life!!!"

Vaughn Brodie left. He didn't know where to go or
what to do. He just wandered off into the Bottoms, hoping
that it would finish the job of eating him alive.

He didn't know that Ollie Gus had followed him. She

had hung around the library for a few minutes but couldn't get interested in anything there. She'd come up to the outside of their place just as Vaughn Brodie, dressed in his Frog Level best, came out the front. She trailed along behind him to the hotel and hung around the dark hallway outside Fay Leigh's door, listening to what was going on inside. She hated Fay Leigh with all her heart. And she hated Vaughn Brodie for letting a female talk to him the way Fay Leigh talked to him. She watched him leave.

In a bit, she tapped lightly on Fay Leigh's door.

"I told you to leave me alone!" she yelled from inside.

Ollie Gus swung the door open. She saw Fay Leigh sitting half-naked on the windowsill of the filthy room. Ollie Gus was shocked at how beautiful the woman she hated so looked in the sunlight.

"Who the hell are you?" asked Fay Leigh.

"Just a nobody," she said, staring.

"If you're not out of here in three seconds—"

"What you do? Call the police on me? Yell for Bobby, whoever he is? Scream for my brother, Vaughn Brodie? Just what you gonna do, huh?"

"What do you want?"

"Just to look at you. Just to see," said Ollie Gus. "Guess I've seen enough." And she left. The Lord Jesus knew how much she hated the female she met that morning.

But that didn't keep her from going home, shutting herself up in her room, and drawing a picture of the beautiful woman she had seen sitting on the windowsill. When she finished, she carried it into Vaughn Brodie's room and put it on his cot. It wasn't just a picture. It was feeling. It was love and hate and dreaming and cursing all combined in a charcoal that captured the inside beauty of a citywise female like Fay Leigh.

When she finished she stretched out on Vaughn Brodie's cot and went sound asleep. The effort of feeling and putting that feeling on a sheet of paper had exhausted her. She slept for the rest of the afternoon without a single dream.

It was late again when Vaughn Brodie got home that night. He stopped in the hall, waiting for his mama and papa to say whatever they wanted to say to him. But they were both silent, sitting at the kitchen table as if they expected him to break the ice. But he didn't. He went into his room instead and shut himself off from his folks. It was easier to shut himself off than to do anything else. Ollie Gus was still sleeping on his cot. At first his anger rose at her intrusion into his private life. Then he found the drawing.

As he sat on the floor in the quiet of his room admiring the incredible work of his sister, Vaughn Brodie slowly began to realize what it really meant to be alive. To hate and be hated and not much else.

"Reckon I should have a talk with the boy," Killie Willie said.

"Not much of a boy any longer," said Cora New.

"No, don't guess so."

"Vaughn Brodie, he's right square in the middle of growing up. What can you say to him?"

"I don't know, Mama. I feel like I've lost touch with him somehow. I don't rightly understand it."

"You moved him to the Bottoms."

"It ain't changed Ollie Gus none."

"Nothing could change Ollie Gus," she said.

"Yeah, don't reckon so."

"But Vaughn Brodie, he's in the middle. Not yet a man, no longer a boy. You got to make yourself available to him, Killie Willie. He needs you."

"How?" he almost pleaded. "He won't take no truck from me, Mama. So how'm I supposed to make myself available to him? I gotta work—"

"I know."

"And then he don't come home. And when he does, it's all busted up like he's been in a fight with a Mack truck. I wasn't like that when I was a boy."

"My papa was."

"Your papa never changed either, not till they put him six feet under."

"Mama used to not feed him when he come home late. And she'd make him eat out in the woodshed when he come home bleeding."

"We ain't got no woodshed."

"And she'd go a full week without talking to him, without having nothing doing with him at all. And he'd get so you'd think he had ants in his pants or something. Then she'd make him swear never to get himself drunk and into a fight ever again. Oh, he'd swear all right. Swear till he was blue in the face. And they'd make it up. Wouldn't last, though. It was his nature, I guess. Vaughn Brodie's something like my papa."

"You saying it's Vaughn Brodie's nature to be doing like he's doing?"

"Might be."

"Then what good would it do to talk to him?"

"Probably none." Cora New touched her man's hand. "You ain't talked to me in a long time, Killie Willie."

"Sure I have."

"I mean, talked in your way."

"Guess I ain't."

"What's the matter? Cat got your tongue?"

"Oh, you cussed woman," he said and leaned over to kiss her. But she was up and away from him, smiling big and sexylike. She slipped into her room and quietly closed the door.

Killie Willie knew the game. He'd give her a few minutes to do whatever it was that she did, and then he'd ease his way between the sheets.

He looked in on his son and found him sitting on the floor

with a drawing in his lap. "Whatcha got there, Vaughn Brodie?" he said softly so as not to wake Ollie Gus.

"Something." Vaughn Brodie held the drawing up to his papa.

"She real pretty, son. Somebody you know?"

"You might say that."

"She look like she real . . ." But he couldn't find the right word.

"Yeah, she real all right," said Vaughn Brodie.

"Somebody special." Killie Willie gave the drawing back to his boy. "You draw real good." Vaughn Brodie didn't say anything to that. "You got anything you want to talk to me about, Vaughn Brodie?"

"No."

"You gonna tell me who it was what busted you up?"

"Weren't nobody. Just an accident."

"Accidents don't carry razor blades, son. You don't get sliced up like you was by accident."

Vaughn Brodie didn't say anything.

"Sometimes," said Killie Willie, "sometimes I need to talk to somebody. There come times when I feel like if I don't say something out loud, I won't be able to understand it and won't be able to deal with it. Know what I mean? I guess I'm lucky cause I got your mama to talk to. But sometimes there're things that I can't talk to her about, things that a woman just couldn't understand. Then I need somebody else. I guess I need you." Vaughn Brodie sat without moving. "You gonna let me talk to you when I need to, Vaughn Brodie?"

"Guess so."

"I'd appreciate that. It'd be a real help to me."

He didn't know what else to say. Vaughn Brodie sat staring at the portrait of Fay Leigh. Ollie Gus slept soundly on the cot. Killie Willie stood there wondering if his boy would have gotten himself busted up the way he was if they had stayed down home in Frog Level. He knew the answer to that. He knew that a body's nature is the same whether it lives in Frog Level or Buttermilk Bottoms. In Frog Level it probably would have been moonshine instead of drugs. Just as bad, either one.

"A family's a lovely thing," Joe Wiscovich said. "You don't know how lucky you are, Frog Legs, having you a family."

Killie Willie merely nodded. Sometimes he wasn't so sure.

"I almost married once," said Joe. Business was slow, the dishes were washed, the supplies were laid in, and the two leaned casually on the counter watching the parade of life outside in the street. "She was a real looker, let me tell you. Yes, old Josef Daniello Wiscovich almost tied the knot. But we decided that it might be best to wait a few months. I don't remember what it was we were waiting for. Isn't that nice? We waited. She met someone else. And now she lives upstate with a bank vice-president and has five children. Count them, five."

"Two's enough for me."

"All girls. That could have been me," said Joe. "Except that I wouldn't be a banker. And I wouldn't be living upstate. I like what I do. And it's not a bad business either. A decent living. I saw her once, three years after her marriage. She was in the city doing some shopping. She had one child by the hand, another in a stroller, and a third in the cooker. And I said to myself, self, there but for the grace of God go I."

"Hmmmm," said Killie Willie.

"I've often wondered what kind of old man I'd make. My old man was the best that ever lived. He never learned to speak English, he never saw the need to learn it. When he died, nobody knew it but me and a couple of his old cronies. He was a good man, but nobody ever knew it. Wish I'd had me a son—somebody to know that I was a good man when I come to die."

"You can have my boy," Killie Willie said.

"Yeah. Why not? Everybody's dream to take over another body's problems." He laughed lightly, as was his way. "You ever thought of sending the boy to college?"

"No," said Killie Willie. He didn't say how dumb a suggestion that was. Joe Wiscovich hadn't met his son.

"If I'd had a boy, I would have put him through Dartmouth. And he would have been a doctor and taken care of me in my old age. Or maybe he would have been a politician and become mayor of this town. There's no end to what a citizen of this great land can accomplish. Isn't that right, Frog Legs?"

"Wouldn't know."

"Well, hell, look at me. Do you think that a man like me would have had an opportunity to own his business and make a decent living in the old country? No. Triple times no. You have never seen the old country. You have no idea about the restrictions put on a man over there. Here. Here is the place to live."

"Guess so," said Killie Willie, though he wasn't convinced that his friend Joe believed what he said.

"Yes, a wonderful land, this U.S. of A."

Three men came in from the street. Each was dressed in a long raincoat, with sunglasses, and one had a fake mustache stuck under his nose. They stood facing Joe Wiscovich from across the counter.

"What—" Joe started to say.

He stopped. He was suddenly staring down the barrel of a .44 Magnum, tensely resting two inches from his nose. One of the men forced a canvas flight bag into his hands as the third guarded the door to the street.

"Fill it," the man with the fake mustache said.

Killie Willie had frozen in his shoes when he saw the pistol pointed at his boss' head. But when he heard that voice, a voice that filled the deli with two simple words, he could not restrain himself. The sound came from his throat without his wanting. He wanted to sink away from what was going down, just slide out of sight behind the counter and pull the grill in on top of him. Instead his voice betrayed him.

"Junktown," he said in a hoarse whisper.

The pistol snapped around until the barrel was pointed right between his eyes. Killie Willie could see the points of the shells aimed straight for him. He couldn't stop shaking. He had to hold on to the edge of the counter to keep his knees from buckling under him.

"You," Junktown said, gesturing with his free hand toward Killie Willie. "Hurry."

Killie Willie tried to gather his nerve long enough to pull the cash from the register and drop it into the bag.

"No," Joe said.

The man near the door was growing more and more nervous. "Hurry!" he yelled. "Ain't got all day!"

"Coins too?" Killie Willie asked with a shaking voice.

"Just fill it!" said Junktown Buck.

If Killie Willie could have gotten the words out, he would have shouted No! Don't!! Stop!!! But the words wouldn't form. He stood frozen inside his cook's apron as Josef Daniello Wiscovich pulled a small revolver from somewhere underneath the counter.

Joe had never used his gun. He'd never had cause to use it. Never before had cause to take it from the shelf just out of sight. But he pulled it, nonetheless, and pointed it at Junktown Buck's chest. The revolver popped like a cap pistol and a puff of smoke came from the puny thing.

Junktown looked surprised. He sort of gasped. For a time he stood amazed. You damn fool idiot, he seemed to say, but he didn't say anything. He collapsed to his knees as his pistol-toting arm sank to his side. Joe Wiscovich might not have known how to use his gun, but the single .22 slug found itself a home in the very heart of Junktown's vitals.

Joe stood like a sightseer, gaping at what he had just done. He didn't see the shotgun come from beneath the raincoat of the man at the door. Killie Willie saw it. His mouth flew open. But there was no time for more than a whimper as both barrels exploded like something out of an old-fashioned Western. Both barrels discharged their nasty loads into the center of the deli. Joe was thrown like so much lifeless meat against the grill, where he crumpled into a heap on the floor.

"Goddamn, goddamn," the third man whispered. And Killie Willie recognized the voice of Hungry Sam.

Killie Willie didn't move. He saw the shotgun pointed directly at him. He saw the blue haze of smoke hanging in the air from the double blast like the pride of the morning rising off the land after an overnight frost. Such thoughts, he heard his head say inside itself, such thoughts at a time like this . . .

"Hey, Toadface," he heard himself say out loud.

The shotgun clicked as the firing pins struck against the empty shells in the chambers. It clicked again and again as Killie Willie stood transfixed by the pointed barrels of the gun.

Then Toadface was gone out the door. Hungry Sam left Junktown and raced out the door into the street and away. The bag of money hung like a dead heap in Killie Willie's hand. He dropped it. Coins scattered across the room, a couple of them landing at Junktown Buck's feet. Oh, such a thing, he thought, such a thing.

And he prayed that his friend and boss Joe Wiscovich would be all right.

His prayer went unheard.

PART TWO

Killie Willie Matt strutted out of the station and headed north toward his place in Buttermilk Bottoms. He wore a smile on his face so broad that he felt sure that everyone he passed must know exactly what he carried beneath that giant black coat of his. He didn't care. For the first time in six months, Killie Willie Matt was feeling good. In fact, he felt like a honeybee in a field of red clover just before a June gully washer. That smile of his crinkled up his mouth and wrinkled up his eyes. He carried with him—tucked away inside his coat—something of a prize, something that he had longed for from the first day he had spent in the city, something that would once again bring some meaning to his life. And he felt good all over.

In the six months since his friend and provider, Josef Daniello Wiscovich, had been left dead in his own deli, Killie Willie Matt had lived through what he could easily call his own personal hell. There had been the questions from the police, and then from the press, and then from the lawyers and judges. He had answered them all in the only way he knew how: it was him, Killie Willie Matt, and not Josef Daniello Wiscovich who should be dead. It was his fault that Junktown had let his attention stray from Joe. It was Killie Willie who had looked down the two barrels of that shotgun and heard the click of the firing pins. It was his inability to clear the register of cash that had created panic in the deli. So to his way of thinking, Joe was dead because of his personal failure.

The deli had closed. Joe Wiscovich had no will, he had no surviving kin. So the city closed the tiny shop and put a "For Sale" sign in the window, claiming that the sale would barely pay Joe's back taxes.

Out of work, Killie Willie Matt had had to search elsewhere, but there was nothing to be found, no work for a man like him to do. He wandered the streets, stopping in every deli that he could find. But nothing. If Joe had lived, he tried to convince himself, if Joe Wiscovich had lived . . .

There were huge lines day after day at the employment offices. Cora New did all she could by taking more homes to tend and spreading her day over a twelve-hour period. It helped, everything helped, but not enough. No work. Killie Willie's idle hands left him forlorn.

But there was more to it than that. Not having work was one thing, but to see two friends snuffed by one another before your eyes, to feel so helpless, so unable to prevent what was happening from happening—and to know deep down that both men had died because of him—well, Killie Willie Matt had a lot to deal with in his life after the shooting.

He applied for and received unemployment benefits. The money was good, as far as that goes. It kept his hands idle, but at least his family was able to eat in the same style as before. Then sometime after the trial and after the deli had been sold and turned into a flower shop, his unemployment benefits ran out and Killie Willie Matt had to turn to welfare.

There was nothing more hateful to him than the idea of being paid not to work. He couldn't take sitting at home alone all day. His children were involved in their things. His wife had her six-day-a-week and twelve-hour-a-day work schedule. The only thing he had to do with his time was to go down to the welfare office every two weeks and get his government check. He didn't understand why it was that they were so eager to pay him for doing nothing. But he didn't question it. He didn't know where to put the questions if he had any.

So Killie Willie spent his days out back. One day he cleared away enough of the rubble from the middle of the back lot to reach the ground. It was hard and gray, not at all like the ground back home. It had probably never been tilled, he determined. Folks in the Bottoms probably didn't even know what a tiller was. What a garden he could grow out back. He could raise him some tomatoes and carrots and turnips and radishes out back if he only had a tiller and if the weather held and no cold snap came in and killed everything off while in the cradle, so to speak. He contemplated it, but it only made him more homesick for Frog Level and the open fields freshly turned and ready for seeds. Besides, he had no tiller, he had no tomato plants or seeds, he had no real desire, only dreams.

Then one day while he was out back he had a new dream. He envisioned a different seed, one that was likely to take root. He didn't talk about it. He thought it out all on his own. When it was time, he sat Ollie Gus down at the kitchen table and had her write a special letter back home to Frog Level, addressed to his younger brother and successful pig farmer Montgomery Matt. Then he purchased himself a sixty-dollar money order, made it out to his brother and put it in the envelope with the letter, posted it, and waited. It was while he waited that Cora New noticed that maybe after such a long time Killie Willie Matt was ready to come forth out of his deep, deep depression caused by idleness.

That was why Killie Willie smiled so big as he left the station that day. His brother Montgomery had honored his wish and sent the "seed" by bus. And Killie Willie strutted on his way home with the "seed" tucked away inside his great coat.

The "seed" kicked at him and squirmed as he moved with ease through the crowded streets of the city. He didn't care. He didn't care that it was too heavy for him to tote such a distance as he had to walk. He didn't care about the stares he got from the folks he passed along the sidewalk as his "seed" squealed out in a high-pitched voice that sounded more like a baby than the special prize he was toting home. And then it stuck its snout out the end of the tow sack in which it rode and through an opening in the black coat. It didn't squeal much after that, but the sight of that pink snout and little black dot eyes drew more stares and points from people on street corners.

Killie Willie couldn't help but laugh a little, because he knew that the joke in the long run was on all those city slickers who didn't recognize the "seed" when they saw it. He nodded to those who stared. He grinned and said such things as "Howdy" and "Nice day, ain't it" and "Real pretty this spring" and so on. Once when he was waiting for the streetlight to change, the thing started nibbling at a lady's cashmere coat. The woman gave Killie Willie the strangest look he had ever seen. And he laughed right out loud, causing the lady to storm off in a huff. One thing kept racing through his head as he closed in on his place in the Bottoms. That thing was simple enough to appreciate: if he couldn't go back home to Carolina, then he could ship a bit of Carolina into the Bottoms just for him. And he felt damn good all over because of it.

"You ain't really gonna do this," Cora New said the day before he posted the letter to Montgomery.

"My papa's done lost his nut," Ollie Gus said as he dictated the letter to her. But she wrote it for him even though she hated doing it.

"Jesus Christ," Vaughn Brodie said when he heard what his papa had done. "There ain't nothing left to do but shoot the old coot and put him out of our misery. Gimme the gun."

But what his family had to say about sending home for the thing didn't seem to bug Killie Willie Matt. He knew what was right for him. He knew what he needed to return some meaning to his life. That morning as he made his way north to the Bottoms he wanted to sing.

He restrained himself, though, with an effort.

A policeman passed him as he neared the north end of the park. Everything would have been fine if the "seed" hadn't grunted just as the policeman passed. The cop gave Killie Willie a strange look and followed along behind, being the obnoxious cop that the city was famous for.

When they came to a corner and Killie Willie had to wait for the light to change, the policeman strolled up beside him, just as the "seed" kicked Killie Willie directly in the side.

"What you got there, buddy?" the policeman asked.

"Groceries." Killie Willie wasn't lying either.

"You got proof of purchase?"

"Sure do," Killie Willie said and almost burst out with a laugh. He gave the cop a bill of sale which he, the cop, looked over with surprise on his face.

"This is what you have there under your coat?" he asked.

"Yeah."

"Let's see."

He pulled the poke from under his coat and placed it on the sidewalk. "Careful," he said, "it could get loose." He pulled the drawstring and opened the poke for the cop to see.

"Now I done seen it all," he said, shaking his head. "What you gonna do with a thing like that?"

"Told you. Groceries."

"Well," the cop said, "don't let me see you getting any notions of keeping that thing around, you hear me? This city's got laws. You do know what I'm talking about, don't you? Laws?"

"Yes, sir."

"Good. Get along. Don't want you holding up traffic, now, do we?"

Killie Willie strutted the rest of the way to his place in the Bottoms, feeling for the first time in a month of Sundays as if he had the world by the tail and it was time for him to swing it a while.

Perfecta got her name when Killie Willie reached his place. Cora New met him at the door. He almost danced in from the hall and into her folded arms. She hadn't approved of any of this business, not from the start, and she never let him forget it.

"Hey, hey, hey," he said as he clumped the poke down in the middle of the kitchen.

Cora New stood there with a ladle in her hand and a scowl on her face.

"She's come," Killie Willie said, bursting with the pride of a new papa. "And she's a beaut, Cora New. You're gonna love her."

"Doubt it," she said. "Really doubt that." She punched at the thing as it squirmed inside its poke. "Come in this thing?"

"Course not," Killie Willie said. "Come in a crate, prettiest little critter . . ." But the squeals were growing in great proportions.

"I ain't having it in my kitchen, Killie Willie," Cora New said.

"She's as cute as a button—"

"Don't care. You hear me, Papa?" Cora New's eyes got that kind of glow that Killie Willie recognized and feared. When that look came to her eyes, he knew it was time for him to "yes, sir" his way right out of wherever he was at that time. So he picked up the squirming poke and lugged it into Ollie Gus' room. Ollie Gus sat up and exclaimed, "Jesus God! We home in Frog Level?"

"Got us a prize," Killie Willie said, slipping the knot off the bunched-up end of the poke. "And she's damn near perfect!" He stood up straight; he liked the sound his prize, his seed was making.

"How about some quiet, for God's sake?" Ollie Gus yelled. "How's a body to get any damn studying done with all this racket going on in the house?" she yelled.

"Take a look, Ollie Gus," Killie Willie said.

"Hate damn racket," said Ollie Gus.

The racket that Ollie Gus railed at was coming from a twenty-eight-pound Hampshire pig, scampering out of her poke and squealing her lungs out. The pig was a good-sized shoat, with a black head and a black body and a broad white collar around her neck and a couple of bright black eyes that scooted about the room faster than her feet could carry her.

Killie Willie just stood there with a dumb-looking grin on his face. "Damn near perfect," he whispered so that Cora New wouldn't hear.

"Got a perfect set of vocal cords," Cora New said.

"Got a perfect pig smell!" said Ollie Gus. "Hate the smell of pigs."

"Yeah," Killie Willie whispered. "Damn near perfect."

And the name sort of stuck after that.

Perfecta, being the pig that she was, squealed for three hours that first day in Buttermilk Bottoms.

"Shut the noise up, for God's sake!" Ollie Gus screamed. She fumed so that Killie Willie paid her no mind. "How's a body to get any work done with all that god-awful noise going on day in and day out?"

Killie Willie tried to ignore Ollie Gus as much as he could, but the squealing was getting on his nerves too.

When Vaughn Brodie came in from his day on the streets and saw the pig, he just smirked. "Thought we'd left Frog Level," he said, "but guess we ain't." He caught his mama's eye, pointed to his papa, and motioned with a finger pointed to his head that the old man was Looney-tunes.

Killie Willie saw the gesture, but he ignored that as well. Since coming to the Bottoms and since seeing what he had seen go down, he had learned to ignore whatever he liked with no trouble whatsoever. He was used to his son's behavior by now, and there was nothing he could do about it, hate it though he did. Vaughn Brodie since his licking had become a known disrespecter of persons, especially if they were his parents. So Vaughn Brodie's commentary on the idiocy of having a piglet running loose in the middle of their place there in the Bottoms didn't bother Killie Willie like it should have. In fact, Killie Willie had expected exactly what Vaughn Brodie had given him.

Then when Cora New said "Killie Willie!" in that tone of hers, he knew that the pig's time inside the flat was significantly limited.

"Killie Willie!" Cora New said. "What you gonna do with that thing now you got it up here where it don't belong?"

"Well," Killie Willie replied, "I thought we'd raise her up—"

"We?"

"Me then. Not much else for me to do. I figured I'd raise her up so we can have fresh bacon and chitlins and things come first frost."

Cora New crossed her arms. It was law-laying time as far as she was concerned. "You ain't raising no hog in my kitchen," said she.

"Didn't think I would."

"So. Where you thinking of then?"

"On the roof?" Vaughn Brodie said with a laugh. He had something hanging out of his mouth that Killie Willie knew wasn't a cigarette. So Killie Willie didn't care to hear whatever it was that his boy had to say.

"No!" he said. "Not the roof."

"Then where?" Cora New wanted to know.

"Well," but he hadn't really thought about it enough to say for sure, though he knew he was obliged to say something. He didn't care for the way that Vaughn Brodie stood there in the corner, staring at his Carolina prize. There was something about Vaughn Brodie that Killie Willie didn't understand. Something that he knew had to do with leaving Frog Level for the streets of the Bottoms. And it had all come about since that day. Killie Willie thought it had something to do with the fact that Vaughn Brodie's love had been dumped on. But he didn't

know for sure since his son didn't talk to him much anymore. Vaughn Brodie had developed a way of sucking on
his joints and holding the toke inside his lungs so long
that when he breathed it out there was nothing there but
clear air, not fresh, just clear. And the way he stood
there, just stood there not saying much, just standing
with no expression, no thought—it bothered Killie Willie.
But what could he do?

"Guess I'll have to find a place for her out back," Killie
Willie announced.

Vaughn Brodie guffawed.

Perfecta stopped her squealing long enough to put her
snout into the first bucket of fresh old-fashioned back-
country Carolina slop that Killie Willie fixed for her. As
she ate, he took in the back lot from the kitchen window.
He was trying to picture a pigsty out in that mass of concrete and rusted girder work. Gonna be difficult, he knew.
Sure enough difficult.

"Gonna put her out there," he pointed.

Vaughn Brodie couldn't help himself. He laughed so
hard at his papa's stupidity that he had to hold his side.
He had seen the kinds of things that went on out back. To
think of a hog trying to make her way out there with the
teeming life struck him as the height of idiocy. And he
couldn't help himself when his head under the influence
of the stuff he was smoking said, "Out back. I'll be shit-
puke. He's gonna put the damn thing out back!"

Killie Willie was angered. "Nuff, Vaughn Brodie,"
he said.

"Enough!" ordered Cora New.

Vaughn Brodie got control of himself. "Sorry," he said.

But Killie Willie knew he wasn't sorry. He also knew
that there wasn't any reason for him to justify what he
had done, but he tried all the same. "If anybody wants to
know," he said, "I got this here pig—sent home to Montgomery for her—all because of Cora New. Wanted to
please my woman."

"That right, Mama?" Ollie Gus wanted to know. "You want yourself a pig?"

"Course not," Cora New answered. "What you think I wanted to leave Carolina for? Pigs stink."

"Oh, hogs got the prettiest smell . . ." Killie Willie tried to bring the odor to his head.

"They got laws, Papa," Vaughn Brodie put in as he started to head back to Junkie's Corner, the place where he spent most of his waking time.

"What laws?"

"Just laws. You know, laws?"

"Pigs stink!" Ollie Gus yelled.

"Pigs smell like . . ." Killie Willie had to stop and get the right image in his head before he could continue to identify the aroma of a pig in its sty. "Pigs smell like a little bit of heaven. Dearly love the smell of hogs."

And he knelt beside Perfecta as she ate her slop. He caressed the little pig's bristles. He would have hugged the animal except for the fact that he was being watched.

Vaughn Brodie shook his head. It was beyond him to make any sense out of what was going on inside his papa's head. He didn't want anything to do with it. It made his skin crawl just being in the same room with an animal that rightfully belonged in a barnyard. So he left.

Killie Willie relaxed a little. Maybe Vaughn Brodie would take to a pig as being part of the family. He didn't worry about Ollie Gus—she hated everything anyway. But Cora New . . .

"I ain't having no messy smelly swine living in my house, Killie Willie. You want us to live in a sty, we'll live in a sty, but we ain't living in no sty along with any smelly old pig!"

The law of Cora New had been laid. It was impossible for Killie Willie to ignore.

He stroked his prize, considering things. Not that he hadn't considered them before. Out back in the rubble pile was the logical place for her. But maybe, he thought, maybe every once in a while, Cora New would let him bring Perfecta into the flat just for a little—

Cora New must have read her man's mind. She stiffened her back and arched her neck as if she expected something or other to attack her. She shook her head with a firmness that could not be argued with. "No," she said. "Absolutely not," she said. "Not in my house," she said. And she pointed through the back window. "Out!" she ordered. And that was that.

Something was happening, though. Ollie Gus saw it and was disgusted. Cora New saw it and was puzzled. If Vaughn Brodie had been there and if he'd seen it, he'd probably have thrown something through the second-floor window. Killie Willie was too close to it to see, but he felt it. What they saw and what they felt was a full-grown and mature man kneeling down beside a half-grown Hampshire pig in the middle of the Bottoms, stroking her with a tenderness and affection usually reserved for the most precious of God's creations. What they saw and what they felt was True Love. A little bit of Carolina had come back into the lives of the Matts. And all of them—even Ollie Gus, though she would never let on—were pleased.

As soon as Killie Willie wrote home for his pig, he began looking for the right place to build himself a pigpen. He had selected a spot in the rubble pile that, though not ideal, would serve. It was as close to the fire escape as he could get it and still have the pen hidden from sight. He didn't know who owned the empty lot, and he didn't know where to go to find out. So it wasn't like he was doing something wrong by parking his pig in somebody else's yard. He was simply doing something that he had to do.

So Killie Willie shaped what would pass for a pigsty. He attracted the watchful eye of Billo, a kid on the outs with the rest of the neighborhood. Killie Willie dug through the bricks and cinder blocks and trash down to the gray ground until he had cleared him a space approximately eight feet in diameter. Then he came to the problem of the fence. That was the most important part: a fence that would hold a full-grown Hampshire hog. Perfecta was little now, but Killie Willie had great expectations for her growing to significant proportions.

There were a number of large slabs of concrete lying around. Killie Willie figured they would make pretty good fencing, with a little jury-rigging. He struggled with the heavy slabs, making a little progress as Billo watched.

"What we making?" Billo wanted to know.

"A sty," said Killie Willie Matt.

"A what say?"

"A sty." Killie Willie wasn't in much of a position to carry on a conversation, especially when there was help sitting there not making any offer to assist.

"Don't mess with me, man," Billo said. "I know what a sty is." And he winked in an exaggerated way. "A sty's what you get when you look at some broad with the pinkeye."

"Maybe," Killie Willie said. "But this here—it's gonna be a sty too."

He said it with such conviction and earnestness that all Billo could say was "Oh."

"If you ain't gonna help me," Killie Willie said, "then go home, Billo."

"Okay," he said, but he didn't move. He enjoyed watching what Killie Willie was doing too much, and giving directions on how to do it a little better was even more fun. He figured that Killie Willie wouldn't be able to finish work without his help.

When done, Perfecta's place wasn't much to look at, but it was the best that Killie Willie could do with the existing materials. He wiped his hands on his pants and stood back to take in what he had done. The concrete slabs when overlapped formed a passable fence. It would do to keep the pig in as long as the pig didn't care to get out. He found a broken shovel in the rubble pile and used it to dig a hole in one corner of the pen. Then he lugged bucket after bucket of water into the pen and filled the hole. The earth drank the water like it was dying of thirst. It was Billo who found the rusted porcelain basin amid the rubble, and together they buried it in the ground. Killie Willie detested the citified mudhole, but it was the best he could do. Then he built a good old-fashioned V-shaped pig trough out of some boards he found lying about. Finally he threw some weeds and dried leaves in a corner of the sty and stepped back to review his handiwork.

"Well," he said, "what do you think?"

"Looks like shit to me," said Billo.

"Needs some straw. Ground's too hard. Shoot." And Killie Willie stood there feeling embarrassed for his special prize. Maybe it was a mistake sending home for her after all.

"You moving your bed out here?" Billo wanted to know.

"You crazy, boy."

"You and your old lady have a spat? She kick you out of the house? You gonna eat your food out of that trough?"

"Go home, Billo," Killie Willie said. But he didn't.

It looked to Killie Willie as though the sty was the best it could possibly be. There was no way, not in that neighborhood, for him to do any better.

"You forgot something," Billo said. "How you gonna get in and out of the thing? There ain't no gate."

"I told you to go home."

"You ask me, I think you done lost your mind. You forgetting the gate!"

"Who asked you what you think?!" Killie Willie chunked a piece of brick at Billo in fun.

Billo edged away. When folks started throwing things

at his body, he knew he had overstayed his welcome. But he couldn't go, not yet. There was something he needed to know.

"What's it for really, Killie Willie?"

"Won't you get?" Killie Willie was eager to move his pig into her sty, and he wanted to do it when it was just the two of them. He wanted no audience for the ceremony.

"You can tell me, man. It's for Ollie Gus, ain't it?" Billo's young eyes bulged at the thought. "You moving Ollie Gus out of the house? Wouldn't blame you a bit if you did."

He didn't get an answer. Another hunk of brick came close to his skull, so he scooted. Killie Willie was finally alone enough to introduce his Carolina friend to her new humble abode.

So he brought her down the fire escape wrapped comfortably in the poke. He didn't see the dozen or so sets of eyes watching his every move from the tenement windows. He didn't know that his labors out in that pile of rubbish in the middle of the Bottoms were giving some folks their best show in years.

He was feeling too good as he lowered Perfecta into her new sty. The place wasn't much, he knew that, but to him it was the best pigsty in the world outside Frog Level.

But Perfecta didn't take to it at all. She sat in the middle of the open arena, looking more like a piggy bank than a real hog. She didn't fuss. She didn't do anything. She just sat.

Killie Willie's face drooped. "Well, shoot, Perfecta," he said. "What do you expect out here in the middle of the darn city? Cucumbers and raw milk? It's the best I can do!"

So she sat. She didn't give him the first grunt.

For the rest of the day Perfecta sat like a pouty kid in the middle of the pen, eating only when the V-shaped trough, filled with Frog Level–style slop, was pushed under her snout.

That first night, Killie Willie stayed in the pen with Perfecta, keeping a watchful eye. Some darn fool might come along and snatch his prize right from beneath his nose if he didn't take care. The sun went down. Strange shadows moved with freedom through the rubble pile. But none of them came near the new pigpen. None of them seemed to notice that there was a newcomer to the back lot.

That first night was a rough one on Cora New. It was a bit hard to understand as far as Vaughn Brodie and Ollie Gus were concerned, their papa baby-sitting with a shoat from Carolina home.

"The old coot's flipped out," Vaughn Brodie said when Killie Willie took his evening meal out to the sty and shared what little he had with his hog.

"You ain't to talk that way about your papa," Cora New said. "Ain't right."

"Right or not, it's the damn truth. Just flipped out. Zappo like a lightning bug."

"Eat your stew and shut up," said Cora New. She didn't know how to handle her son anymore either. He had gone far beyond her know-how.

Vaughn Brodie shrugged and wandered out to the back lot. He found his papa perched on one of the concrete slabs, watching his shoat sitting there in her pout. Vaughn Brodie leaned over the concrete fencing and spat into the porcelain basin, which had been cooked dry by the afternoon sun.

"You got yourself a pokeful of problem, ain't you, Papa?"

"Huh?"

"Ain't nobody gonna let you keep a pig out here."

"Why not? We ain't bothering nobody."

"Just ain't gonna do it."

Killie Willie had been thinking the same thing himself.

He had wondered about those laws the policeman had told him about. So he asked his son, "Folks got dogs around here, ain't they?"

"Well, sure. Martha Bird's got hers—"

"Fella cross the street says a neighbor of his keeps twenty some-odd rats caged in his bedroom. They got a law against that?"

"Ain't the same thing, you know." Vaughn Brodie had grown unaccustomed to having long talks with his papa, and the one he was having had already gotten out of hand. So he crossed his arms, stoiclike, and with the ultimate authority that comes from being a respected man of the streets he pronounced, "All I can say is they ain't gonna let you keep no pig out here in the middle of this damn trash heap."

Killie Willie sat perched without moving. At first Vaughn Brodie thought his papa was imitating the shoat, sitting in a pout. Or maybe he hadn't heard. Just as Vaughn Brodie was fixing to leave, Killie Willie replied, "Ain't gonna keep me from it, not as long as nobody don't know she's here."

"How you plan on keeping something like a pig a secret?"

"Well." Killie Willie thought for a bit. "I reckon I just won't tell nobody that she's out here. Guess that'll do her."

Vaughn Brodie gave up. He had done his due, and he had better things to waste his time on. So he left his papa sitting there studying what to do with his pet.

Ollie Gus was the next to visit Perfecta in her new home. It took her five minutes to manage the fire escape steps and the layers of rubble that she had to traipse across. She was winded by the time she reached the pen, and she swore as she tried to catch her breath that she would never make the trip again, not if she could help it.

She sat next to her papa, wheezing. After she caught her breath, she snorted and wheezed some more.

"What you want, baby?" Killie Willie finally asked her.

"Mama sent me. You're to come in the house now, she said."

"All right." And he sat.

"Right now!" Ollie Gus didn't have time to waste trying to convince her papa to do what Cora New had told him to do.

"I said all right." He still didn't move.

So papa and daughter sat side by side on the concrete wall. The moon was pretty well set in the sky, and the breeze told of a chilly evening ahead. Ollie Gus liked sitting beside her papa—it made her feel like her papa really was her papa, and she didn't have many chances to feel that way anymore. Sometimes when they were back home in Frog Level, Ollie Gus would sit down beside Killie Willie and pretend she was Cora New and slide one of her hands into his and squeeze it like she had seen her mama do and sometimes if she was lucky he would squeeze back and make her feel like she really belonged, like she really was somebody. Those times had come along rarely in Frog Level. They had not come along at all since moving to the Bottoms. So Ollie Gus took advantage of the concrete wall, the moon, and the quiet of the back lot to slip her hand into her papa's and make like she was somebody really special. Killie Willie patted her hand gently and smiled. Ollie Gus could have crowed, she felt so good.

"Everything all right?" Cora New said. She had slipped up on them, and she stood on a pile of crumbled bricks with her arms akimbo and her chin stuck out like she expected somebody to take a poke at her.

"Jim-dandy," Killie Willie said, "just jim-dandy. The poor thing's homesick, though, I guess. She just sits there."

"Well, can you blame her?" Cora New said, standing there like a true mama. "You put me in a pen like this and I swear to you I wouldn't move around much either."

"What she needs is a man," said Ollie Gus.

"What she needs," said Cora New, "is to be left alone,
for crying out loud. You coming into the house or not,
Killie Willie?"

"In a bit."

"Ollie Gus, you get." Cora New whacked her on her
overgrown rear end as Ollie Gus began the trek back
across the rubble pile.

"Hate damn mamas," Ollie Gus whimpered. But she
loved her damn papa, even though she didn't say so.

"You're not staying out here all night, Killie Willie,"
Cora New ordered. There was as much finality in her
voice as she could put there. But she didn't figure it was
enough.

"I know," he said.

"I mean it, you hear me? You come on into the house."
She trudged her way back to the fire escape.

But Killie Willie didn't move for the rest of that night.
Neither did Perfecta. It was hard to tell just who watched
after whom that first night in the rubble pile.

The next morning Killie Willie climbed through the
kitchen window chilled to his marrow. His eyes were red
from lack of sleep and his stomach growled from having
been mistreated so.

Cora New put her foot down. "They's just so much a
body can stand, Killie Willie," she said, giving a little
hitch to her left shoulder the way she did when she was
really ticked off.

"I know, Cora—"

"It's getting downright embarrassing, you out there
with that hog every waking minute, especially at times
when you should be in bed sleeping—when any decent
and sane person would be in bed sleeping. Fore long folks
in the Bottoms are gonna start in to talking, and then
where we gonna be?"

"I ain't done nothing."

"Lordy," said Cora New. "Talking to you's like talking
to the headboard in yonder."

"Perfecta ain't acting right, Cora New," he said. "She won't do nothing but sit there. She won't budge. What we gonna do?"

"We?" said Cora New. Killie Willie had a mortal fear of his wife's wrath. "I tell you what 'we' gonna do. First, 'we' ain't staying out there with that darn hog again. Second, 'we' are gonna start behaving like normal, for God's sake. You, Killie Willie, you a honest-to-God pig farmer. And here you are behaving like some kind of teenage child with a new toy in his hand and a tick in his rumpus." Her shoulder was hitching noticeably. "Killie Willie, we ain't dirt farmers no more. We put that kind of life behind us and left it in Frog Level, praise the Lord. And I'd hoped you'd put it behind us for good. But you ain't. You gotta bring a truckload of Frog Level dirt up here to us. This ain't no right place, Papa, it just ain't the place for such doings. Killie Willie, are you listening to me?"

"Yes, ma'am."

"Well, you ain't hearing. You're worse than Ollie Gus sometimes. At least she grunts every now and then."

"Maybe it's the water. She ain't taking to the water. Fella once said change an animal's water and you change its entire life. Maybe—"

"Enough!" she almost screamed at him. "I ain't got time for your arguing, Killie Willie. So get that pig out of your head and listen to me. You ain't gonna—" She could see his eyes wander toward the window. "Killie Willie Matt!!"

"Huh?"

"Will you listen to me?"

"Listening, listening."

"You ain't to spend another night out at that pigsty. Now that's gospel." She had her overshoes and coat on ready to leave for work. "I mean it, Mr. Matt. You ain't!" She had the door open ready to leave. "I mean it."

And she was gone.

Killie Willie sat alone. Ollie Gus was already off to her

library. Some guy that she had met there was giving her free drawing lessons, something Killie Willie didn't understand. Vaughn Brodie was sleeping and couldn't be roused until well past noon. For the first time in six months, the first time in what seemed to Killie Willie to have been a year of weeks, he had something to fill his time. He looked forward to what his day held with something akin to good old-fashioned glee.

All day long, Perfecta sat on her haunches, looking like a twenty-eight-pound piggy bank, and no amount of coaxing from Killie Willie could get her off her rear end and moving about. He filled the basin in the corner of the sty with water time and time again. He mixed up the noontime bucket of slop with a can of condensed milk instead of water. But that didn't help. She only nibbled at her food.

That afternoon Killie Willie found a branch from an oak tree, freshly cut and covered with leaf buds. He had no idea where the limb had come from, since there were no oak trees anywhere around; he had found it in the gutter of one of the side streets. He dragged it with him to the back lot, being careful not to lose any of the leaves, and propped it up against one of the concrete slabs. It was just tall enough to give Perfecta a little shade and, he hoped, make it seem like there was a Carolina live oak growing nearby.

But nothing helped. She sat there all day long.

In all his years of pig farming, Killie Willie had never encountered a puzzle like Perfecta. The stubbornness of hogs was well known to him. But normally the cause of the stubbornness was obvious. Like the time that Killie Willie, Montgomery, and another pig farmer name of Primus Smith tried to load up a sow to take her to market. They got the old hog into the loading chute with no trouble at all. But when she caught sight of the truck backed up to the end of the ramp and the men standing all around, that old sow decided she didn't want to go anywhere. Instead she lowered her head and bolted through the chute gate and back to the holding pen. That sow was the definition of stubbornness as far as Killie Willie was concerned. No amount of coaxing could get her anywhere near the chute after she had busted free of it that first time.

Primus Smith wasn't too well known for his mild temper or for his lack of will. He decided that that sow was going into that truck if it killed him. Which it almost did. Killie Willie remembered how Primus Smith first used a rope, hoping to drag the animal into the chute. But she braced her feet, digging in, and the three men could not get her to budge. Then he tried driving her into the chute. They managed to get her up to the gate, but no further. There she balked. Then Primus took his tire rod to her. Montgomery had a hammer, and Killie Willie had a ball bat. They were determined to beat the animal into the truck. That didn't work either. All it did was leave the old sow bloodied beyond recognition and Primus Smith fuming from his inability to control the actions of a stupid pig. Once that sow had made up her mind that she wasn't going to market, there was nothing that could be done to change her. So Primus Smith loaded his hunting rifle and put a bullet between the hog's eyes. They then had to drag the carcass to the slaughtering oak, hoist it up with the singletree, and back the truck to beneath the body. That to Killie Willie had been a stubbornness he could understand. The sow had seen her fate and fought with all her might against it. Killie Willie knew that he would have done the same.

But the pigheadedness of Perfecta, her sitting on her rump in the middle of the sty, defied Killie Willie. He could not understand the cause of her choice. And that was what frustrated him.

That night after eating, Killie Willie and Cora New visited the sty. There the pig sat. She hadn't moved.

"Don't expect she's retarded, do you, Papa?" Cora New said.

"Guess anything's possible." And they stood for a time, Cora New slowly leaning against her man. He slipped his arm around her waist. For Cora New it felt good having her man again.

That night Killie Willie feigned sleeping as he waited for Cora New's body to give its little jerks as she relaxed into a dcep sleep. He slid out of bed, down the fire escape, and made his way as best he could in the dark out to the pen. Perfecta had curled into a tight little ball in the middle of the sty. She looked so forlorn that Killie Willie felt deeply sad. He talked to her that night. He told her of Frog Level, of some of the folks he'd met in the Bottoms, of how he couldn't get work since the deli had been closed, of how much he'd rather be back home than where he was. He admitted to her that they were both alike in that they were both out of place, that they would be happier in a place where folks made their living off the land rather than off the misery of others, a place where folks didn't have to die because they didn't want to give up what they had worked hard to earn. He tried to tell her not to mind the Bottoms too much, that she could learn to live with the strange doings of the place. He told her about how lonesome he got sometimes, especially in the past few months of being on welfare and not having anything to do with his hands. He told her how most folks in the Bottoms found the way he thought and talked sort of silly and even a little bit dumb. He wasn't like most, he told her, and he didn't want to be like any of the others, not a bit. He told her how much he'd like to have a red ripe tomato fresh off the vine, or an ice-cold slice of homegrown watermelon with a heart dripping juice, or a freshly picked peach off one of the trees in the Shealy orchard, or how much he'd like to smell the rich, full-busted smell of a hundred hogs sloshing around in a pasture that had been turned into an ankle-deep bog.

The more he told Perfecta the more homesick he got.

Perfecta didn't seem to listen to any of it. She sighed and put her head into his lap. Pretty soon both of them were sound asleep.

Come morning, Killie Willie sprang awake. He didn't know where he was. It terrified him—he couldn't find his pig, he couldn't find himself.

He focused his eyes. There sat Perfecta, just like the day before: on her rump and not so much as blinking an eye.

Cora New didn't fuss at Killie Willie when he crawled through the kitchen window that morning. In fact, she didn't speak to him at all.

"I sort of fell asleep," he said with a silly little grin on his face.

She flopped a fried egg on a plate and slapped it on the table for him to eat. She put on her coat and overshoes and left for work. Killie Willie was glad that she had not fussed at him like he had expected. He needed the time to gather his thoughts and try to figure things out. He moped around the kitchen, not eating the egg. It was overcooked and cold anyway, his silent punishment for going against his wife's law.

All the talking he'd done the night before had left him lonely for Carolina home. He hadn't thought this much about Frog Level since he'd moved north, and suddenly there in the kitchen of his place, thoughts of the way things had been flooded over him. There was the smell of the fresh spring earth, turned and primed for planting. Get a handful of that good dirt and the odor would hang around for days. There was something magic about such smells. Days on days he would plow with that old Farmall tractor of his, pulling the harrow through the leftover cornstalks and the Johnson grass. Time upon time he would step off the tractor, giving it a chance to cool, and kneel to the turned earth and spit into it, sharing his life and spirit with the land that was his to share. He would prance along with a song in his step as he rotated his way around the plowed land, casting seeds from the sack hung about his middle. He would sing his songs of sowing, filling the Carolina days with a glee that was his to share.

It had always amazed Killie Willie that so soon after the plowing and the singing, the seeds would send up their promise of a healthy crop and fill the land with the fresh green smells of growing things. He would marvel at the likeness of the sprigs of growth, always the same, always predictable. A few times he would have to pull up some mutated plants, but not often. There was something healthy about the land that let it give forth the kind of growth that farmers could count on year after year.

Killie Willie missed it all. But especially he missed the smells of harvest. No smell in the world could match that of hay freshly mowed or corn newly picked or cotton freshly pressed into bales. He loved the hayloft and the corncrib following harvest. Yes, no doubt about it. It was the harvest that caused him his special grief. He remembered it, not willingly, but the memory was not to be removed by time. He had missed the harvest two years running before his move from Carolina home. For two years there had been the smells of spring, of turned earth, of growth and health. But there had been no harvest. One year there had been drought and the growth wilted under the hot Carolina sun. The next there had been more rain than anyone could remember. And then the last year, the one that drove Killie Willie Matt away from the land, the dust had come with the absence of rain. It was as if something on top of the earth wanted to keep the smells of harvest at bay. There had been the promise of work and wealth in Buttermilk Bottoms. Whereas back home there had been no feed for cows or hogs or families. There had been no promise of getting the family through another Carolina winter.

He moped about the kitchen. Had he done right? Or had his brother Montgomery been wise to stay in Frog Level? He didn't know. If only his pig would break loose of her squatting in the middle of her new home. If only she would accept the Bottoms as being a decent place to live. Until she did, Killie Willie wasn't sure he could heal himself of his sickness for his home.

At noontime when he carried out her bucket of slop—decorated on top by a cold fried egg—there she sat, not moving, not wanting to move. He dumped the slop in the trough, put the trough near her nose, said "It's there if you want it," and stormed with his anger showing back to his place, where he sat the rest of the afternoon, feeling cheated by Perfecta's strange behavior.

Perfecta spent her third night in the Bottoms alone.

"Pigheaded, ain't she?" Nate the Wino said on the morning of the fourth day. He had stumbled across the sty the night before and had nearly scared himself out of his stupor. In the morning light, with Killie Willie mixing up the pig's breakfast, Nate sensed the shoat's problem: "Seems homesick to me."

"It'll pass," Killie Willie remarked.

It wasn't every day that Nate found a growing pig biding time in the vacant lot that should rightfully belong only to him. So he hung around. Besides, Ollie Gus was leaning against the concrete fence eating a doughnut and drawing a portrait of Perfecta. Nate had avoided her since that day under the bridge. But now he tried strutting his stuff for her again. "What that pig needs is a man pig," he said, winking at Ollie Gus.

Killie Willie poured the slop into the trough.

"Tell us, missy," Nate said, grinning. "Tell us about how that little piggy needs a mate." His tongue poked through the hole in his teeth and made him look ridiculous.

"Get," Killie Willie said to the stinking bum.

"Yeah, get!" yelled Ollie Gus. "Hate damn bums."

Nate grinned his possum grin. And he wandered off toward the row of cans that lined the street.

Killie Willie waited for Perfecta to move out of her pout, but she would have nothing to do with him or the food he put in front of her.

"She's really sick, Papa," Ollie Gus said, making Killie Willie wince. "You ain't gonna keep no sick pig, are you, Papa? They find this pig out here sick like she is and they gonna lug you off to Bull Street."

"Bull Street's Carolina," Killie Willie said.

"You know what I mean!"

"What we needs," said Killie Willie, "what she needs is some corn shucks and melon rinds. We gotta make her feel at home. What do you say, Ollie Gus?"

"I didn't say nothing," she said, working on her line drawing.

"Gonna have to find her some melon rinds," Killie Willie said. And off he went, stumbling over the rubble in the empty lot.

Ollie Gus drew. After a bit she looked at what she had done and then at the pig sitting like a porcelain vase. She kissed her hand to Perfecta like she had seen Ava Gardner do in her number one favorite movie in all the world. "We'll find you a sweetheart, little piggy. Don't you worry yourself about that."

She smiled to herself. She had never talked to an animal before, not even back home in Frog Level. Oh, she had said a few words to the pot roast or to the bacon as it was being fried in the morning. She knew that the cuts of meat couldn't hear her, but Perfecta—it tickled her to think that maybe the pig sitting in front of her understood what she said.

"Do you?" she whispered. "You understand?"

But Perfecta didn't move.

"Homesick," she said, "homesick and Carolina's a million miles away."

She closed up her drawing pad and made her way back to the second-story tenement that somehow felt akin to Perfecta's sty. Ollie Gus was hungry. Time to eat. And the tenement was Ollie Gus' own personal V-shaped trough.

In Frog Level it was the season of early corn and good juicy honeydew melons. The weather in the Bottoms had been just right for a bumper crop. But search though he did, Killie Willie couldn't find a single used melon rind or discarded corn shuck.

He looked everywhere.

"Melon rinds!" a busboy in a Piccadilly Cafeteria said to him. "Who the hell keeps melon rinds? What the hell do you think garbage disposals are for?"

He called on a deli just up the street from Joe's old place. "You wanna buy?" the fellow said from the other side of the counter. "You wanna buy?" But there were no melon rinds to be bought.

There was a fancy French restaurant on the east side of the park that Killie Willie passed every time he walked to and from midtown. He stopped in there. Only one person in the whole place spoke English, and the English he spoke didn't resemble what Killie Willie used. So they got nowhere. Killie Willie finally had to bow his way out of the French restaurant.

A few blocks over he visited a normal, everyday, all-American-looking cafe that seemed to welcome just about anybody, even a Killie Willie Matt who was living off welfare. "Shit, man," the Puerto Rican waiter said too loud for Killie Willie's sensibilities. "We don't get watermelons in this joint! What do you think we are? Sardi's?"

Killie Willie didn't give up, however. It wasn't in his nature to give in to what some might call adversity. Instead he continued his search for melon rinds and corn shucks.

If he had been home in Frog Level, he would have known where to go to find them. But he wasn't home.

Sometime midmorning of the fourth day of Perfecta's pout, it rained. It wasn't much to speak of, just a drizzle. But it was a nice gentle rain that did a job on Perfecta and her mood.

With the first few drops from the clouds, her head came up. She sniffed. She grunted. Soon the gentle rain swarmed over her. And it washed the stink of freight off her bristled back.

Nobody was there to see it, but her instincts got the better of her. The ground was softened just a bit by the rain, and there were treasures to be found under the earth. She waddled to the buried basin that held a little water and rooted. She dug her snout into the ground and turned the earth much like Killie Willie would have done with his tiller. The idea of rooting caught on in her head. Even after the rain stopped and the sun came out to dry things, she continued the fun of her rooting. And oh, the treasures that pig found!

Killie Willie came home that night, slipping in from the hall like a worn-out shoe. His search for corn shucks and melon rinds had been more than he had thought it could be.

"You gonna feed that hog of yours, Killie Willie?" said Cora New.

"What for? She ain't gonna eat none of it."

"Maybe not," she said, "then again, maybe she will."

Cora New realized something he didn't, Killie Willie could see that. For some reason it scared him. He knew how much his wife hated his new pet. He didn't know what could have happened, he hadn't been away from Perfecta for so long since she had come into his life.

"What's the matter with her?"

"Oh, nothing." Cora New sort of winked. It was a dead giveaway for her when she was trying to keep a secret.

But Killie Willie didn't wait for her. He raced like he hadn't done a bit of walking all day down the fire escape and out to the pigsty. And what he saw did his heart more good than if he'd seen the Lord himself making his way to earth for the Second Coming. There was Perfecta, coated with mud and smelling for the first time like an honest-to-goodness Frog Level hog. She was rolling with delight in a small mound of mud. If a pig could smile, Perfecta was smiling.

"Gee-golly" was all Killie Willie could say. He said it over and over. "Gee-golly . . . Gee-golly . . ."

The first treasure that Perfecta unearthed in her rooting was a broken whiskey bottle. She flipped it over, and it nicked her snout. A spot of blood oozed out one of her nostrils. She didn't seem to feel it. And Killie Willie didn't mind. To him that broken bottle and speck of blood were pure delights. And he was more determined than ever to find his beautiful prize Hampshire shoat those promised corn shucks and melon rinds.

Killie Willie turned to scrounging through garbage cans. Nate the Wino accused him of horning in on his trade until he found out what Killie Willie was looking for. Then Nate turned a hand to help. But he didn't have much hope of Killie Willie finding any melon rinds. Every bum in town's looking for melon rinds, Nate told him, for himself.

Then one afternoon Killie Willie found his first melon of the season: a huge eighteen-pound Kleckley's Sweet. It was on the fruit shelf in Michael Pogo's grocery store.

"How much?" Killie Willie asked.

"Five dollars," Michael Pogo said.

"Give you three."

"Make it four."

And Killie Willie brought home a store-bought melon.

"Lord, looky here!" Ollie Gus squealed.

"I done scrounged my last garbage can, Cora New," said Killie Willie. "I ain't Nate the Wino and I ain't gonna dig my way through trash heaps for corn shucks and watermelon rinds."

He thumped the melon down in the middle of the kitchen table, drawing Vaughn Brodie's glazed stare.

Vaughn Brodie laughed. "Now that's kinky!" he said, rolling the melon about on the table.

"Killie Willie," said Cora New, "have you lost your mind? What do you mean, bringing a thing like that home with you?"

"First melon of the season," he said. He thumped it with his middle finger and scratched the rind with his thumb. "Good melon," he said.

"Gimme some!" screamed Ollie Gus.

"Ten bucks." Vaughn Brodie was weighing the melon in his hands. "That's a ten-buck melon if it's a dime. Where'd you get this ten-buck melon, Papa? Steal it?" And he giggled like an eleven-year-old.

"It's for Perfecta," Killie Willie said.

"I want melon!" Ollie Gus squalled.

"Killie Willie, you ain't about to feed that hog no whole watermelon!" said Cora New, her shoulder starting to hitch.

"Ain't a hog. Just a shoat."

"She's a stinker, that's what she is." Vaughn Brodie giggled.

"Don't care what you call her," Cora New said. "You ain't feeding no pig no watermelon and that's all there is to it." Cora New's law had been laid.

"If you say so, Mama." And Killie Willie got a butcher knife from one of the kitchen drawers.

"Gonna have me some good stuff." Ollie Gus watered at the mouth. Killie Willie sliced the melon into four equal pieces. Ollie Gus couldn't wait. She reached both hands into the melon, grabbing its red, sweet, juicy heart. The juice oozed down her chin and onto her dress, but she didn't care.

Killie Willie offered a piece to Vaughn Brodie, but he refused it, mumbling to himself about embarrassments and damn pig farmers. He left. He wanted no part of what was happening to his people in the Bottoms.

Cora New didn't care for any watermelon either. "Too early in the season," she said.

Killie Willie tasted it. He spat the pulp into the kitchen sink. "Ain't no Kleckley's Sweet," he said. "Tastes like grit."

But Ollie Gus loved it, even though it was a hothouse melon with hothouse taste. She ate her fill, three-fourths of the whole. And what was left Perfecta got.

The pig relished every morsel. And Killie Willie relished it along with her. He watched his happy shoat as she nosed every speck of red from the green rind and then chased the residue around and around her sty. After a bit, she stopped long enough to look up at her master. Killie Willie and Perfecta caught each other's gaze. She seemed to say "thank you" with her jet black eyes. She grunted, a short spurt of sound that came from deep inside her chest.

"You're welcome," said Killie Willie Matt.

The kids of the neighborhood discovered Perfecta in her jury-rigged shebang out back, and none of them was sure what she was.

"I ain't asking him," a kid named Gregalee said to all. The others were poking at him and calling him names, but he wasn't about to ask that crazy man from a place called Frog Level what it was he had in the rubble pile.

"Well, I don't give a shit," the biggest of the bunch, a kid named Jimmy, said.

"Mo'll ask him, won't you, Mo?"

Mo shook his head. That was all Mo ever needed, that and his bright grin.

So it was decided: nobody was going to ask Killie Willie what the animal was. They left it at that.

Except Billo. He would ask Killie Willie. Hadn't he helped build the pen? Besides if Billo, the kid on the outs, found out what it was for the rest, maybe the gang would accept him. Well, it was worth a shot, to Billo's way of thinking.

"Damn thing likes mud," Billo said to Killie Willie as they leaned against the concrete fence, watching Perfecta chase her last remaining melon rind across the sty.

"Guess so," said Killie Willie.

Perfecta tossed the rind away from her and then pounced on it, splashing mud as high as Billo's elbows.

"Getting sassy, ain't she?" Killie Willie said.

"Guess so. What is it you call that thing?"

"You don't know?"

"We got this bet, you see. I know what it is, I just needs to make sure. For the bet."

"Uh-huh." Killie Willie had a glint in his eye, one of pride and mischief. "Let me tell you, Billo. That there is a purebred one hundred percent Hampshire gilt that's gonna breed me and the rest of the Bottoms a whole passel of ham, bacon, and chitlins." His mouth watered at the thought of stuffed and roasted chitterlings. Then he looked down into the deep eyes of his pig and felt ashamed of himself.

"What's chitlins?" Billo wanted to know.

"Boy, you downright dumb about some things, ain't you? Chitlins is battered and deep-fried rat turds served with sour cream and chives." Billo's eyes almost popped, and Killie Willie couldn't help his belly laugh.

"You messing with me, man—"

"Okay, tell you what," Killie Willie said. "Chitlins is pig entrails, fried crisp and sweet."

"Entrails?"

"Yeah, you know, the guts." Killie Willie stretched; the thought of the delicious treat was making him hungry. "Down home in Carolina, there's this place called Salley. Salley, South Carolina. And every summer they have this sort of festival, the Chitlin Strut. They must fry up to ten tons of pig guts in one day. You talk about a good time, boy—that's it. Ain't nothing in this world quite like the good ol down-home Chitlin Strut of Salley, South Carolina." Killie Willie was getting lost inside his memory. "You can smell them chitlins all the way to Orangeburg. Just floating up there in the air . . ."

"I ain't gotta stay round here to be shit on, man," Billo said. "Ain't nobody I knows eats guts—"

"Well, then, you ain't lived, have you?"

"Don't nobody know how to eat down there in this Carolina place you're always talking of?"

"Best eating in the world," Killie Willie said.

"You got many of those animals down there?" Billo asked, pointing at Perfecta.

"That's a pig, Billo," Killie Willie said. "A pig. Ain't you ever heard of pigs before?"

"Sure, I ain't stupid. She's a pig." Billo stared at the animal for a bit. "But she don't look much like the pigs they have on the TV."

"Ain't never seen a pig on the TV," Killie Willie said.

"You ain't never watched the Muppets?"

"What's a Muppet?" Killie Willie asked.

With that, Billo guffawed, too hard and too long. He pointed a wagging finger at Killie Willie and sneered. "You the stupid one," Billo said. "Miss Piggy? You ain't never heard of Miss Piggy?" And he went into a brief imitation of Miss Piggy's quest for Kermit the Frog.

"Must be some kind of farming show," Killie Willie said.

"Shoot," Billo said. Perfecta tossed the melon rind again.

"She likes her games, that's for sure," Killie Willie said. "You really never seen a living pig before?"

Billo shook his head. "Where you expect me to see a thing like that? All they got in the zoo is lions and tigers. You got a tiger you bringing in?"

They stood shoulder to shoulder, watching the pig play her game with the melon rind. "That all it know how to do?" Billo asked. Killie Willie just shrugged. "Well, what's the thing good for? Can't bark. Too slow to catch many rats. What's it for?"

"Well," Killie Willie said. "You like bacon?"

"Course."

"Well, that there is bacon on the hoof, Carolina-style. Uncooked, of course."

"Shoot," Billo said. "You shitting me, man."

"Truth, swear to God."

"Ain't no such thing as bacon on the hoof. You the craziest old coot."

"Well, where do you think bacon comes from then?"

"The grocery store." When Killie Willie laughed, Billo changed his source. "From cows, that's where bacon comes from: cows."

"Nope." Killie Willie pointed. "That there's the only source you got for bacon. I ought to know. I've raised enough in my day."

Billo thought for a bit. "Bacon, huh?"

"And ham."

With that, Billo was off to tell all the kids in the neighborhood about bacon and ham on the hoof. He didn't expect any of them to believe him, but it was worth a try. Maybe his choice bit of news would be all it took for the guys to like him. He raced across the rubble pile as best he could.

"And chitlins!" Killie Willie called after him. "Don't forget the chitlins! And pickled pigs' feet!!" He laughed hard at the way Billo scooted. He laughed so hard that tears came to his eyes and he had to brush them away. Perfecta gazed up at him and tried to talk, making contented little sounds. She flipped the mud-coated melon rind at him and rolled lazily in the mud. "Chitlin Strut," he said to himself, remembering. And the memory made him sad even as his pig flirted with him. "Shoot," he said, "too long . . . too darn long ago . . ."

And he left Perfecta to strut her stuff alone.

"You as sick in the head as my dodo sister, Billo," said Jimmy, the big kid with the flat nose from an early life run-in with a sidewalk following a two-story free-fall.

"Truth, swear to God," Billo said. But he could see it was no good. If Jimmy didn't believe him, none of the others would. He turned to his last resort. "Ain't I right, Mo?"

Mo grinned and shook his head. The rest jeered.

"That what that old man told you?" Gregalee said. Gregalee was the feisty one, always ready for a round or two. "If that's what that old man told you, Billo, he fulla shit, man," he said.

"Billo the one fulla shit," said Jimmy. "Go get your bat, Gregalee, let's play us some ball."

"He also said they have them a Chitlin Strut back down where he comes from," Billo said.

That stopped the kids. What's a Chitlin Strut, they wanted to know. And when Billo told them that it was something like a big fish fry, only they use the guts from pigs instead of fish, all the guys burst their sides with laughter.

"That's the biggest damn lie I've ever heard tell of," said Yul, the kid who was as bald as his papa. And Gregalee poked Billo's belly, saying, "You gonna strut your chitlins for us, mister?" And all laughed the harder.

"I ain't lying," Billo almost begged. "That's what he told me."

Mo didn't laugh. He looked about him at the full sets of teeth making fool's-meat out of Billo.

"Them folks down south done all gone queer," Jimmy said amid the taunts aimed at Billo's head. "They eat pig guts down south. Ain't that the cat's pussy tail?"

"I knew there was something a-matter with them Matts," Gregalee said. "Every one of them is done gone all queer. Same as poor old Billo!"

"Billo a queer," Yul chimed in.

Billo wasn't in the mood to take that off Yul, and since they were almost the same size, Billo gave him a hefty push. And Yul pushed back. The third push was being readied when a new voice was heard, one that the rest of the kids hadn't heard much from. It was soft and high-pitched, and it came from the silent one, Mo the mute.

"I had me some chitlins once," Mo said.

The whole bunch was dumbstruck. Jimmy couldn't believe his ears. Mo had spoken! The first time in nobody knew how long. Jimmy had protected little Mo every day of his life, and the boy had said maybe five sentences in all that time. So Jimmy, forgetting poor Billo, who was on the edge of getting his ears raised, stepped over to Mo and put a paternal hand on the kid's shoulder.

"You did?" Jimmy said.

Mo nodded.

"When?"

Mo shrugged.

"What'd they taste like?"

"Real good," Mo said and flashed his broad grin.

"They really made from pig guts?"

Mo nodded.

"You ain't shitting us, are you, Mo?"

Mo shook his head as hard as he knew how.

"You see?" Billo yelled out. "I told you, didn't I?" And he took his turn to taunt the others, too loud and too long.

"If Mo says it's true, then it must be true," Jimmy pronounced. The rest agreed.

And the wad of kids started off down the street.

"You guys gonna play some streetball?" Billo called after them. They all continued walking. "How about letting me play? Hey, fellas, how about me playing with you?"

They walked on. Billo, in spite of his information and in spite of being right, was still the kid on the outs.

Word spread.

There was a pig in the back lot.

Perfecta wasn't meant to be a secret. Killie Willie wasn't trying to hide her. He just didn't want folks around pestering her and causing her mental turmoil. He knew how the folks in the Bottoms were. And he knew that sightseers would be a real problem once word was out.

But Killie Willie was surprised. Most folks didn't care that there was a newcomer in the neighborhood. A hog wasn't unique enough to cause much concern. Folks knew there were stranger things than pigs living in the Bottoms. Killie Willie had heard of some weird pets hanging around the neighborhood. He didn't believe all he heard, but there was always room for possibility. A woman two tenements down from the Matts had had five boa constrictors in her one-room flat. She had become sick and tired of being broken in on. Once word was out that she had those snakes roaming loose in her place, there wasn't a soul in all the Bottoms who had the nerve to pay her a visit. Then one day, so it is told, one of the boas escaped, crawled down one of the heat vents, and disappeared. No one found the thing, but the rat population in the tenement took a nose dive for about five months.

Then there were the rumors that some crazy bum had dug a huge hole in the basement of a dilapidated tenement and kept it filled with water. Some folks claimed that he grew the biggest crocodiles outside Florida right there in the middle of the Bottoms. One day the bum disappeared, and some swear even today that he was eaten by one of his pets.

There were even tales of a drunk who became confused one night with all the pink elephants running loose in his head and visited the zoo down in the park. It's hard to believe, but some folks claim that the drunk stole a baby elephant out of the zoo and kept it on the roof of one of the tenements until it died—pecked to death by all the pigeons.

So Perfecta's living out back didn't draw much attention to her or to Killie Willie Matt. Still, there were a few folks who visited the sty for the sight, folks like Martha Bird Blotchley and Michael Pogo and Killie Willie's number one bother, Nate the Wino.

"What are you gonna do with that thing?" Nate asked one afternoon as Perfecta ate her bucket of slop. He had come into the habit of hanging around the sty when he was sober, which, thank the Lord, wasn't all that often. It was at the sty that he felt sure he would run into Ollie Gus again. Nate wasn't the kind to give up on any woman without at least six or seven tries.

"Raise her up," Killie Willie said.

"What then?" Nate was so sober he was hungry. He seemed to be licking his chops as he gazed at the pig.

"Just gonna keep right on raising her up."

"You gonna slaughter her?" Nate wiped his mouth with his dirty sleeve.

Killie Willie hadn't really thought that far ahead. Somehow he didn't think that such a conversation should be carried on in the hearing of the growing pig.

"You ever slaughtered a hog?" Nate asked.

"Well, sure."

"How do you go about it?"

"Simple enough," Killie Willie said, "if you know what you're doing." And his head was filled with images of Slaughter Day down home in Frog Level. He didn't want to talk about such things, not to the likes of Nate the Wino.

"Couple of fellas was talking the other day," Nate said, "down near Junkie's Corner, talking about the killing that took place a few nights ago over near the park. They said the fella'd been stuck and bled like a pig. Bled like a stuck pig. What's that mean, Killie Willie?" Nate was more sober than Killie Willie had ever seen. For some reason he liked Nate more when he was drunk—he seemed less dangerous then. So he merely shrugged in answer to Nate's question.

But that didn't stop Nate from asking, "You ever stuck a pig, Killie Willie?"

"Guess so," he said. The images of the fall slaughter were growing too strong in his head for him to deny. And the thought of his pig, Perfecta, being stuck and strung up on Slaughter Day gave him reason to pause. Then he told Nate all about that special day down home in Carolina.

"Slaughter Day," he said, "usually comes the Saturday after the first frost. Folks from all over truck in their finest boar and park out under one of the biggest live oak trees I've ever seen, and then everybody pitches in and helps everybody else. Something of a party, if you know what I mean. Biggest party day in Frog Level excepting the Fourth of July.

"Well, that live oak tree is in the barnyard of old Captain J. W. Stafford, but before that it was in the keeping of the Reverend Claude Bedenbaugh. Preacher Bedenbaugh started Slaughter Day way back when and as far as I know there'll be Slaughter Day come again this year. I took one of my prize herd every year as long as I had me some hogs. But it had to be a full-grown boar fitten for slaughter. You couldn't truck in no scrawny little thing. Why, you'd be the laughingstock of the entire county if you came in with a suckling shoat."

"How do you kill the hog? Pigsticker?"

"Shoot. You gonna come at a seven hundred–pound boar with teeth three inches long and him knowing exactly what you've got in mind and all you've got in your hand is a puny little old pigsticker? You lose a hand and maybe an arm if you try that. First, you hit the hog square between the eyes with a custom-made sledge-hammer; there's this fella name of Gromarisey who was the expert with the hammer. He knew just where to hit and with just the right force. I mean, you hit the boar too hard and you crack his skull like an egg and ruin the brains. You have to hit him just right. I can see him now, old Gromarisey with his hammer. It'd come down swift and clean on the hog's front snout, taking the thing down to his knees, stunned, you know. And then this fella name of Primus Smith would be in there on top of the hog quicker than spit and he's the one with the pigsticker. In'd go the blade, quick as a wink. Old Primus Smith knew what he was about. He never missed. In'd go the blade and a river of blood would flow. There ain't nothing that bleeds like a pig stuck with Primus Smith's steel blade.

"Only you don't let the blood just spill out, you know. For one thing, the Captain don't like for his barnyard to be all littered with hog blood come end of day. I mean, you might butcher upward of twenty hogs in one afternoon. That's a mountain of blood, if you ask me. For another, the stuff's too useful to let go to waste. There's a kid—we call him the Bucket Boy—whose job it is to hang around Primus Smith with his five-gallon-aught tub and catch the flow. You take the blood home, boil it, and you've got one of the best treats you can come up with. Blood soup. That is, unless you're Primus Smith. Primus always claims the first blood bucket of the day. To my way of thinking, he only does it for show—Primus is the kind who wants to impress the womenfolks, being the ugliest darn fool I ever saw. Anyway, Primus Smith claims the first bucket of drawn blood and he drinks it right there on the spot like it was water or something. Gulps it down. Oh, just for show, he lets some of it ooze out the sides of his mouth and drip down his overall front and then he struts around with his chest puffed out like a bantam cock. I never had much use for the likes of Primus Smith. But I have to give it to him: he knows how to handle a pigsticker."

"Sounds like a messy business."

"Ain't, though. Everybody knows exactly what to do and how to do it. Hanging down from a limb of the oak tree's a heavy-duty rope and chain that's hooked to a windlass that's so big it takes two grown men to manage. At the end of the chain's a singletree, oh, about three feet long, made of wood, colored dark gray by all the smoke, and at each end of the singletree's a hook. What you do, you see, once the pig's stuck and ain't in no mood to give you a kick, you slice its back legs here"—and he demonstrated by showing Nate the section of his lower leg near the ankle—"between the tendon and the bone. Then you slip one of those hooks in the slit and with two men on the windlass, the pig—it's still bleeding, you know—is hoisted off the ground and left hanging, ears dangling and the last of the blood dripping in the Bucket Boy's tub.

"There are three fires all going. They're built far enough away from the oak to keep from doing it any damage, but close enough to keep from having to lug the hot water too far. Then there're these three-legged caldrons, each filled with water. All day long, these caldrons are kept full of boiling water. It's the job of the younger kids to keep the well water coming. Well, when a hog gets the knife, one of the caldrons is lugged to the singletree and left to cool a mite. Then when the carcass is high enough off the ground to clear the top of this huge oil barrel and the barrel is in place, the hog's lowered into the barrel headfirst."

"How come?"

"Hold your horses, I'll tell you. Then the Test Lady comes along. Her job's to test the water in the caldron. If she can brush her finger across the top of the water without jerking her hand away, the water's ready. The water can't be too hot, you see, or too cold. It has to be just right, otherwise you can cause all sorts of problems in the scraping. So when the Test Lady says the water is right, the whole caldron is poured into the barrel over the carcass. Oh, steam and hot water go every which way. That's what you call a baptism. A hog is truly ready for the Sunday table when it's been baptized.

"Just as soon as the water starts pouring, the men set in with the scraping, and the water runs everywhere, full of hog hair, lice, hide, blood. You can't keep the hog in the water too long without the bristles starting to set. So after a bit, the men on the windlass have to hoist away, pulling the carcass out of the barrel. Once the barrel is clear the water is dumped, the barrel's rolled out of the way, and the caldron's lugged back to the fire and refilled with water.

"Even as the hog comes out of the barrel, there we all are, scraping away like crazy. Bristles and hide and everything else fly all over. And all that water from the barrel runs down the hill and by the end of Slaughter Day, Hog Lake's a perfect place for kids to splash and cool themselves. You can't lose time in the scraping, though—it's hard work and you've got to do it fast and clean. Some folks scrape with knives, others with a large piece of slate, honed just perfect for the job. Me, I always used a handleless garden hoe. It's the best for work on the pig's back and underbelly. The knife's best for the tighter places. While we're still scraping, off come the hog's ears and tail. Oh, that hog's tail is something of a prize. It's usually given to one of the kids too young to help. By the end of the day each little kid has himself a pig's tail, and they wear those things as Slaughter Day bracelets for weeks until their mamas throw em away.

"With the scraping done and the hog still up in the air the way it was, we'd start in on the butchering. First of all the head comes off. It's dumped into a tub. Then we slice open the belly and out fall the innards. They're dumped in a tub too."

"Why's that?"

"They's good eating in pig brains and tongue and such things."

"But the innards?"

"I'll tell you about that in a minute. Well, the hog is still hanging there from the singletree, balanced. Then the fellow who owns the hog comes in with the saw. It has to be the owner—it's a matter of pride. He has to cut the animal exactly in half so that the singletree—when it's left hanging with half a hog hooked at each end—hangs balanced, perfectly balanced. It ain't and there's no end to the ribbing that the fellow gets. Once the sawing's done, the two halves are lowered into the back of the owner's truck. The halves are covered with pieces of canvas, and one of the kids sits on the tailgate as a sort of guard against dogs and cats. Then the whole thing's repeated. Oh, each hog takes all of thirty minutes unless somebody's trucked in a hog that's oversized. All day long, we hammer, stick, boil, scrape, and split those carcasses apart. And the womenfolks work on the innards, doing they darnedest to keep pace. Then off to one side there's this one other fire, this one covered with a grate, and on that grate is a pot of boiling water for coffee and tea. When the last pig of the day's taking its licks, a bushel tub worth of chitlins is spread over that grate and fried. That smell is the sweetest smell on earth, I swear.

And when that smell starts coming, we start working harder. There's that promise of chitlins once the work is done."

"Chitlins?"

"Something real special, let me tell you. But you got to look out you don't find yourself a piece of corn!" And he laughed.

"Don't understand," Nate said.

"Didn't figure you would." Killie Willie missed such things as Slaughter Day. He longed for the company of folks like himself, men who knew what he knew and could talk about it and share the fun of it all. He wished in his heart (though he'd never speak of it) that he could go back home, just for a visit, stick his fingers in the dirt, smell the glory of the land. But he never let on to anybody about such things. He didn't even tell Perfecta of his longing. He didn't feel that he had to.

Nate took an unmarked bottle of liquor from his hip pocket, unscrewed the top, and drank. He smacked his lips and licked the rim of the bottle. "Want some?" he offered, holding the bottle out to Killie Willie.

"Got no need for that stuff, thank you," he said. "What's it you got there anyway?"

"This and that." Nate's eyes showed the effect of his pull. "I pour everything I can find into this, shake it up some, and there it is. Mostly beer. Hate beer myself, but enough liquor to give it some punch. Sure?" he offered a second time.

"Sure."

"Well, when you gonna learn me about pig farming?"

"Ain't," said Killie Willie, and that was the final word as far as he was concerned.

"Well, now, that ain't all that neighborly." Nate took a second pull from his bottle and burped like a baby. "Goes down even. Just trying to be a neighbor, Killie Willie."

"Why don't you go be a neighbor someplace else?"

"Fraid I'll stick your pig, ain't you?" Nate said, a wicked-looking grin on his face. Killie Willie hated that toothless smile of Nate's. Gave him the shivers. But he said nothing. The wino has the evil in him, he thought, and it's all coming out of that bottle of his. He just didn't want Nate around, that was all.

"Well," Nate said, getting a little wobbly in his knees, "I just might do it, give me half a chance. Yes, sir, I get hungry sometimes for some good honest-to-God fresh meat . . ." He giggled as he wandered off across the rubble pile toward the street.

It was a good world, Killie Willie figured. And why it had to be populated with the likes of Nate the Wino he couldn't understand.

The sky was hanging heavy with a needed rain. A good early spring shower. There was nothing better for the world than a clean washing every so often. Besides, Perfecta loved rain. Nothing whatsoever better in all the world.

Martha Bird Blotchley hung around Perfecta's sty too.

Martha Bird Blotchley was a crowd in herself, Killie Willie told Cora New. Get Martha Bird out to the sty and there wasn't room for much of anybody else, he said.

From her third-floor tenement window, Martha Bird had a clear view of all that took place out back. She was one for knowing all comings and goings, even those revolving around the pig out in the rubble pile.

Martha Bird visited out back as often as she could. She loved the way the shoat could eat. She identified with that. It was something that she and Perfecta had in common. And the way that all the eating seemed to edge its way to fresh fat. That was another thing the two had in common. Martha Bird didn't talk to anybody about it, but she found the way that Perfecta ate her slop to be exciting. She wished deep inside her that she too could grapple with her food the way that hog did. Just get in there on all fours and wolf the slop down, quick and easy. Martha Bird slobbered all over herself every time she watched the pig enjoy a meal.

She had another reason for visiting out back. His name was Michael Pogo.

Even with Cora New's advice that she would be better off letting go of her fascination with Michael Pogo, that there was no hope of her getting him, Martha Bird continued. Cora New tried in vain to get Martha Bird to recognize that Michael Pogo was the ugliest man she'd ever set eyes on. His face, she said in her prejudiced way, was that of a boxer dog. Vaughn Brodie once remarked that if Michael Pogo should go downtown on New Year's Eve, he'd be arrested for wearing a mask! Ollie Gus smacked Vaughn Brodie for that remark, because she too, like Martha Bird, found much in Michael Pogo to admire.

Maybe their attraction for the man was due to the fact that he stocked so much good food in his grocery store. Another was the man's quiet shyness. Martha Bird liked quiet in a man. As long as he was quiet, it gave her more time to talk. And how the woman could fill an ear! She also admired a man who could make his way in the world without making a big to-do about it.

Another thing about Michael Pogo was that he had never been married. He wasn't sullied (that was her way of putting it). No woman had had a chance to get to the man and teach him a set of bad habits. That was Martha Bird's ambition in life: to sully the man herself.

Michael Pogo visited with Perfecta every chance he got, that being whenever Killie Willie or no one else was about. He would slip out to the sty with a couple of peck baskets full of rotting vegetables from his store, feed them to the pig—which delighted Perfecta no end—and then slip away, trying his best not to be noticed. Of course, Martha Bird from her third-floor window noticed it all. And her heart, in her words, would melt every time she saw the man out back with his baskets of rotting veggies.

So that was what drew Martha Bird to Perfecta's sty: to tell the hog of her deep, deep love for Michael Pogo and to be around when he made one of his quiet visits. Perfecta made a good listener. She would stand in the middle of the sty and stare up at her secret admirer and listen with rapt attention. Perfecta knew that when Martha Bird showed up she would get a feeding of goodies. Martha Bird always brought something to eat with her, usually more than enough to share, things like popcorn or Cracker Jacks or a bunch of grapes or maybe a candy bar or two. She would lean against the concrete fencing, talk to Perfecta, and feed her bits of whatever she brought with her.

It seemed that Martha Bird's visits became more and more common, so much so that Killie Willie couldn't hold his peace.

"I don't like the way that woman hangs around Perfecta," he told Cora New one night.

"How come?"

"I don't know," he said. "She's your friend, I know that, but it just don't seem healthy to me, that sow of a woman slobbering all over herself over a growing hog." Killie Willie shuddered when he told of it. "Makes me nervous, having a woman like that watching every bite that Perfecta eats."

"Martha Bird Blotchley wouldn't hurt a fly," said Cora New.

"It ain't flies I'm worried about," said Killie Willie.

"Besides, it's Michael Pogo that Martha Bird's really interested in."

"What's that got to do with Perfecta?" he wanted to know.

"Michael Pogo dearly loves all animals. That's why he refuses to stock fresh meats."

"So?"

"Well, think about it, Killie Willie. Michael Pogo's bound to come calling on Perfecta and Martha Bird's just hanging around until he comes."

"Shoot!" Killie Willie said. "She'll wait until Judgment Day before she gets a decent shot at that man."

Cora New supposed that Killie Willie was right.

But to Killie Willie that meant that he had to put up with Martha Bird Blotchley hanging around his pigsty day in and day out for the rest of Perfecta's natural life. That to him was a fate far worse than death. He had to do something. He couldn't figure out what.

One morning Martha Bird was leaning over the concrete fence, dropping bits of stale popcorn to Perfecta as Killie Willie mixed up a bucket of slop.

"You ain't feeding that animal enough," Martha Bird said, munching on popcorn and spitting kernels into the sty.

Killie Willie tried to ignore her.

"That pig looks sort of peaked to me," she said.

It was getting harder to ignore her. Nobody was to find fault with his prize Hampshire shoat.

"Looks puny about the eyes," said Martha Bird. "Hmmmm. Must be the runt."

"What's that?"

"I said your piggy's obviously the runt of the litter."

Killie Willie stood fuming. He didn't have to take that, not off one of the fattest human beings he'd ever known. But still he didn't speak his mind.

"No need getting angry with me over a thing like that. I mean, you can't help that you got stuck with the runt. And it sure ain't her fault, poor thing."

Enough was enough. Killie Willie stormed across the rubble pile as he heard Martha Bird call out a final, "You ought to feed this hog more! Give her a chance to be somebody!!"

He rummaged under Ollie Gus' cot. There he found what he was looking for: a felt-tipped pen and a good-sized piece of cardboard. It was one of the few things that Ollie Gus hadn't drawn on. Killie Willie took the materials with him out the front, down the street, and into Michael Pogo's store.

"Here," he said to the grocer.

Michael Pogo looked up at him, confused.

"Write me something," Killie Willie said. "Big letters too. I want everybody to be able to read what I want you to write."

"All right," said Michael Pogo.

And Killie Willie dictated his message.

Once he had his laying-down-the-law sign written out, he took it to the pigsty, found a stick with a sharpened end to it, tacked the sign on, and rammed the stick into the hard-packed ground with a brick.

The sign stayed in place for the rest of that week and would have been up longer if Jimmy and Gregalee and the others hadn't used it for target practice. While it was up and even after, the sign did its job. It read: "No Trespassing—That Means You, Martha Bird Blotchley!"

When Martha Bird saw it, her feelings were so deeply hurt that she locked herself inside her room with her little lapdog and refused to come out for three days. (She gave up her pout when she ran out of food.)

Cora New scolded Killie Willie for doing such a thing to a sensitive woman like Martha Bird. But his conscience was clear. He had done what he had to do. Martha Bird had pushed him to it. When Cora New went calling on Martha Bird, the woman refused to let her in, telling her to go away and leave her alone since she was special enough for the whole world not to like.

Martha Bird watched from her third-floor window and cursed Killie Willie Matt. Michael Pogo crossed the rubble pile to the sty and dumped his baskets of rotting vegetables, and she hadn't been free to be there to greet him and thank him for his good-heartedness. Once after dark, she crept out to the sty and talked quietly to Perfecta. It made her feel better. But she couldn't stay long. She had no idea when Killie Willie might slip out back to check on his hog.

After a week of pouting and after she saw what the kids had done to her name with their target practice, she walked out to the sty, tore the sign down, and burned it. She made a vow to herself that she would stay as far away from Killie Willie Matt as she could. But her vow didn't apply to his pig. She couldn't deny herself the pleasure she got from her heart-to-heart chats with her new friend. Nobody listened to her the way Perfecta did. So once or twice a week, every chance she got, Martha Bird slipped out to the rubble pile and hand-fed the gilt. She took Perfecta such things as brussels sprouts or fresh ears of corn or large ripe cantaloupes. Martha Bird was Perfecta's very best secret friend.

What Perfecta didn't know was that Martha Bird, in order to feed her corn or cantaloupe, had to buy the produce from none other than the grocer Michael Pogo. He remained the number one man in Martha Bird's life, only he didn't know it. Oh, if only he knew . . .

One night a late spring storm hit the Bottoms.

Killie Willie was shaken from his sleep by a blast of thunder that rattled the springs of his bed.

"Where you going?" Cora New asked as he slipped on his work britches.

He couldn't tell her. She would keep him inside. That was Cora New's way. So he said, "Hungry."

"Your pig's all right," she said, turning over and pulling the bedding under her chin. The storm was putting a slight chill in the air.

"We don't know that."

"Come back to bed, Killie Willie. You'll get sopping if you go out in this."

He sat on the edge of the bed. He could see out the

second-story window. The wind was whipping the rain as it fell by the tubful so that the spray was nearly parallel to the earth. A few drops oozed through the cracks in the windowsill and ran down the inside of the wall. Killie Willie itched to be outside tending to his shoat.

"Remember that time back home?" he said.

"I remember."

"Same kind of storm as this."

She remembered all too well. So did Killie Willie. It had been one of those things that no human could prevent. There was no way to predict how such a thing could happen, and once done there was no call to bemoan it. Seven out of eight in one litter and all nine in the other— the future of the Matt pig farm had been nearly wiped out by a storm such as the one raging. In Killie Willie's memory, it wasn't all that long ago.

"Perfecta's over half-grown," Cora New said. "There's no need to worry about her."

"Maybe so," he said, not believing his own words. Try as he might, he couldn't go back to bed, not as long as the storm flashed and flooded outside.

Cora New stretched her arms to the headboard of the bed and pulled herself awake. "Guess I can't sleep neither." And she went into the kitchen, where Killie Willie could hear her putting a pot of coffee on the stove. He didn't want any coffee. There wasn't anything that he wanted except to know that his hog was weathering the storm. It couldn't last long, he told himself, knowing that a rain with such large drops was usually short-lived. The night was too much like the one he had suffered through back home in Frog Level . . .

Losing sixteen little pigs in one night was more than enough to shut down a small-time pig farmer like Killie Willie Matt. The event had come pretty near to cleaning him out, but he had been determined not to let the elements do him in. That was the way he had felt at the time, but here in the Bottoms, where he didn't know the ways of the weather, he wasn't sure at all.

Besides, back then he had had the sows and his trusty old boar to keep things going. Here there was only Perfecta, and if anything happened to her, well, he just didn't know if he'd have what it takes to start over once again.

He made circle after circle around the kitchen table with his two thumbs between clenched fists. And when Cora New put a cup of coffee on the table, he took it out of habit, not from want.

"Should have built her a lean-to," he said as Cora New settled down at the table.

"That's a good idea. I know that I'd welcome a roof over my head on a night like this."

"Ain't fitten," said Killie Willie, soft and quiet.

"What ain't?"

"Just ain't fitten," he said again. He was thinking back. The morning after the big storm back home, he had hurried down to the sty and seen what the Lord had heaped on him. So much mud had filled the pen that the water had been unable to run off. It held, and it became deeper and deeper until the whole pen was like a giant lake. And the little pigs, all less than two weeks old, had stood no chance. He had to dig with his shovel to find some of them. They had been covered by muck, some buried alive. Sixteen out of seventeen, drowned. And the two sows, their screams still echoed inside his memory. They fought each other over the one remaining little barrow. Their undersides hurt from the pressure of the milk in their udders, and it made them cry out in pain. And there was not a thing for Killie Willie to do but pray that the Lord in his wisdom would soon cause the milk to dry up and the pain to ease and the boar to do his duty.

This time as the wind whipped around corners and down alleys and streets and tossed a month-long collection of junk about the neighborhood, Killie Willie didn't know what the good Lord had in mind for him. He sat patiently. There was nothing else for him to do until the storm eased.

"Drink your coffee," Cora New suggested. She knew that as soon as possible her man would be trekking out to the sty, and she wanted something hot inside him to keep him braced against the wetness of the night.

"I guess I can find a few old boards and fashion some sort of lean-to tomorrow. What do you think?"

"We had us a lean-to down home, remember?" she said. "Didn't do much good."

"Everybody needs a shelter from the elements," he said.

Cora New's skin crawled. Here was her man putting a pig in the same category as herself. Her neck hair bristled at the thought of him giving equal consideration to his animal. Because if there was anything she knew it was that she and her children were far more important than a whole passel of pigs. That had been one reason why she hadn't put up much of a fuss when Killie Willie announced that he was selling his stock and moving his household to Buttermilk Bottoms in search of a better life. It was the idea that maybe, by starting somewhere anew, she might be given a chance to take her place in Killie Willie's life a little bit above that of a smelly, ignorant hog.

So she said, "That pig ain't a body, Killie Willie. Just a pig and that's all."

"One of God's creatures, ain't she?" he replied.

"Still . . ." She wanted to slap his face, but she knew he wouldn't understand. She also knew that she didn't have the words necessary to share her meaning. It was a frustration. It was a bother. But she tried. "She ain't a body. A body's got a soul. A body can go to heaven. Can't you see that?"

Killie Willie knew there was no need to debate such a thing. "You just jealous," he said. And passed it off with that. He knew Perfecta wasn't a body. He knew she was a good sight better than a body. She was a being and that put her in a special place as far as he was concerned. He couldn't expect Cora New to appreciate that. He had no reason to expect her to grasp a thought so filled with meaning and importance. Because Perfecta as a being needed him above all else. For her to continue being was his personal responsibility. No way could Cora New understand such a thought. No way would he try to explain it to her.

But Cora New understood well enough. That word "jealous," like iodine on a fresh wound, stung her deeper than he could ever guess. It made her madder than a dog after a flea. And like that dog, all Cora New could do was bide her time, hoping the pest would find another place to bite. That word "jealous" killed whatever conversation the two of them might have had for the rest of that night.

The thundercloud moved on. The wind idled. The rain dwindled to a drizzle and then stopped. Killie Willie slipped out the kitchen window and stood on the fire escape, smelling what he could have sworn to be the smells of Frog Level, fresh, clean, clear, almost sweet. The air was clean for a change. And from somewhere he caught a whiff of honeysuckle. For a moment he was transported back home to Carolina. And he stood on his front porch looking across the plowed fields that showed the sprouts of his planting.

But he didn't hear any hogs. Where were his pigs? He was jarred from his dream by the silence. There wasn't a sound coming from the sty. He almost ran down the fire escape.

The rain gave a glisten to the rubble out back. It almost looked pretty under the faint lights of the Bottoms. The old bedsprings that were rusted and brittle sparkled like they were trying to get clear of the dark and be made gold. They tripped Killie Willie as he raced across the rubble and sent him sprawling.

It was too dark for him to spy his pig. He wished that he owned a flashlight for times like these. But since he was out of work he didn't feel comfortable spending money on anything but the essentials.

"Perfecta," he called out. "Sooey."

He was answered by a grunt that spoke of sheer pleasure. The sty was the lushest it had been since Killie Willie built it. The place was a giant bog, and Perfecta was in hog heaven, having been given the best washing she'd had since moving to the Bottoms. She sat in her personal swimming pool and grunted her greeting to Killie Willie. It was as if she was trying to tell him how wonderful her life had become and she wanted to thank him in some way. He sat on the edge of the concrete fence and contemplated where he could find the materials to build a lean-to inside his pigpen.

Because he became one of her most dependable customers in terms of money up front and times a week, Fay Leigh charged Vaughn Brodie less for the time she spent with him than she charged anyone else. She enjoyed having a boy around who obviously adored her—he made her feel as if she was the most beautiful woman in the Bottoms, a feeling that she had always suspected to be true. She treated him special. She wore her best clothing and her most expensive perfume when she knew he was coming around. There was something about his style (or lack of it) that pleased her. Since he knew nothing about lovemaking, it was her privilege to teach him. All in all he was an easy forty bucks three times a week. And he didn't put any pressure on her to marry him, now that he understood her relationship to her work.

One night when his time was nearly up, she pulled him down close and kissed him long and wet. Then she broke free of him and stared at him in a strange way.

"I hear that your old man's a kinky one," she said.

"How do you mean, kinky?"

"You know. Has some weird habits. He has a strange way of thinking, so I hear."

"He's not so bad."

"Is it true that he has a pig farm here in the Bottoms?"

"Course it's not true."

"You sure?"

"All he's got is one measly little shoat. One shoat don't make a farm," Vaughn Brodie said.

"How many does it take?"

"A hundred or so. That'd be a farm."

"He just has one shoat? What's a shoat?"

"Female pig that ain't had a boar."

"Poor thing." She giggled. "Why is it she ain't had her a boar yet?"

"Far as I know there ain't one this side of Frog Level."

"Where's he keep her? This shoat."

Vaughn Brodie didn't want to talk about Perfecta, not when he was paying good money for his girl's time. "In a pen," he said, moving in on her breasts.

"Where's it at?"

"In a vacant lot near our place."

"Leave me alone, Vaughn Brodie. I've had enough." She pushed him away. "Take me there."

"Where?"

"To see her. I'd like to see a shoat."

"Maybe sometime."

"Now, Vaughn Brodie." She gave him a look she knew he couldn't resist. "Okay?"

"What's to see, Fay Leigh? A pig's a pig. This one's nothing special."

"Would be to me."

"My time's up. What would Bobby say?" He remembered the last time he had overstayed with Fay Leigh. Bobby had warned him then that he wasn't in the business of giving his girls away.

"I need some time off. I've already told Bobby that you were taking me to see your sick grandma. He understands."

"I don't have a sick grandma."

"But you have a pig I want to see."

"You're crazy."

"Please?"

So Vaughn Brodie took Fay Leigh to pay a visit to Perfecta on a night that was made especially for lovers. The moon was right. The stars were actually shining in the sky. And the lovemaking that night at the pigsty was the best that Fay Leigh had ever had. She told Vaughn Brodie so. There he was in his element, there he was in charge.

From that night on, Fay Leigh was Vaughn Brodie's for free, as long as they made it at the pigsty.

Killie Willie pounded the final nail in Perfecta's new lean-to. It wasn't much to look at, but what could anybody expect, building a house out of materials that had no business ever being considered for a house. The top was two pieces of bent tin. The sides were made out of pieces of burlap tacked to the crossties. He stepped back to admire his handiwork. So did Perfecta. She grunted and sloshed her way to the other side of the sty and lay in the mud in protest.

"She don't think much of her new house, does she?"

Killie Willie turned and saw the skinniest female he had ever seen.

"You must be Killie Willie," she said.

"Guess so."

"I know your boy. Him and me came by here last night to see your pig. My name's Fay Leigh."

He liked her right away.

And she genuinely liked him.

Killie Willie first noticed the man on the subway. He was on his way to the lower south side, looking for work. Word was out that there was good money to be made on a new building going up, and even though Killie Willie had no talent for building, Cora New had urged him out of the house. Get yourself something to do, she said. We didn't move up here for you to be a bum, she said. We ain't living much longer off welfare handouts, she said. There had been no arguing with her.

The man stood behind Killie Willie, staring at him. The city was full of strange people, but this man wore the finest three-piece business suit Killie Willie had seen. And his shoes were spit-polished. And his graying beard was trimmed close around his chin, very neat. Given his looks and the way he stared, the man made Killie Willie anxious to be off the subway and back on the streets. That's why he got off five blocks early.

He came into the bustling street from beneath the earth and heaved a long sigh. Having somebody stare at you is one thing, but to stand on the street and turn and see the fellow behind you still, this time with a broad grin on his face and still staring, well, that's another.

Killie Willie felt a strange kind of panic rising in him. What if the man was some sort of government agent? What if he was following Killie Willie to find his pigsty? What if he was going to charge Killie Willie with some sort of crime? The policeman, and Vaughn Brodie too, had told him there were laws. He didn't know what those laws were, but he was sure he was breaking several of them by having a pig in the Bottoms. And now this stranger in a three-piece suit . . . His panic forced him into the busy street, hurrying away. He didn't know and he didn't care what direction he took.

He came to a traffic light. "Don't Walk," the sign flashed as the traffic rushed past the corner. Killie Willie looked to his left. Nothing, just people and vehicles and normal big-city madness. He looked to his right. There stood the man, a big grin on his face, a welcoming glint in his eyes.

"Hello," the man said.

Killie Willie rushed across the intersection. A cab slammed on its brakes and would have slammed into him if he hadn't leapt out of the way and run across the street. He walked as fast as he could, visions of losing his pig rushing through his head. He wanted to hide, but the street was a strange one to him, and he didn't dare stop, not for anything, even though he thought he heard his name being called from behind him.

His heart did a flip-flop when he felt the man's hand on his shoulder and heard his voice in his ear: "Will you stop for a minute?!" He broke into a run, bumping into a bag lady and brushing past a couple of policemen. He wished he was younger—he longed for the days when he could run like the wind and leap hedgerows and take a whole terrace in three maybe four strides. But there was no spring left to his running. There was nothing he could do when he heard the voice call out from behind him: "Stop! Thief!!" There was nothing for him to do but huff and puff as he was grabbed from behind by a grasp as strong as any he had ever felt. He was yanked around, he was forced against a building, his arms and legs were spread apart, he was frisked, and he was being read his rights by the cop as the man in the three-piece suit puffed his way to the scene, holding his hand over his heart like he thought it was going to burst out of his chest.

"Let him—" the man tried to say, but he couldn't catch his breath. The policeman was putting handcuffs on Killie Willie's wrists when the man finally blurted out: "He didn't do anything."

"You yelled—" The policeman stood in amazement.

"I know what I shouted. I wanted him stopped. He's a friend of mine," the man said.

Killie Willie had never seen the man before in his life and he tried to say as much, but no one gave him a chance.

"Strange way to treat a friend, if you ask me," the cop said.

"Take those things off him," the man said, referring to the cuffs. "I'm sorry, Killie Willie, I tried to get you to stop."

"You know this man?" the policeman asked Killie Willie.

"No, sir."

"Don't you remember?" the man said, letting Killie Willie get a close look at his face. "I'm Keister, Gus Franklin and Laurie Wertz' boy."

Killie Willie stood stunned.

"Yeah! It's me! Keister Wertz."

"Well, I'll be hog-tied . . ." They forgot all about the two cops, who were enjoying what they were seeing. "Why, you were no bigger than—you're that little Keister?"

"Yeah. Weird, ain't it?"

"Well, I'll be."

"Keister Wertz. How about that?" one of the cops said to the other.

"Weird, ain't it, Hank?" the other cop replied.

"Real strange, let me tell you."

"Hey, fellas, thanks for your help," Keister said. "We come from the same hometown—Frog Level. Christ, I haven't thought about Frog Level in years!"

Hank the cop looked at his partner and shook his head. "Frog Level. My wife told me when I got up this morning that it was going to be one of those days." And they wandered off, hoping to catch a real thief the next time.

"Hey, listen, Killie Willie. How about letting me buy you a cup of coffee or something? We've got a lot to talk about! Come on, man." And Killie Willie was led down the street by a man whose only feature recognizable from his past was his name.

Keister took his friend to work with him and had Killie Willie wait for him in the coffee shop on the first floor of his office building. He had to check in with his secretary, he said. He'd be right back, he said. Wouldn't take but a second, he said, and they would catch up on old times.

While he waited in the coffee shop, Killie Willie called forth the memory of Keister Wertz and Keister's father, Gus Franklin Wertz, the man who owned the land Killie Willie had worked all his life. Keister had been born in the back of Gus Franklin's pickup truck as he was rushing his wife into town. When he arrived at the hospital, his mother, who had been riding in the back of the truck along with his wife and sister, held up the newborn baby for the proud father to see, and Gus Franklin had shouted out: "Would you look at that keister?! It's a boy!" And the name had stuck with the boy from that day on. Killie Willie remembered how Keister had grown up learning all he could about truck farming, how he had graduated from high school, gone off to college, come home six years later declaring that he was heading out to make a life of his own. And that had been the last he had heard of Keister Wertz. Until that day. Killie Willie marveled at how small a world he lived in.

They talked for an hour, covering the time between Keister's graduation from the state university with a master's degree in finance to his present position as vice-president for internal affairs for the third-largest savings and loan institution in the entire city. Killie Willie could tell that Keister was pleased as punch over his advancement in life. To Keister bragging about how he had raised himself out of the dirt in a place called Frog Level made his accomplishment all the more meaningful. It made good conversation, Killie Willie could tell, because as Keister told his story Killie Willie felt that he was being told something that was practically memorized.

Keister, it turned out, had lucked into the mother lode when he moved to the city. He was married, had three kids, all girls, a penthouse overlooking the river, a car in storage, a cabin in the mountains upstate, a mass of money invested in stocks and an even larger mass stored away in real estate, a mistress on the side, and a membership in one of the best junior executive country clubs in the area. Oh, Keister Wertz was doing himself proud.

Finally Keister asked about Killie Willie and his life. Killie Willie played with the cloth napkin in front of him as he said, "Ain't much to tell."

"Where are you living?"

"In the Bottoms," said Killie Willie.

"No kidding? I've never ventured into the Bottoms. Is it as bad as they say it is?"

"It ain't bad at all, once you get used to it. Took me a while to get used to staying home nights. You know how it was down home. Finish your day's labor and then take a walk with your woman down to the creek and wash your face and hands, that sort of thing. In the Bottoms, well, you learn to stay in close."

"I'd like to visit with you one of these days. Say hello to Cora New. What are you doing with yourself now that you're in the city?"

"Oh, nothing much. Raise my pig mostly."

"No, I mean in the Bottoms. What do you do?"

"I told you. Raise my pig."

"You have a pig up here?"

"Guess so."

"Shit, man." Keister leaned in close. "You're not lying to me, are you?"

"A Hampshire shoat. Weighs about sixty pounds. A good-natured hog."

"I've not been around a pig in so long . . . My daddy used to keep pigs down in the holler, and I'd go down there and slop them and talk to them. I swear sometimes I think they were talking back to me, you know? It's been fifteen years. Where do you keep this pig of yours?"

"Out back."

"And they let you do it? I mean, the city hasn't tried to stop you keeping a pig?"

"Guess they don't know she's there."

"Damn," said Keister Wertz. Then he stood up, almost knocking over the table in the coffee shop. "Let's go."

"Where to?"

"To Buttermilk Bottoms. I want to see this pig of yours, Killie Willie. It's been too damn long. I want to see your sixty-pound good-natured Hampshire shoat!"

Killie Willie learned that morning how to hail a cab. The light on top was the key: if it was lit, there was no way the cab was going to stop. So you look for the unlit cab and hail it. He also discovered that taking a cab into the Bottoms was a lot more inconspicuous than toting a pig home under your overcoat.

The cabby was a man much like Killie Willie. And he spoke English, thank the Lord. His name was stuck on a piece of cardboard along with his picture and registration, a fellow who went by the name of Sam Smith. Killie Willie smiled to himself when Keister tallied off the name, putting it and the registration number into his little black book. Killie Willie knew a whole passel of Sam Smiths, most of them back home, and most of them not really Sam Smiths at all.

During the ride to the Bottoms Keister drank from a flask he had tucked inside his suit coat. The more swigs he swallowed, the more he railed against the traffic and the poor driving of Sam Smith. He offered the stuff to Killie Willie, but he wasn't about to have anything to do with whatever it was that was making Keister Wertz act so tickled about going into the Bottoms.

As they rode, Keister told Killie Willie about the last time he had been home in Frog Level—seven years before, when he had gone back for his father's funeral. Gus Franklin Wertz had been helping one of his tenants clear a piece of land. His huge John Deere was chained to a giant stump, chugging away, trying to yank the stump free of the ground. The chain had snapped, one end of it catching Gus Franklin in the middle of his forehead. He was dead by the time he hit the ground. Killie Willie remembered it well. The death of Gus Franklin Wertz was the beginning of all his trouble back home in Frog Level. The Wertz family (probably Keister himself) had sold the land and moved out. It was then that Killie Willie had borrowed the money from the bank to buy the land he had tilled for Gus Franklin. It was then that Killie Willie had come up against such things as taxes and interest and payments and land banks and assessments and everything else that he knew nothing about. It was that death more than anything that led to Killie Willie's having to give up his home and move all he held dear to a place like Buttermilk Bottoms.

But he didn't say anything about that to Keister Wertz. He let the fellow ramble on about how he had moved his mother and lone surviving aunt into town, sold the land that his father had so dearly loved, and got out of Frog Level as fast as he could, hoping, he said, not ever to go back. He hated Frog Level, he said. The whole place stank of carrion, he said. He said that if God ever wanted to give the earth an enema, he'd put it in somewhere near Frog Level. Killie Willie didn't argue with him. He knew it would make no difference. Besides, said Keister Wertz, he shouldn't hate the place so much. It had been the sale of the land down there that had given him the financial start he needed to build the fortune he had growing under him. Oh, he had made a killing on the land sale, he said. Those folks down there hadn't known anything about buying land, he said. And then all the droughts and floods, well, it had really done him up right, he said. Of course Killie Willie Matt didn't say a thing. He let Keister Wertz drink from his flask and ramble on about whatever crossed his mind.

The cab pulled up to what had once upon a time been a curb, and Keister Wertz gave Sam Smith a fifty-dollar bill and told him to wait for him. He knew the cabby wouldn't wait, he told Killie Willie as they started across the rubble pile. Let the cabby bug off with his fifty-dollar bill, he said. He had his name and registration number and the serial number off the fifty-dollar bill, he said. He'd track the son of a bitch down, he said, and have his ass on the rack. Serve him right. They stepped out of sight of the cab and waited a few seconds. Then they stepped back to the street just in time to see the taxi turn the corner. He'd get the son of a bitch, Keister said. And he laughed. He'd get his fifty dollars back, he said. With interest. No trouble at all.

"So," Keister Wertz said. "Where's this pig of yours?" The flood of neighborhood kids that seemed to be coming from nowhere followed along behind as Killie Willie led Keister across the rubble pile.

It was strange to Keister Wertz. He admitted that. He felt like he was in a whole different world there in the Bottoms. The kids trailing along behind made him feel uneasy, but he didn't mention that. He knew that they were waiting for the right time to do whatever it was they wanted to do to a man so far out of his place.

They came up to the sty. Killie Willie wanted to apologize for the way the place looked, but to Keister Wertz there was a sort of magic about it. He felt right at home, standing beside the concrete fencing, looking in on a pig in the middle of her mud pen. Just as he in his three-piece suit was out of place in the Bottoms, so was the hog. He sat on the edge of the concrete and wheezed a little from the exertion of climbing over the rubble. And Killie Willie sat with him, proud of his shoat, even a little proud of his jury-rigged pigsty.

"Bout time for her afternoon feeding," Killie Willie said. "Be back in a bit."

"Can I help?" Keister said.

"Nothing to help with. Just need to bring out the slop bucket. Be right back."

And he was gone up the fire escape.

The kids lost their hesitation toward the man in the wrong part of town. They inched closer and closer. Keister noticed them, but he didn't say anything. He was enjoying the memories that seeing and smelling a pig put in his head, and he didn't want to let anything from the outside mess his memories up. He wished he had something to offer the pig, something to make her come a little closer to him so he could reach out and touch her bristled back.

"Hey, man," Billo said, coming up close to Keister, so close that he could smell the man's Old Spice after shave. "You like my pig?"

Keister ignored him.

"Hey, man," Billo said again. "You know what that thing is, loving that mud so much?"

Keister ignored him again.

"That there is real live bacon and ham on the hoof. And chitlins. Ain't that right?"

Nobody said a word. The rest of the kids, Jimmy in the lead, inched closer.

Jimmy touched the sleeve of Keister's suit coat. "Real nice cloth, you like it?"

Keister almost toppled into the sty, he was so startled by the touch. He laughed. "When I was a kid," he said, a bit too loud, but he wanted to be heard. "Yeah, when I was a kid, I fell into a sty once. Nearly scared me right out of my tree."

"No shit," Jimmy said. "You hear that? The man lives in a pigpen."

"The old lady sow must have thought I was after her little ones or something," Keister said, "because she came at me like a mile a minute. I was trying my best to get up, you see, but the mud was like an oil slick and I couldn't get my footing. Well, that old sow hit me full blast, knocked me up against the fence, and stood over me all sprawled out, glaring at me, just daring me to make a move toward her litter of pigs." He laughed.

Jimmy, Billo, and the kids didn't say a thing. "I didn't know what to do, so I just stayed there as still as I could and screamed my head off. My uncle heard me and came running over and found me lying there in the mud with that mean old sow straddling me, teeth bared, ready to rip me to pieces if I so much as twitched a leg muscle. Scared my uncle too, pretty bad." He laughed again. The kids just stood there.

"What's a sow?" Billo finally put in.

"You don't know what a sow is?"

Billo shook his head.

"Well, that there's a sow, or she will be as soon as she has herself a litter of pigs. She's gonna make one beautiful sow, that's for absolute sure."

"That pig can't never be no sow," Jimmy said. The rest of the kids nodded. Jimmy was always right.

"What's that?"

"You think I'm stupid or what, mister?" Jimmy said. He wore a chip on his shoulder big enough to fall off of its own weight, Keister Wertz could tell. So he shook his head, not knowing what it might take to tip the chip off and cause a problem. "You see any other pig around here?" Jimmy asked.

Keister shook his head, no, he didn't.

"Then you know more than me. Cause how's this pig gonna get herself knocked up if there ain't no other pig around to get it in her?"

Billo, Gregalee, and the others sniggered.

"You've got a point there," Keister said, smiling in spite of himself. "That's a real good point."

"How'd you get away from that sow, mister?" one of the other kids asked. He was a little fellow with huge eyes who loved stories with snappy endings.

"Well," Keister Wertz said, "my uncle—he owned the pig and had raised her up from a shoat—jumped over the fence and whopped that old hog with a pole that must have been five inches thick. That old sow was knocked a good six feet backward by the wallop. My uncle jerked me out of the mud and literally threw me out of the pen, and he came over the fence right behind me. But that old sow was a mean mother. She was after my uncle by then. She grabbed his heel as he was climbing over the fence and ripped his boot right off his foot. Lucky thing for him the boot was on his foot, otherwise my uncle might have lost it instead of the boot. That old sow chewed on that boot for thirty minutes before she buried it in the mud."

"You jiving us, mister," Jimmy said.

"Listen to me," Keister said, "a pig can be a mean and ornery critter if you start messing with her litter. Pretty much like your mamas, I bet, if anybody started messing with any of you. Right?"

The kids cackled. Keister Wertz didn't know anything about it, but Gregalee's mama that morning had lit into her old man for backhanding Gregalee at the washbasin, and Gregalee had told everybody about it. Some of the kids poked him in the ribs and oinked at him and the others pushed him a bit, all in play, and Jimmy said, "I always figured your mama to be a hog, Gregalee," and they all laughed.

Killie Willie was back then with a bucket of slop. He tried to shoo the kids home, but they were having a good time—all at Gregalee's expense and to Keister Wertz' enjoyment. Killie Willie poured the slop into the trough, and all of them hung around the edge of the sty watching Perfecta slurp at the slop, which was mostly water anyway.

"They's soap bubbles in that slop, Killie Willie," Billo said, pointing.

"Ain't nothing wrong with that, is there?" Killie Willie asked.

"Who wants to eat soap?" Gregalee said. He could remember the time his mama had doused his mouth with a bar of Ivory, and the taste hadn't been all that bad.

"Dishwater?" Keister asked.

Killie Willie grinned. This fellow might know his hogs after all. He nodded.

"You feeding that sow dishwater?" Jimmy asked.

"Makes the bristles on her back soft as a baby's bottom," Keister said. And Killie Willie just nodded. "Best thing in the world for a hog."

"Might be filthy on the outside," Killie Willie said, "but on the inside she's as clean as a china plate." And he laughed. Mo, the silent one, laughed too. Pretty soon, all of them were laughing, having a grand old time as the kids seemed to forget that Keister Wertz was out of his element there in the middle of Buttermilk Bottoms.

Cora New remembered Keister Wertz as a stuck-up college boy who came home with all sorts of new ideas and notions that had little to do with what was right or good for the tenant farmers of Frog Level. In other words, she had never liked the fellow. That was why she was so civil to him when he stayed that evening for dinner.

Keister shared their meal, not noting that his portions were double those of anyone else except Ollie Gus. He carried on a continuous babble of words, all aimed at the way he remembered Frog Level. Once during his ramblings Cora New caught Killie Willie's eye and shook her head. She was ready for the man to be on his way. Ollie Gus sat completely quiet as Keister shared memory after memory with the Matts. Her silence disturbed Cora New. It wasn't like Ollie Gus to sit for such a length of time without interjecting at least one hating remark. In a bit she left the kitchen and locked herself away in her room.

Keister was in the middle of the third telling of how his uncle had saved him from the angered sow (Vaughn Brodie had staggered home and he hadn't heard the tale) when Ollie Gus unlocked her door and reentered the kitchen. She carried her drawing pad.

Even as Keister Wertz spoke, Ollie Gus approached

him. She ripped the top sheet from the drawing pad. That stopped Keister in midsentence. She moved as close to him as she could without bumping into him and dropped the paper in his lap.

"Something from Frog Level," she said and returned to her room.

Keister turned the paper over in his lap. There, staring at him from the sheet, was himself, drawn to perfect scale in heavy-leaded pencil. The eyes were his, as were the hair, the nose, the receding chin. But there was something out of sync about the etching. At first Keister couldn't make it out. Then he noticed the mouth of the drawing. It was slightly askew, slightly cocked, slightly demented. The drawing sent shivers up Keister's spine. He saw himself, not with his eyes, but with those of Ollie Gus. He saw himself as a cocky, insecure, awkward, menacing individual. And it shocked him.

"Well, uh," he said, letting the drawing slip from his fingers to the floor. "Guess it's time . . . I was on my way. Mind calling me a cab, Killie Willie?"

"Don't have a phone," he said.

"Well, who does?"

"Nobody round here."

"How'm I supposed to get back downtown?"

"Same as the rest of us, I guess," Killie Willie said. "Walk."

Keister glanced out the kitchen window. It was already nearly dark.

"I'll walk with you down to the park," Killie Willie said. "There you can catch a cab easy."

Keister Wertz didn't have much to say as they made their way out of the Bottoms. The image of his face as seen through Ollie Gus kept raging through his mind. He couldn't get away from it. He wished that he had the drawing with him so he could take it home and show his wife. Only he didn't think that his wife would understand.

Finally, when the park was in view, Keister spoke: "Are you gainfully employed, Killie Willie?"

"Well . . ."

"I want you to come work for me," he said.

"What kind of work?"

"Oh, you know, janitorial stuff. It ain't easy work, eight hours a day, but you'll be your own boss. Interested?"

Killie Willie waited a bit before he nodded that yes, he would be interested in work. He didn't want to seem overly anxious for a well-paying job. Nor did he care for this fellow from down home knowing that the Matts were making ends meet by way of welfare. "I'd be interested, I guess," he said.

"Good. Come down to the office first thing Monday morning. I'll fix you up." And with that Keister Wertz caught a cab and sped away, leaving Killie Willie to manage the streets of the Bottoms on his own.

When he got back to his place, Cora New gave him a big robust hug, one like she hadn't given him in over a month of Sundays.

Less than a week later, Killie Willie was working full time as head janitor at the midtown office of the third-largest savings and loan institution in the city. The hours were good and the pay was such that for the first time in his life, Killie Willie felt like he just might be able to get ahead in this world. Add his earnings to those of Cora New, and the Matt family was doing downright grand.

It scared Killie Willie a little. He didn't want to think about how well things were going. It might jinx him if he thought about it too much. But Cora New thought about it every day. That's why she opened up her first ever savings account. That account gave her an awfully fine feeling, knowing that the folks down at the bank were overseeing her money, keeping it safe and secure for the next rainy day.

Wilbert Sease entered Ollie Gus' life through the back door. He was a tall, slender, rangy-looking fellow with a full beard that needed a trim. He came to the Bottoms with his palette, paintbrushes, and a desire to capture the essence of the place in oils. He came into the Bottoms each morning, bright and early, found himself a spot, put down his easel, and began his work. He was the most conspicuous person in the Bottoms, with his bushy beard and his face smeared with a rainbow of colors. Besides, not many artists dared venture into the Bottoms. And when this one did, he was an instant celebrity.

Wilbert Sease painted as long as he had light. After the sun sank out of sight, he disappeared. Nobody knew where he came from or where he went. But word spread that the artist fellow was really something, and in the second week of his tenure in the Bottoms, Ollie Gus found him.

She was marveled by the brushes and paints. The artist at the library was trying to teach her more about how to handle a pencil. She longed to learn about color, about brushes and oil paints, but he wouldn't help her with that. So when Ollie Gus discovered Wilbert Sease and his paints, she was enthralled.

She gave up the library in favor of hanging around Wilbert Sease's easel and watching every brushstroke he made.

He wasn't bad, she could see that. Sometimes she got in his light and he had to brush her aside. At other times she sat half a block away, drawing what he was painting, and then left him just before sunset. And then there was the time she asked him where he got his palette of paints.

At first he wouldn't talk to her, so she asked a second time. She wanted some for herself. She had watched him for a week and knew that she could handle the color.

It wasn't that he didn't hear her or that he was trying

to ignore her. He looked at her, his lips moved as if they were trying to respond, but no words came, not at first.

"What's the matter? Too damn good to talk to a person like me?!" Ollie Gus nearly screamed at him.

His lips moved again. A bit of sound came out, nothing she could understand. Finally he forced the words out. "Art store," he said and smiled.

She liked his smile. She liked his art. She liked the fact that he actually spoke to her. And suddenly she felt a little embarrassed.

He nodded toward her drawing pad. That made her even more self-conscious. "Ain't nothing," she said. Then he reached for it. And she let him take the pad from her.

She had only two drawings in it: one of a shadow on the pavement, the other of him sitting on his stool painting. He studied the drawings, his lips moving as if trying to speak. Finally he said, "Nice."

"Ain't much," she said and snatched the pad away. "Where's this damn art store where you get the kinds of things you've got?"

He shrugged and offered her the brush.

"Shoot," she said and backed away. It wasn't her way to take anything from anybody. But he smiled and made the gesture a second time.

She took the brush.

He stood up, motioning for her to take his stool. She did. He took her hand in his and showed her how to hold the brush. And Ollie Gus painted.

Her strokes were wild but true. Broad and filled with passion. Her colors blended and shocked themselves with contrasts. She painted with a whirlwind, adding to what Wilbert Sease had started in such a way as to alter what was his, making it better, more expressive, more complete. And he watched her. His awe at her talent was obvious to anyone who could see deep into his eyes. If Ollie Gus had only known how sincerely he longed to be able to do exactly what she was doing.

She finished the canvas, stood up, handed the brush back. She had captured more than the street of the Bottoms that Wilbert had started. Instead she had put all of the Bottoms into that one street and onto that single canvas. Wilbert smiled and frowned and groaned and wept, all at the same time. He tried to take her hand in his, but she slapped him away, her anger glinting in her eyes. "Ain't interested," she said and stormed away.

Wilbert Sease watched her go. Then he sat down at his easel and etched his signature on the bottom of the painting.

The next morning he was back. So was Ollie Gus. She brought along her best drawings to show him if he asked to see them. She stood at a distance, not knowing if she should come near him or not. He had chosen a spot near a bombed-out building that would have been hard-pressed to make a cockroach comfortable. Yet it was populated by several families, all of whom were hanging around the outside, not caring that Wilbert Sease was there to paint them.

Ollie Gus finally got up the nerve to approach him. She stood watching as he outlined the scene in pencil. She learned from him as he mixed his paints. Finally she tapped him on the shoulder. He turned and smiled. He gave over the easel with gratitude and he became the student as Ollie Gus recreated the scene before her in such vivid color, in such incredible detail, that Wilbert Sease could only admire her craft.

By midday, Ollie Gus had captured the building and its inhabitants, all of whom were pleased by what she had done. Wilbert Sease etched his signature in the lower right-hand corner of the canvas and offered Ollie Gus part of his lunch, which he carried in a paper bag. As she ate, he browsed through her drawing pad. He rubbed his forehead as he moved slowly from drawing to drawing.

His lips moved with an effort and he finally said, "Good."

"Shoot," said Ollie Gus.

Then he came to the series of etchings that Ollie Gus had made of Perfecta in her sty. Suddenly, there in the charcoals of the half-grown hog, Wilbert Sease recognized a new passion, one that had not been present in any of her other work. He couldn't put a name to the passion he felt, but it came close to deep, deep love. In each etching, Perfecta was eating. In each, she was enjoying her food with tremendous passion. In each, the pig was smiling.

Wilbert tapped a drawing and held it up to Ollie Gus. "That's my pig," she said. Even the tone of her voice was different when she spoke of Perfecta. She wasn't aware of it, though. But it was something that he picked up on right away. He rubbed his forehead and contemplated the strange enigma that was this multitalented female whose name he didn't know.

His lips worked feverishly as a string of words came out of his mouth in a broken, almost unintelligible flow. "Can . . . I keep . . . these?" he said, tapping the drawing pad.

"Guess so," she said. She couldn't figure the man out. It was like he wanted to talk more than anything else, but for some reason he couldn't. It was as if the words became hung up inside his mouth. She liked that. It made her want to crawl inside his mouth and pull the words free. So she touched him on the arm. And he responded by gently caressing her hand.

She didn't know why, but she led the man to her place. She knew that her mama and papa were away at work and that her brother was hanging around Junkie's Corner, selling his stuff and hoping to earn enough to pay for Fay Leigh's attentions. She led Wilbert Sease home, into her room, and locked her door.

It wasn't necessary that Wilbert talk with Ollie Gus inside her room. And it wasn't possible for her to hate. Rather, for the first time that she could remember, it was possible for her to love.

When Wilbert Sease left late that afternoon, he took with him every drawing that Ollie Gus had done. He had dollar signs in his eyes as he left the Bottoms that day.

Work at the savings and loan as head janitor took up more of Killie Willie's time than he wanted. It gave him too little time for Perfecta. And even less for Cora New.

His rising in the morning would take him with the slop bucket out to the sty, where he would stay until almost time for him to leave for work. And when he came home his first thought was of his hog, and out to the sty he would go with her evening meal of scraps and slop and he would hang around until it was well past dark.

Cora New became irritable. She didn't know why. She had no control over how she felt or reacted to things. She wasn't aware of the lack of time she had with her family anymore, what with her work and with each family member's special interests. She was, though, aware of her growing resentment of Perfecta the pig.

When Perfecta first arrived, Cora New would venture out on occasion to see how she was doing. But those visits gradually diminished until finally, now that Killie Willie was working as well as she, she didn't go out to the sty at all. Until that night.

That night, as was his custom, Killie Willie dragged in from work, mixed up a bucket of slop, swallowing his evening biscuit and ham as he mixed, and lugged the bucket down the fire escape to the sty. Billo, Mo, and a couple of the other kids were already there, pelting Perfecta with bits of broken bricks, and Killie Willie had to shoo them off. His shooing seldom worked. The kids sat on the piles of rubble, admiring the hog as she ate her evening meal. It was that night that Cora New finally broke down and visited with Perfecta. It was that or not talk to her man at all.

She stood on top of a rubble pile, hands on her hips, shaking her head with something of a scold. "Billo?" she said with a sternness that he hadn't heard from her before.

"Ma'am?"

"You kids get home."

"But—"

"I ain't taking no buts off you, baby. You and the rest—get." The way she said it meant that Billo and the rest had to get or else. They didn't know what the "or else" was, and they didn't want to find out. They left.

That meant that Cora New was alone with Killie Willie for the first time in God knew when. That is, along with Perfecta, who was giving full attention to her evening meal.

"Growed some, ain't she?" Killie Willie said.

"Some." There was a fire brewing inside Cora New that Killie Willie didn't want to see or couldn't see or both. There was no way of telling. Cora New kept things to herself mostly, buried deep inside her strength that was the strength of the ages. But sometimes, and Killie Willie had seen it on a number of occasions, the strength that was unique to her would weaken a bit and some of the true emotions that kept Cora New alive and well would slip forth. But that night—Killie Willie had no way to be prepared for what happened, for what Cora New revealed to him that night.

"I've had my fill," she said, more of a pronouncement than a piece of conversation.

"What of?" said Killie Willie.

"Of you uprooting this family of yours from our home, of you shipping this family of yours way off up here in this hell of a place, of you then bringing that home that we left up here to make what we've now got nothing more, nothing better than what we left. And I'm telling you here and now, Killie Willie Matt, I've had my fill."

That was it. She turned on her heel and marched as well as she could back to the fire escape and disappeared inside their place.

Something was bugging her, Killie Willie figured. He didn't understand what, except that for some reason Cora New was unhappy with their life in the Bottoms. He left Perfecta to her slop even though there was still light in the sky.

Back inside, Killie Willie drew a tub of hot water, took off his shoes, and sat in the middle of the kitchen, soaking his feet. The work that he did wore him out, he said. Never got a chance to sit down, he said. Kept him going from the time he got there till he left, he said. Only time he got to rest, he said, was when it was time to eat somewhere around noon. He rubbed his feet together in the hot water. Cora New busied herself with the dirty dishes in the sink. When they were all squeaky clean, she cleaned the stove top and the sink and the icebox cabinet. And didn't say a word.

"Well," Killie Willie finally said, "reckon it's time to go to bed."

"You go on," said Cora New. "Got too much to do around here."

"Cora New, something bothering you?"

"Done told you all I got to tell you."

"That so?"

"That so."

"Well," said Killie Willie, "maybe you can tell me why it is you had to tell me what you told me."

"I'm just ready to leave this place, Killie Willie, ready to pack it in and head back to Frog Level where you and me and Ollie Gus and Vaughn Brodie belong. I mean, look at Ollie Gus. You seen her happy here? I know, Ollie Gus ain't happy nowhere. But how about Vaughn Brodie? You think this place is any good for your only son? Shoot."

Killie Willie sat with his feet dumped in a tub of water. He thought for a bit before he said, "What about you?"

"What about me?"

"You ain't happy here?"

"Oh, Killie Willie," she said, a sigh in her voice, a tear fighting to get clear of her eye. "I lost me a house today."

Killie Willie didn't have to ask. He knew what that meant. In all her adult years, Cora New had always given the best of service. She had left every household she had served with the families begging her to stay, giving her all sorts of gifts to try to entice her to remain in service. But for her to lose a house, regardless of the cause—well, it was unheard of for a woman like Cora New. He wanted to ask her why, but he held the question at bay. If it was important for him to know, she would tell him. Until then, he would have to bide his time.

"You can get another house," he said after a time.

If looks could kill, the look she gave him then would have left Killie Willie in a smudge like a swatted fly. She didn't say a word but left the room with her head high and her feelings intact. She shut the door to her room. Killie Willie heard the dead bolt slide into place.

After a bit, he dried his feet and dumped the water down the sink. He didn't know what to do. He didn't know if he should demand access to his room so he too could get a good night's sleep, or if he should go out back and bed down with his pig. Or maybe he should rip the bedroom door off its hinges and demand admittance to his rightful place in his own home.

What he did was tap gently on the bedroom door.

It swung open slightly, and Killie Willie eased into the room, shutting the door behind him.

Cora New's crisis passed. And so did Killie Willie's. She attracted two new houses to replace the one she had lost. Why she lost it was kept a secret from Killie Willie. But deep inside she knew she had been wronged by the

family that had accused her of lifting five dollars in coins
from the little girl's piggy bank. She hadn't liked the family anyway, she rationalized, and the new families were
far better than the one she had lost. But she couldn't help
but feel a twinge of hurt pride deep inside her. Pride
goeth, she knew, before a fall, and she soon put her vanity behind her.

Sundays, Killie Willie's one day free of janitorial work,
he enjoyed spending with Perfecta. Sundays were her
days of rest too, he soon discovered, because on Sundays
Perfecta would find herself a special mud puddle (and if
there was not one readily available, Killie Willie would
make her one), lie on her side, and play her game with
the pigeons.

To Perfecta, the pigeon game was the most pleasant
one she played. She would purposefully leave some uneaten slop in the bottom of her V-shaped trough, knowing that the food would lure the birds in. She would lie in
the mud beside the trough and wait for the pigeons to
swirl over her head, edging lower and lower with each
swoop. Perfecta would lie without moving. The birds
would become bolder and bolder, and soon one or two
would light on the ground or on the trough and lay into
the food as fast as they could. No sooner would they start
pecking at the wet meal than Perfecta would let out an
ear-splitting squeal, leap to her feet, and lash out at the
invaders, grinding her teeth and snorting. The birds
would swirl away in a flurry, lighting on the wires and on
the ledges of the buildings, and fuss at Perfecta for her
trick. Then the game would start all over again.

Once Perfecta tickled Killie Willie so that he nearly
rolled off his perch with laughter. One of the birds, a
dumb one, he supposed, lit right on Perfecta's snout. She
snapped her mouth open and shut so fast that she caught
the pigeon's foot in her teeth. Oh, the birds swirled everywhere. They flew in her face. They swooped at her from

all directions. But she clung to her captive. They pelted her with wings and feet and beaks, but she would not relinquish her catch of the day. She thrashed the bird about. It fluttered as best it could. It did all that it could, all that its puny little body could do to free itself before it was too late. She killed it. It didn't take much for a sow her size to kill a pigeon its size. Once it stopped its fluttering and lay still in the mud, she buried it. And the flock of pigeons swooped away, none of them wanting to take on such a mean old hog.

But there was no end to the pigeons. In half an hour there were swarms of new birds, ready to take part in Perfecta's game.

It was on a Sunday, when Killie Willie sat at the sty admiring his hog as she tempted the swarm of pigeons into her reach, that someone spoke behind him.

"One day that pig's gonna cook them birds' goose," the voice said.

Killie Willie turned. Fay Leigh stood behind him, her hip cocked in such a way as to tantalize him into thinking thoughts she knew a man like him had never thought.

"Guess so," he said.

Perfecta stood in the middle of the sty with her feet spread over the trough, staring after the birds. She stood that way, guarding her food, for a long, long time.

"What do you suppose that hog's thinking?" Fay Leigh said.

"I think that she's thinking about birds, about how nice it would be if she could fly."

"I think so too," she said and settled down beside him.

"You really think a pig can think?" Killie Willie asked.

"I read somewhere that a pig is one of the smartest of animals, that chances are a pig can feel emotions just like human beings."

"Folks write about pigs?" Killie Willie said. "I mean, in books?"

"All the time," she said. And Killie Willie wished more than ever that he had the skills to make sense out of the symbols that defied him.

"You ever wish you could fly?" he asked Fay Leigh.

"Sure, but there ain't no way."

"Why not?"

"Just ain't no way. You see any wings on me?" she asked.

He smiled. Yes, he did, sort of. "Ain't it a shame?" he said. "Over there's a pig that's wishing she was a bird and here sits a sweet-smelling young woman wishing she was a pig. Ain't it a shame?"

"You're crazy, Mr. Matt," she said.

"Got me a cousin, not only wished he was a bird, but once he actually thought he was one."

"Your whole family is crazy, Mr. Matt."

"My cousin, his name is Buick," Killie Willie said, assuming his storytelling posture. "Called Buick because that was where he was thought up, in the back seat of a '28 Buick. That old Buick had no wheels, up on blocks, you see. No wheels. And that's why some folks thought old Buick lived without his full set of wits, because the old car didn't have any wheels."

"You're making this up."

"Oh, no, I swear. My cousin Buick is still living down home in Frog Level. He's considered the town eccentric—every town has one. Well, Buick woke up one morning and claimed he'd become a hawk overnight. So he fastened some turkey feathers to the sleeves of his long johns, climbed up to the top of the barn—"

"Whose barn?"

"What does it matter, whose barn? It was a barn, one of the barns we had back home in Carolina. Well, that barn was thirty feet at the peak if it was an inch, and that was where old Buick decided he'd perch. Well, everybody came running. My old man, my papa, he yelled up to Buick, 'What you figger on doing up on top of that barn, son?' And Buick didn't say a word. He chirped instead. Then my papa, he said the wrong thing. He yelled up, 'Don't you wanna come on down now?' And old Buick nodded his head and chirped real loud." Killie Willie chuckled as he remembered this story about his cousin. "Dumbest fool jackass thing I've ever seen, beg your pardon. 'Then come on down then,' my papa said." He watched as pigeons swooped into the pigsty. Perfecta squealed and the birds fluttered away to the ledges and the wires.

"Well?" Fay Leigh prompted him. "What did your cousin Buick do?"

"He come down. Started flapping his arms as best he could with the feathers stuck to them and he jumped straight out into the air. That barn was a good thirty feet high, too, from where he was perched. Chirped his head off all the way to the ground."

"What happened to him?"

"Well, he didn't fly, if that's what you're thinking." He whistled and gestured with his hand to show the path that old Buick took in his flight.

"That must have killed the son of a—"

"Oh, no, not old Buick," Killie Willie said. "Buick was too smart to kill himself. He knew what he was doing. He landed headfirst in the manure pile down below. He squished all the way up to his waist. Would have drowned if my papa hadn't pulled him free."

"You're shitting me, Mr. Matt," Fay Leigh said with a smile.

"Oh, no, I ain't. But old Buick is!" And he guffawed. "He came up with a mouthful of wet cow patty and spewed it all over everybody. And man, did he laugh at us! Laughed his fool head off for days after that."

"Your cousin's a crazy son of a moron."

"It's God's truth, Fay Leigh. You can ask Cora New if you don't believe me. She was there." He turned serious for a moment. "Now the point of my story is this: if you ever stop wishing a thing, like wishing to fly or something, and start into thinking it as a thing to do, you make sure that you've got a big fat manure pile close by to catch you when you fall."

Fay Leigh looked deep into his eyes. He was sincere. She could see that. But that didn't matter to her. She liked him too much not to get drawn into his fantasies.

"One good thing, though," Killie Willie said. "Before he became a bird, the selective service was after old Buick. They wanted him to go into the war and fight along with the rest of all those smart people. But after his shit trick, well, the selective service left old Buick alone. Today, he's one of the richest men in all of Frog Level, and that's God's truth."

"And I think that you, Mr. Matt, are one of the richest men I've ever met." She moved in very close to him and whispered, "If you ever want me, I won't charge you a thing."

He didn't understand. Or if he did, he didn't want to. "What do you mean?" he asked.

"I think you know what I mean," she said as she stood and stretched, spreading her arms and taking in the air. "It is such a beautiful day, don't you think? It's wonderful to be alive."

She touched his hair with the back of her hand and then left him there with his pig. He didn't see Vaughn Brodie standing above them on the fire escape landing. But Vaughn Brodie had seen them. And he was confused.

Vaughn Brodie avoided Fay Leigh the rest of that week. He didn't understand at all what was happening to him, he had never been in love before, and he had no means to handle the problem that plagued him. How do you deal with a woman who costs an arm and a leg just to be with her? And who has so little time for you? And who likes your own father so much that she is willing to give freely to him what she charges others so much for? It puzzled him deeply, so much so that he didn't care to see her at all, not for a while.

He saved his money instead.

There was a fellow he knew, a fellow who hung around Junkie's Corner every once in a while. This fellow, named Freeload, dealt in firearms. It had become obvious to Vaughn Brodie that one needed a firearm of some sort if one was to deal on the Corner. So he saved his money and sought out Freeload.

The gun he wanted, an M-16 semiautomatic rifle, wasn't a cheap purchase. It would take weeks, maybe even a month or more, to save up enough to make such a purchase.

But it was what he wanted. There was no other firearm for him. By not seeing Fay Leigh for a night or two, he discovered that he was making faster progress toward having the needed cash. It lessened the pain somewhat from not seeing Fay Leigh, knowing that the cash he saved was going toward something he needed for his own protection.

His body longed to be with Fay Leigh. Spending time with her had become something of a habit for him. When the time came for him to seek her out, his feet automatically turned him in her direction. But when he saw her standing under the streetlamp in her special provocative way, he felt cheated. She had offered herself to his father for nothing. He didn't hate her. He didn't hate his papa. He just did not understand. And he could not spend time with her with the same freedom that he had before, not for a while at least.

And the M-16 would have to wait, too, until he had the needed cash. Enough to purchase the piece along with at least a thousand rounds of ammo.

Then he would be a man. No doubt about it. None at all.

One night when Killie Willie and Cora New were two blocks away giving aid to an ailing neighbor, Vaughn Brodie came home the back way, crossing the rubble pile toward the fire escape. He was halfway across the vacant lot when he heard the first crack of a gun coming from somewhere near the pigsty. Guns going off in the Bottoms didn't seem that odd an event, not for Vaughn Brodie. So he waited a bit without moving. Then he heard it again, a single pop. This time it was followed by a strange sort of yelp, not loud but frightened, as if something somewhere was bewildered without the ability to control its bewilderment.

"By sweet Jesus," Vaughn Brodie whispered, and he raced across the back lot toward the pigsty.

He saw the kids right away, four of them, just punks. He knew them all. The tallest of the four held a small pellet gun that he was giving some extra pumps. Jimmy. Probably the lousiest kid in the Bottoms as far as Vaughn Brodie knew. He couldn't be trusted. Once Jimmy had tried to rip off Vaughn Brodie's stuff, stuff that Vaughn Brodie kept for emergencies. And he had had no use for the likes of Jimmy since that day.

And there he was, raising the pellet gun to his shoulder and taking aim at Perfecta, who cowered as far from the kids as she could get. Vaughn Brodie stood aghast as Jimmy squeezed the trigger. Perfecta flinched and screamed her high-pitched wail. It sounded to Vaughn Brodie like a cry for mercy, a plea. The hair on his neck rose up as tight as springs in a car seat. An urge screeched through him, the urge to take that damn punk kid Jimmy and break every bone in the kid's two good feet. Wouldn't be hard to do, no, sir.

"My turn, Jimmy," Gregalee said, reaching for the gun.

Jimmy gave the gun a few extra pumps and handed it to Gregalee. "Shoot for the eye," he said.

Vaughn Brodie stood behind the kids. They had not

heard him come up. "I think it's my turn, Jimmy boy," he said.

The sound of his voice sent a shock wave through all four kids. Gregalee almost dropped the gun into the mud.

Jimmy regained his position as leader of the gun party. "What you want, man?"

"Well, for one thing, I want you to leave my pig alone."

"That so?"

"Guess it is."

Vaughn Brodie's laid-back attitude sparked Jimmy on. "So how you gonna get us to leave your little piggy alone, huh?"

"Just don't like you messing with my hog, man," Vaughn Brodie said. It was the first time he had used the possessive when thinking about Perfecta. Maybe she was part his, he didn't know. Regardless, it was an attack against him if anybody attacked his hog. That much he understood, and he was more than willing to protect that which belonged to him and his.

"How you gonna keep me from it, Mr. Cool?" Jimmy said.

"Me? I ain't doing nothing. But no telling what little Bertha might do." The kids heard the click and saw the glint of light off the blade as the shiv stopped half an inch from the point of Jimmy's chin. "Bertha," Vaughn Brodie said, "just loves fresh meat. So does my hog. You want me to feed you to my hog tonight?"

Jimmy was afraid to swallow. He was afraid to move. "No," he said. The rest of the kids were backing away. They wanted no part of Bertha or Vaughn Brodie. Still, Gregalee held the pellet gun. It could go off anytime, Vaughn Brodie knew, and it was pointed at him.

"You tell your friend to lay that gun on the ground. If it goes off and hits me, I'll probably slit your throat and it'd be an accident. You see? I don't want to slit your throat, not really. So don't make me, all right?"

Jimmy gulped. He wasn't sure about Vaughn Brodie. He could be high and capable of doing just about anything.

"Best hurry it up, Jimmy boy, cause my hand's getting kinda shaky. No telling what Bertha's gonna do if my hand gets kinda shaky."

"Gregalee," Jimmy whispered, "why don't you do like the man say?"

Gregalee put the gun down.

Vaughn Brodie was enjoying himself. It had been a long time since he had felt so much in control of a situation, and it made him feel more of a man. Besides, he had no use for these punk kids. They were scum. Had no money to buy his stuff, and that was bad news to him. He brought the point of the blade to Jimmy's Adam's apple. "You know who I'm feeding to my pig next time I catch him hanging around here?"

"Who?"

"Dumb, ain't you?" He leaned in very close. "You, Jimmy boy. And you know something else?"

"What?"

"You owe me one, Jimmy boy. You owe me one."

"One what?"

"Oh, you'll find out. Now get the hell away from my pig's house." Vaughn Brodie was grinning. He was having the time of his life.

Jimmy and the rest scampered across the rubble pile as fast as they could.

Vaughn Brodie sat on the concrete fencing for half the night, or so it seemed. Perfecta groaned from the dark pit of the sty. She was in pain, but he didn't know that. He sat there and smelled the smells of the mud and the rotting vegetables that Michael Pogo had dropped over the fence and he remembered what it had been like back home in Frog Level. After a bit he spoke to the pig: "You some damn lucky hog, you know that? And my old man's some goddamn lucky man."

Perfecta groaned. She was in too much pain to do anything else. Vaughn Brodie smoked his best stuff that night. He was trying to get the memories of Frog Level out of his brain.

The next morning, Killie Willie cried. Tears streamed down his face, and he wasn't shamed by them. He was too heart-torn. His prize Hampshire gilt wasn't perfect any longer. The damn punk kids had seen to that. He wanted to take a horsewhip to their backsides and beat them and beat them and beat . . . But regardless of how his heart bled and how rapidly the tears flowed and how effectively he blistered the backsides of the punk kids, there was nothing he could do to reverse what had been done to his pig. Oh, it hurt him so deeply when he saw what damage there was. It was as if they had shot out one of his own eyes instead of one of Perfecta's. Yes, shot away by one of the pellets. And in the eye's place was a dark red scab that oozed a poison-smelling white pus.

Killie Willie bandaged it and coddled it, but it made no difference. She was scarred. She was imperfect. And she seemed to know it too, to know that maybe she wasn't worthy of Killie Willie's adoration any longer.

He found the pellet gun where Gregalee had dropped it. He shattered the beast against the concrete and buried the pieces deep in the rubble.

Perfecta moped about in her sty. She was skittish and shied away from anyone who came around. Killie Willie tried to soothe her. He put all kinds of ointments on her injured eye, but she wouldn't let anything stay on the hole long enough to do any good. He would smear the wound with something Cora New concocted and bind her head as best he could with bandages of all types. But no sooner were the medicine and wrappings in place than Perfecta would roll in the mud and waste all his efforts. By late afternoon, Killie Willie was at a loss. Not only had he missed a day of work, he couldn't seem to do his pet any real good. The wound festered and there was nothing he could do about it.

Billo wandered by late that afternoon. Perfecta groaned when he showed up and hid inside her lean-to. In fact, that was where she stayed most of the day, hidden from the kids who might come lurking around again.

Killie Willie wanted to take a brick to Billo's head, but what good would that do? He didn't know. All he knew was that he didn't want Billo hanging about.

"What happened to your pig?" Billo asked.

Killie Willie gave him a look. "You don't know?"

Billo shook his head slightly and then changed his mind. "Might have heard something about it," he said. The look on Killie Willie's face made Billo feel ashamed of being a kid on the block, even though he had had nothing to do with the pellet gun or the target practice. Billo was still the kid on the outs. And from the look on his friend's face, he was somehow glad that that was his station in life. "You got yourself a real messed-up pig, ain't you?"

"Go home, Billo. Don't need you hanging about. Don't need any of your kind hanging about today . . . or ever."

"Didn't have nothing to do with this, man," Billo said. He sounded hurt that Killie Willie would even think that he, Billo, could be a party to such a thing.

Killie Willie clucked to Perfecta and coaxed her out of her lean-to so he could work at the wound on her head. The pig wheezed and snorted in an unusual way as Killie Willie worked.

"She gonna die?" Billo asked.

"Course not," said Killie Willie. But he wasn't all that sure. He had seen pigs die from stranger things than a pellet wound in the eye. But it didn't seem fitting to him that a hog as healthy and rambunctious as Perfecta had been could be done in by a bunch of punk kids with a puny little pellet gun.

"Hope she don't die," Billo said.

"I told you to get, Billo!" Killie Willie hadn't hit a kid since Vaughn Brodie was eight and deserved far worse. There was a meanness in his tone that told Billo it was time to be off. So he scooted out of pelting range and sat on the rubble pile.

Killie Willie caressed Perfecta's head. The last time he had done anything like that had been a long, long time ago, when he was a kid himself. He had been no older than Billo when his papa gave him his first pig, a ten-week-old Poland China barrow named Shucks.

Shucks was the first thing that Killie Willie had ever owned, and to him Shucks was the smartest critter God had ever created. He babied Shucks like he was the only pig in the world. He made a special brush and used it every day on the pig's hide. Shucks loved it and grew like a bean sprout. The growth came from all the special leavings that Killie Willie was able to scrounge from the kitchen table.

Shucks and Killie Willie worked out their own primitive language. The pig would snort and Killie Willie would match him. Even though Shucks was kept in the pasture with all the other hogs, a hundred or so head, all Killie Willie had to do was snort in his way and Shucks would come scurrying. The snort meant something good to eat. As the pig ate, Killie Willie talked to him, sharing all the events of his life. It didn't take long for him to share things because there weren't many events. But then it was the talking that counted.

In the eighteenth week of Shucks' growth, a strange thing happened: some of the herd took sick. It wasn't much to start with, just a listlessness in half a dozen or so of the older hogs, followed by a strange drooling and an even stranger dizziness that kept the animals off balance. At first so few pigs were affected that Killie Willie's papa passed it off as coming from the heat. Then he said it was probably the water and there was nothing he could do about the water. Then as twenty some-odd hogs caught the dizziness, the first of the hogs to take sick died. Killie Willie had been in the tomato patch next to the hog pasture when the first of the animals flopped over dead. He saw the pig and at first thought it was Shucks. The only pleasure of the day came when he found Shucks rolling in the mud down at the creek.

That afternoon Killie Willie started digging the graves.

His papa was puzzled when the fourth hog hit the ground. Maybe it wasn't the water. He had seen nothing quite like it. More and more of his pigs, a herd that he had given the better part of his life to building up, were taken by the strange dizziness. Killie Willie dug the holes as deep as he could. The earth was packed hard from the long, dry summer, and the red clay was more like cement than earth. And he buried the dead pig flesh as fast as the earth would let him.

A new problem arose. The pigs were dying faster than Killie Willie and his three brothers, Montgomery included, could bury them. Before long there were so many graves that the Matts ran out of space to put more. So, on the fourth day, they built a bonfire and kept it blazing, using the dead bodies of pigs as tinder.

The vet was called in from town. He didn't know what was going on. He'd not seen such a thing in his life, he said. No telling what was the problem, he said. Probably the damn Russians poisoning American pigs with some sort of chemical, he said. Just have to destroy the rest of the herd, he said, to keep the disease—whatever it was—from spreading all over the county.

Destroy the herd. The idea had been a heavy load for the young Killie Willie to manage. His pig, the only pig that really mattered, was fine, had no signs of illness, and probably wouldn't get the disease. He was too healthy to get sick, Killie Willie knew that. But then his papa scratched his chin and said, "Guess we'll have to do it. Guess so." And that had been that. Just destroy the rest of the herd.

They did it.

The bonfire was kept going for over a week. It was fired by the healthy and the sick alike. On the Sunday after the destroying had begun, the fire was kept going with the remains of a very special Poland China pig.

The stench of burning pig flesh was something that Killie Willie knew he would never forget. The smell had hung in the air long after the fire was out. And the ashes had been buried under a ton of earth. Buried with the ashes were the charred remains of the pigs whose bodies wouldn't burn. All the rest of that summer the dogs kept dragging pieces of charred pig into the yard and chewing on them. Killie Willie took it on himself to lug the pieces back down the hill. The worse part of the summer was the carcasses that had been buried without burning. The dogs dug them up too. It kept Killie Willie busy all summer long.

The pasture was empty when the herd was gone. Killie Willie tried not to think too much about Shucks and the way that he had been shot. He had cried then, too, he remembered. His papa had shrugged and put the rifle barrel up to the barrow's head and pulled the trigger. Killie Willie decided then as he watched his pet crumble into a pile of meat and bones that if he ever got sick, really sick, he wanted to have his papa around so he could put the rifle to his head and put him out of his misery same as Shucks. The act seemed so painless, so impartial. And his feeling sad seemed so out of place. It hurt too much to get too close to things, that was something else Killie Willie decided. And he determined to keep his feelings at a distance from then on. Safer that way. Less potential for hurt. Besides, his papa had given up pig farming after that. He took up with the county road crew and died at the early age of fifty-nine.

"I should have joined the road crew myself," Killie Willie said aloud as he rubbed his pig's wounded head.

"What say?" Fay Leigh called to him from her sexy perch on the concrete fencing.

"I said I should of joined up with—" He saw the female propped in such a way as to reveal a sight down her blouse front. Killie Willie sat down in the mud. Nothing turned out the way it was supposed to. This thing of bringing a piece of Frog Level up to him in the Bottoms was all wrong. The idea of making a sty in the middle of a godforsaken hellhole was simple stupid foolishness and downright selfish. What had he been thinking of when he had had Ollie Gus write home to Montgomery? Didn't he have any sense in him at all? God, Killie Willie Matt felt like a pokeful of cattle crap. That oozing scar on the side of his Perfecta's head made him think of his papa's rifle, if only he had it with him, if only he had one well-placed rifle barrel . . .

"I think your pig," Fay Leigh said as a tear glistened down her cheek, "is gonna be just fine, Mr. Matt. I do believe that she is." She had climbed over the concrete fence and was standing ankle-deep in the mud beside the man and his pig. She placed a well-decorated hand on his shoulder and knelt beside him.

"Shoot," Killie Willie said, turning away lest she see that he was nearing tears. "I just betcha," he said, "I just betcha she ain't."

"Vernadetta Hope can heal your pig for you," she said.

"Vernadetta . . . ?"

And Fay Leigh told him about Vernadetta Hope, about how the woman could heal almost any ill. She also told him where she lived.

With that Killie Willie came out of the pigsty and beelined it across the rubble pile toward the tenements.

Fay Leigh reached out and for the first time in her life touched a pig. The bristles on Perfecta's right shoulder weren't nearly as coarse as she had imagined them to be.

Vernadetta Hope was the best midwife in the Bottoms. Killie Willie had heard of her often but hadn't needed her services before now. If it hadn't been for Fay Leigh, he wouldn't have thought of her in his time of need. It wasn't anything that he would ever consider on his own.

Vernadetta lived on the edge of the neighborhood near a section of the Bottoms that gave Killie Willie the shivers. He avoided the area whenever possible. There wasn't much good to be said of the kind of folks who peopled that section where Vernadetta Hope lived. And Lord knows that Killie Willie would have kept his distance if the midwife was not the only person he knew of to call on for help.

Folks from all over, even from downtown and the richer sections of the city, leaned on Vernadetta for help when it came to illnesses and things. But they stayed away from her otherwise. Rumor had it that she was more than a midwife. Some said she was a voodoo woman too. She could cast spells. Evil spells. Such rumors protected her from the scummy kinds of folks who lived around her. Her whole tenement was a sanctuary from the pimps, and whores, and junkies, and beanies who wandered the streets and demeaned life all over.

A mad-dog pimp could drop dead a block or so away from Vernadetta Hope's tenement and word would spread that the voodoo woman had done him in. Or a clap-ridden whore could wake up cured and word was that Vernadetta had cast a spell. A body didn't go to Vernadetta Hope unless it was a matter of life or death. She had cured Martha Bird Blotchley's house dog that had suffered from a bad case of the jerks. Killie Willie had seen it. Vernadetta had come in, taken a look at the dog that couldn't hold itself still, put out her right hand, and sent the evil in the dog screaming through the window. Killie Willie hadn't been around to see it, but Vernadetta had done the same for a mutt that had been crushed by a taxi in the street. Of course, the mutt had died two days later and so had Martha Bird's dog, but the pain had been taken away when Vernadetta put her hands on them.

Killie Willie didn't know what it was he wanted from Vernadetta Hope. All he knew was that no one else had the strength to help him and his pig in their time of crisis.

So he pushed himself out of the comforts of his home neighborhood and into the scummy area not so far from where Vaughn Brodie perched atop a crate in a state of zombiism and not too far from where Fay Leigh hung out her shingle for selling her wares. Killie Willie passed within hailing distance of his son, but Vaughn Brodie made no move to speak. In fact, Vaughn Brodie hardly moved, even as one of the pimps lolling against a graffitied wall hailed out "SOOEY!" in Killie Willie's direction. And Killie Willie didn't stop. He plunged deeper than he liked into the land of the evil folks.

A female—he guessed she was female, since she was wearing a skirt and high heels—pushed up against him as he passed down the street and tried to grab hold of his arm and pull him into a nearby dump. But he jerked free, warding her off with a whispered "I'm on my way to the voodoo lady." It was hands off him after that. But Killie Willie quickened his pace. There weren't many folks like that whore back home in Carolina, none that smelled like her, like she hadn't taken a bath in five months after wallowing in a dungheap every day. He could still feel the woman's hand on his arm as he ran up the front steps leading to Vernadetta Hope's place. There was something about the whore's painted mouth and missing front teeth that nagged at his innards. A little voice inside him seemed to be trying to take hold of his thoughts and say, "What the hell're you doing in a damnable place like this?!" But he didn't listen. Instead he tapped politely on Vernadetta Hope's door. He knew it was her door because it was the only door in the entire tenement still on its hinges and not all painted up with streetwise garbage.

The door stayed shut. Through it came a deep voice, deeper than any man's Killie Willie had ever heard. The voice seemed to articulate "go away," but then it could have said "come in." Killie Willie didn't know. So regardless, he blurted out his mission.

"My Perfecta's hurt bad, Miz Hope, and we need your help."

Nothing came from the other side of the door. A large rat scurried across Killie Willie's foot as he stood there waiting for some sort of response. It wasn't the rat that startled Killie Willie so—he was used to rats, even the size of the one that scurried across him. It was what the rat had in its mouth that shook Killie Willie. It was dark in the hallway and he couldn't swear to it, but it looked as if the rat had the better part of a small human hand in its mouth as it scampered over his foot. Cold shivers ran through Killie Willie's body. But he couldn't leave. He tapped at the door again.

"Miz Hope? This here's Killie Willie Matt from ten blocks over." He waited, but again no response. "We need your help, Miz Hope, something bad, me and my Perfecta."

The door creaked open. Killie Willie edged into what was to him the neatest place he had seen since coming to the Bottoms. He hadn't seen such a place since the time he was thirteen or so and had wandered uninvited into the living room of a rich family in Frog Level. He stood now in the midst of a white shag carpet, feeling ashamed that he had tracked his mud-caked shoes and pants into the neatness of Vernadetta Hope's home. He took off his hat and waited.

Some folks claimed that Vernadetta was part Haitian and thus had true voodoo arts. Others said she was a witch with evil potions. But Killie Willie knew better. She was a staunch Southern Baptist from somewhere below the Mason-Dixon line, living where she was because she couldn't make a go of it back home, same as Killie Willie. By the looks of her place with its cotton white furnishings and crystal glassware, Vernadetta Hope had found the mother lode in the Bottoms.

Then Vernadetta herself made her appearance. She was a waif, a spirit dressed in white gauze, a terribly small, frail, pale-looking woman with deep blue eyes. Those eyes seemed to see deeper into things than people wanted or needed. She came into the room, stood looking at the grimy Killie Willie, and said, "I've been expecting you, Mr. Matt."

Killie Willie stood turning his hat round and round in his hands.

"What can I do for you, Mr. Matt?" said Vernadetta Hope.

He told her all about the target practice and the damn punk kids and Perfecta's spoiled eye and his inability to give her comfort. She listened to every word. And when he finished, she looked at him a long, long time. Then she spoke: "You're a good man, Mr. Matt. I'll pray for your Perfecta. I'll send a spirit over and pray every night for three nights. Will you do the same?"

"Yes, ma'am," he said.

"You're a good man, Mr. Matt," she said as she turned and moved back into her inner room. "Your friend is going to be really fine." And she was gone. She left behind her the strangest odor of mint. And Killie Willie felt relieved. Little Detta Hope sure knew her stuff.

Killie Willie almost danced his way back to his place. He tipped his hat to the gap-toothed whore who smelled of a hundred dungpiles and greeted Vaughn Brodie with a cheerful "sooey" as he passed him.

Two days later, Perfecta's wound was scabbed over and healing fine. She was a strange-looking animal, missing an eye, but that didn't prevent her from growing fat and sassy. Fat and sassy. Losing her eye didn't seem to bother Perfecta all that much. Her sty wasn't so big that she needed both her eyes anyway. And she learned to make do with just the one.

It took her a while, though, to get over her skittishness when strangers or kids came around. But that too passed.

Killie Willie grimaced when he was taken by surprise by the hole in Perfecta's head or when the sunlight caught the scar just right. But that was to be expected. Killie Willie wanted his hog to be happy, and it tested him some to figure out how she could be happy with such a gash in the side of her head.

It was Ollie Gus who suffered most when she saw Perfecta's wound. Ollie Gus had been acting strange anyway, but when she saw Perfecta, even though the gash was healing, she wept. She grabbed her midsection and sobbed. There was something ailing Ollie Gus, but she couldn't talk about it.

She hung around Perfecta a lot during the day when Killie Willie was at work. She wanted to draw but saw no reason to, not since her time with Wilbert Sease. She cooed to Perfecta instead and sang little songs to her in a pure, high-pitched voice that eased whatever pain Perfecta had left.

"What you need," Ollie Gus said in a soft, pleasant voice, "is a man."

In some ways, Perfecta's loss of physical perfection was a boon to her respectability. Any hog that could survive such a neighborhood with all its built-in hazards deserved the admiration of folks who came around. And the scar proved to be a real conversation piece for Killie Willie. But not for Ollie Gus. It hurt her too much to see it, much less talk about it.

Late one Sunday, after the gash in Perfecta's head was

healed, Keister Wertz dropped in for a visit. He had been by a couple of other times to admire how much Perfecta was growing. But that Sunday when he noticed the ugly scar on the side of her head, he was shocked. How could Killie Willie let such a thing happen to his pet? What the hog needed, he said, was a mate. Hell, he said, why stop with one or two? Why not shoot the works and start a full-fledged pig farm there in the Bottoms, he said. Killie Willie could build another sty not far off, he said—just clear away the rubble and stuff and a second sty would be perfect for a whole herd of pigs, he said. But Killie Willie said that he couldn't afford any more pigs. And Keister Wertz said as how it was a shame, that they were sitting on top of a gold mine, what with the price of pork these days.

"How much would it take to have a boar sent up from Frog Level?" Keister asked.

"Well, a boar pig would be cheaper, I guess, less weight, and he'd grow. Oh, he'd grow just the same as Perfecta," said Killie Willie.

"How much for a boar pig then?"

"Enough so I can't afford it," said Killie Willie.

"Well, hell," Keister said, taking out his billfold. "How much you think it'd take?"

"Ah, now, Mr. Wertz—"

"I'm serious, man. You got yourself a real opportunity here to make some real money."

"Couldn't do that."

"Would a couple hundred do? Get a real nice pig for a couple hundred, don't you think?"

"No, Mr. Wertz," said Killie Willie, hoping the man would put his money away.

"Consider it an investment." Keister was proud of himself for thinking of it. "All I want in return is the pick of her first litter. Want to take it home to the kids. I've told them about your hog—"

"You've told about Perfecta? You ain't to do that, Mr. Wertz, never. Don't tell nobody about this here pig."

"Why not?"

"Cause they got laws, that's why." Killie Willie wanted to take the man by the shoulders and shake him so he wouldn't forget. Leave it to Keister Wertz, he thought. "Don't say a word to nobody. And we ain't getting us another. That's all."

He marched away from the sty, leaving Keister Wertz in the rubble pile to find his own way out.

Nobody noticed Ollie Gus sitting to one side, munching on a homemade biscuit. She had heard it all and she agreed with Keister Wertz—Perfecta definitely needed a man of her own. And a tear swelled in her eye. The figure ran rampant through her head. Two hundred dollars. Just two hundred dollars and they could have a man pig for Perfecta. If only she had two hundred dollars, she'd send home to Montgomery herself.

The second time that Wilbert Sease came into Ollie Gus' life it was through the front door. He stood in the hall, dressed much better than before, new shoes, new pants, new shirt, new cap on his head.

"Who are you?" Cora New asked.

Ollie Gus pushed past her mama. "He's looking for me," she said and pulled Wilbert Sease into her room and slammed the door. She shoved him down on the cot and sat beside him, gazing with deep affection into his eyes down to his deepest insides. Since they had spent time together, Ollie Gus had not put pencil to paper. But now she grabbed her pad and began drawing at a frantic pace. Wilbert's face appeared on the pad. Only it wasn't his face at all but his face seen through the love that Ollie Gus felt for him. He didn't speak. He didn't know how.

She finished the drawing and placed it in his lap. He shook his head and handed it back. He wanted nothing more to do with her art, only he couldn't say that. There were so many things that he wanted to say to her and that she wanted to say to him. But neither had the words to phrase such things.

He took an envelope from inside his shirt and placed it in her hands. She ripped it open and a small fortune of cash, all in bills, fell in her lap.

"What's this for?" she said.

His mouth worked. His throat tensed. His lips struggled to form the words. "You," he said. He took a letter from inside the envelope and opened it for her to read.

"These are your earnings," the letter said. "I kept what I consider to be a modest commission. The public outside Buttermilk Bottoms dearly loves and approves of your work. May God bless you and keep your talents well oiled. Sincerely, Wilbert Sease."

She offered him her lips. But he stood up instead. She reached for his hand. But he pulled away. He rushed to the door, eager to be gone, anxious to never see Ollie Gus again. At the door he smiled, waved in a shy sort of way, and was gone.

She stopped in the door and screamed after him, "Hate damn men what—" But she stopped. She didn't hate Wilbert Sease at all. Not at all. She slammed her door and tore Wilbert's note into twenty bits and ate every one of them.

Cora New could only wonder about the strange man who showed up for Ollie Gus one day. She never knew who the man was.

In her room, Ollie Gus counted the stack of money. Close to seven hundred dollars! She was shocked. Wilbert Sease had sold her drawings for so much money? She found it impossible to believe. He had made a mistake. Besides, had she given him permission to sell her stuff? Hell, no. Had she wanted to see him again ever? Hell, no! Had she wanted anything from him at all? "Hate damn men," she whispered over and over.

Then she stopped. The thought came to her head like a sudden explosion. Of course. Two hundred dollars was all it would take. The fellow in the three-piece business suit had said so himself, and he ought to know. It would be a simple enough thing to do, just write to Montgomery Matt and tell him . . . tell him to send them a boar! Love, Ollie Gus.

ain't tending no damn pig," Ollie Gus said when Killie Willie asked her about it. "Hate damn pigs what stink," she said.

"Just once a day, round noon. Just mix up the slop and pour it in the trough. Ain't gonna hurt you none."

"How much?"

"How much? What do you mean, how much?"

"This ain't Frog Level, Papa," Ollie Gus reminded him. "Here you want somebody to do something, you gotta answer to how much."

"Where you learn this sort of thing?"

"On the streets."

"Only thing you ever learned."

"It's enough. How much?"

"Two dollars a week." And Killie Willie felt that that was far too much for what service he was to receive.

Ollie Gus considered it. When her hog arrived (which she still hadn't told her papa about), he would be her responsibility, that much she knew. And feeding him would be a real pain if she didn't have the means to do it. She had decided to keep the rest of the money from Wilbert Sease for a rainy day, though she didn't know what a rainy day was exactly. So she said, "Five dollars."

"Five? Dollars?"

"Five dollars. In advance."

Killie Willie wanted to forget the whole thing. But he really needed the help. Besides, he had noticed how much Ollie Gus hung around the pigsty. And it was time at her age, all of twenty-three, that she took some sort of responsibility in life. So he scratched his chin and ran his hand through his thinning hair and said, "Five dollars."

"In advance," she said with her hand outstretched.

He took a five-dollar bill from his pocket. "See that Perfecta gets a good brushing every afternoon."

"Shoot!" said Ollie Gus, snatching the money. "I ain't about to brush no damn pig. Hate damn pigs!"

But Ollie Gus tended to Perfecta, and she didn't mind

it a bit. She could buy herself an awful lot of sweet stuff with what was left over from the five a week that she didn't use to stockpile meal for the pig she had ordered from Montgomery. That's why her mouth watered when she mixed Perfecta's slop every noon. It reminded her of all that was good to eat in the world. Even the slop got to looking awfully good to Ollie Gus, especially when she saw how the hog lit into it. She stirred it with a flat stick until it was just the right texture. It looked even better when she added the leftover biscuits from breakfast. And a little jam added just the right touch of color, to her way of thinking.

Once she put the flat stick aside and put her arm all the way into the slop bucket and stirred the meal and water that way. The slop felt cool and soothing. When she withdrew her arm, the wet stuff stuck to it and she smelled it, the clean, earth smell of wet meal mixed with the goodies from the kitchen. Not bad, she said to herself. So she tasted it.

"Not bad," she said aloud. "Needs some salt."

She added salt.

Vaughn Brodie came in from his trek down to Junkie's Corner. He threw the empty biscuit tin across the room in disgust.

"I told Mama to save me a biscuit. Where's the damn biscuits, Ollie Gus!?"

"Soon to be in the pig's belly," she said.

"Be damned. You know I like my cold biscuit with ham this time of day."

"Well," said Ollie Gus, "the ham likes your cold biscuit too, Bubba."

"Damn hog eats better than any of us," Vaughn Brodie snapped. Ollie Gus grinned. She knew it to be gospel.

Ollie Gus took her time tending to Perfecta. School was out, so the library was closed, which was just as well since she had gotten about all she could from the place. She was ready for something more, something that would truly challenge her. She had bought her some oil paints and brushes, but she usually made a mess of things and threw her canvases away. So taking her time tending to the pig was just what she wanted some days. She mixed the slop, poured it into the trough, leaned against the concrete fencing, and enjoyed the way her hog ate. Ollie Gus envied Perfecta's appetite; it hadn't been affected by losing her eye at all. In fact, since she became the one-eyed wonder, Perfecta's appetite had increased. That was why Killie Willie needed Ollie Gus' help. As she watched the pig eat, Ollie Gus longed to enjoy her eating half as much. With the kind of eating that Perfecta did, if Ollie Gus could only duplicate it she would be the biggest female this side of Carolina. And everybody already admired Ollie Gus' size.

It was her eating and her size and her growing that made Ollie Gus long to touch the pig. So she did, with a brush in her hand. Every afternoon she gave Perfecta a good firm brushing with the whisk broom she found in her mama's closet. She brushed and watched the flecks of dried mud shower in all directions. It was in one of her brushings that Ollie Gus noticed the little nicks for the first time. The nicks were not very big. In fact, she probably wouldn't have noticed them if one of them hadn't had a speck of blood oozing out.

The nicks were all over the soft belly of Perfecta's underside. Ollie Gus looked closer. She couldn't be sure, but the nicks looked as if they had been made by some sort of teeth.

What in the world, she wondered without saying it. And she ran as best she could up the fire escape into her place to tell somebody of her find.

Vaughn Brodie wasn't inclined to believe Ollie Gus' tale of teeth marks on Perfecta's belly. He had to see for himself, which she urged him to do. Sure enough, there they were, tiny little scabs as if the sow had a litter of carnivorous piglets nursing on her.

"What causes them?" Ollie Gus wheezed. All the scurrying back and forth had almost done her in. She could hardly catch her breath.

"Rats," Vaughn Brodie said. "Damn rats the size of house cats."

"Hate damn rats," said Ollie Gus. "What are we gonna do?"

"How you mean, we? This pig ain't nothing to me," he said. But he stood there. Perfecta's one good eye caught him in a vulnerable spot. He couldn't understand himself, but he knew deep down inside that he couldn't let such a thing pass. He had to do something, if only he knew what. His head was clouded with dope. The only thing he saw clearly was that eye of the pig, staring at him, almost pleading.

"Where do they come from, Bubba?" Ollie Gus asked.

"God knows." They looked about the sty, saw a few rat pills in the mud, but that was all. Then Ollie Gus spied the hole in back of the lean-to. It was no bigger than a hole that would be made by a mole. She squealed and pointed it out. Vaughn Brodie took one look and was off over the rubble pile.

"Where you going, Vaughn Brodie?"

"Be back!" he called. And disappeared out of sight.

Ollie Gus brushed the pig's back and sang her a song of the Gullah that she had learned a long time ago from her great-grandma.

Vaughn Brodie was back in a bit, carrying a large red gasoline can and followed at a respectful distance by Billo. The two could be heard approaching the sty from a long, long way off because of Billo's constant flow of questions like "What you doing, man?" and "You got real gas in that tank, huh?" and "You gonna burn down the neighborhood?" and "Cops gonna put you *under* Attica, man, they catch you with that stuff—whatcha gonna do?" and on and on.

Vaughn Brodie stopped when he neared the sty. Ollie

Gus was still singing her Gullah song to her friend the hog. He had not heard his sister sing before and he was shocked, or perhaps the better words for it would be blown away, by the sounds that came out of her mouth. It was the song, one that he hadn't heard since he was a tyke near his grandma. But more than that it was the tone of her voice, light and free, like a hummingbird floating above a cluster of azalea blooms. The voice tinted the back lot with a beauty that Vaughn Brodie had never suspected as being part of his sister. Usually her voice would shake a cadaver into motion. That's why he stopped. That's why Billo stopped and was left questionless for a moment. They both listened. They didn't quite know how to appreciate what they heard, but they knew that they liked it—though they would probably neither one ever let on that they did.

Ollie Gus must have felt them standing behind her, because she ended her song in midphrase and without turning said as loudly and as stridently as she could, "Hate damn folks what sneak up on me! Hate em!!" That broke the spell.

Vaughn Brodie climbed into the sty and sank up to his shoe tops in the mud. He pulled the gasoline can in behind him. Billo and Ollie Gus could do nothing but watch. They were afraid that maybe Vaughn Brodie had taken an overdose of something and that he was going to douse the pig with gas and set the whole place on fire. Even Perfecta must have sensed something like that, because she clung as close to the far corner of the sty as she could, keeping as much distance between him and her as possible.

Vaughn Brodie closed in on the rat hole in back of the lean-to. He looked into it. He listened to it. He straightened up with a strange smirk on his face. "They in there," he said, and he unscrewed the spout of the gasoline can.

"What's in there?" Billo said. "Who's he talking about?"

"Rats!" Ollie Gus said. "Hate damn rats!"

And Vaughn Brodie poured the gas down the hole.

After a bit, when the can was emptied, he stood up and turned to his audience and said, "Well—here goes."

He struck a match and dropped it into the hole. The gas almost exploded. It was an instant bomb. A flame like that from a torch spat out of the ground, followed by a billow of fire that hung above the hole like a bright rain cloud. Then it was gone. There were no sounds from the hole other than that of something burning deep in the ground. Nothing came from the mouth of the hole except smoke and flame. The extra gas burned for a minute or two and then was extinguished by the mud.

"Well, shit," Vaughn Brodie said. He threw the empty can as far as he could into the rubble pile.

"What's a-matter, Bubba?" Ollie Gus said.

"There weren't nothing in that damn hole," Vaughn Brodie said as he climbed out of the sty. The mud caked up on his sneakers and made his feet twice as heavy as they should be. "Damn, look at this!" he said, kicking his feet against the concrete and rubble. "Smell like a god-damn pig now."

"They weren't there, then where are they?" Billo asked.

Vaughn Brodie just gestured about him. That was where they were, out there, in the rubble, in the ground, in the tenements, in the streets, in the whole stupid world. And Vaughn Brodie felt like an idiot for thinking that he could help his papa's pig by burning out one silly little hole.

"What we gonna do now?" Ollie Gus said.

"Hate damn rats," Billo said.

The three of them sat on the concrete. Vaughn Brodie scraped his sneakers off as best he could, but the mud was clogged in the treads on his soles. Billo tried whistling the Gullah song he'd heard Ollie Gus singing, but he couldn't remember the tune. Nobody could have recognized it anyway even if he had remembered it. And Ollie Gus reached into the sty and rubbed her pig's back. They must have stayed that way for a good long time, each thinking singular thoughts.

Then Vaughn Brodie stood up. He stretched. "Well, I know one thing we can do," he said. The other two just looked at him. They had hoped he'd come up with something, they both hated rats so. "Billo, you know a punk kid name of Jimmy?"

Billo considered his answer before he said, "I don't know."

"You know him," said Vaughn Brodie. "I want you to get a message to him. You tell that punk that he's to have his ass here tonight at ten. You tell him that if he don't, I'm gonna feed him piece by piece, bit by bit to my hog. You'll tell him?"

Billo nodded.

"Good. Just Jimmy. Nobody else."

Billo scooted in one direction. Vaughn Brodie sauntered off in the other. And Ollie Gus sang her song of the Gullah to her girlfriend, Perfecta, the pig.

Jimmy showed up at the sty that night just as Vaughn Brodie had ordered. In fact, he had been too frightened not to show up, though he would never let on. Billo and Gregalee and Mo and a small handful of others showed up as well. Vaughn Brodie was the last to arrive.

He looked over the small gathering and waved all the others off, and they hid in the nooks of the rubble pile as Jimmy and Vaughn Brodie settled against the concrete fencing.

The two sized each other up. Jimmy was ready with his blade if that was what Vaughn Brodie had in mind. But Vaughn Brodie didn't. All he had was a flashlight and a couple of joints. He lit up and offered the good stuff to Jimmy.

It was a coolish night. There was the smell of rain coming from somewhere. It felt good to Vaughn Brodie to hang about like that with his best stuff going into his hide. It made him almost like the rest of the world. He almost liked the punk who was standing out there with him. Vaughn Brodie looked at Jimmy, who was leaning with his upper torso hanging in space over the pigsty. In the dark, Jimmy could have been anybody in the world. It didn't matter. He could have been the Lord Jesus himself for all Vaughn Brodie cared right then. That's why he laughed to himself and said, "Shit."

"What you want me for, junkie-man?"

"Just shut up." And the two smoked and kept their mouths shut.

In a bit what Vaughn Brodie knew would happen happened. First there was a slight rustle in the sty. It was followed by a faint grunt from Perfecta, who was hanging loose in her lean-to. Vaughn Brodie leaned against Jimmy and whispered "shhhhh" as quietly as he could. And Jimmy kept his mouth shut.

Then they heard the first little squeak, something like a mouse or maybe a baby toy that made silly little noises when squeezed. Then there was another squeak and another. Perfecta moved uneasily in her lean-to. Then she was in the middle of the sty, grunting and complaining. She gnashed her teeth and started roaming about the sty faster and faster. Every so often she would stop, then grunt and thrash at the dark and rush about the outer edges of the mud pen.

"What is it?" Jimmy said.

Vaughn Brodie held his forefinger to his mouth. And they listened as the squeaks came more frequently and with more insistence from inside the sty.

Perfecta was getting more and more irate. The two couldn't really see her in the dark, but her grunts were growing and her thrashing was more defined. Then she bellowed in rage. That was when Vaughn Brodie turned on his flashlight.

At first all they saw was darting shadows in the pen. Once or twice a flash of a red eye could be seen, and

Jimmy said, "Good God." The light found Perfecta. She was moving as fast as she could round and round the edges of the sty. And right with her were a dozen or so opossum-sized rats, nipping at her underside. She fought against them, but they were too many and too quick for her. And the light didn't faze the rats one bit. Those rats would have stayed after Perfecta all night if Vaughn Brodie and Jimmy both hadn't leapt into the pen and begun flailing at the darting shadows with whatever they could find.

The rats were gone as fast and as quiet as they had come. "Jesus," Jimmy said. He was coated with mud and he felt good and ready for the next rat to come along.

"Never seen rats that big," Vaughn Brodie said.

"Thought the damn things were gonna eat that hog alive!"

"Might do it one of these nights," Vaughn Brodie said.

Perfecta nudged up against Vaughn Brodie's leg. Without even thinking, Vaughn Brodie scratched her behind the ears. When he realized what he was doing, he didn't feel ashamed at all.

"Ain't never seen such rats," Jimmy said as he crawled out of the sty.

"Where you going?" Vaughn Brodie asked.

"I don't know," Jimmy stammered. "Home, I guess."

"Listen, punk." And Vaughn Brodie drew him in close. "You owe me and my old man one. You know that?"

"Yeah?"

"I ain't got time for none of your cooties, man," Vaughn Brodie said. "You got a debt and I'm calling it in. You got a gun?"

"You took it, junkie."

"Then get you another. A real one this time, one that shoots more than spit." Vaughn Brodie climbed out of the sty. "I want you here again tomorrow night."

"What if I ain't interested—"

"You're interested. Bring every damn kid you can find,

and make sure you all got yourselves a gun. And plenty of ammo. You guys can shoot straight, can't you?"

"Shit, man," Jimmy said. He thought about pointing to Perfecta's eye but decided that might be salting a fresh wound.

"Then be here. Ten o'clock. We gonna have us a grand old time." And Vaughn Brodie lit another joint.

"We gonna have us a shoot-out, huh?"

"You got it." And Vaughn Brodie turned his attention to his weed.

That's how the Great Shoot-out at the Pigsty came about.

The letter arrived the morning of the Great Shoot-out. It was addressed to Ollie Gus from Montgomery.

"What's it say?" Killie Willie asked as Ollie Gus snatched the letter out of her mother's hands.

"Mine!" she squealed and rushed to her room, slamming the door.

"That daughter of yours," Killie Willie said to Cora New, "gets stranger and stranger every day."

He tapped lightly on the door to Ollie Gus' room. "Gussy?" he called. "You gonna let me in?"

The door swung open and he slipped into the room. There were drawings of Wilbert Sease strewn about the floor, each one with a different kind of smile on Wilbert's face, each one not quite right.

"Who's he?" Killie Willie asked.

"Nobody."

"What's Montgomery say?"

"It's to me."

"I'd kind of like to know," he said, sitting beside her on her cot.

"Promise me you won't get mad at me," Ollie Gus said.

"You done something to make me mad with you?"

"Might."

"What is it?"

"You gotta promise."

"I think I've got a right to know what my own brother Montgomery has to say," said Killie Willie.

"You got to promise me first that you won't be mad at me."

"I promise."

"Well," Ollie Gus said. She was up from the cot and pacing about the room. She stopped over one of the drawings and pointed to it. "That's Wilbert. A friend of mine, I guess. Hope he's my friend. I don't know. Anyway," and she was pacing again, "Montgomery says I ain't sent enough money. Says I need to send a hundred dollars more. Says prices are up. I can't afford no hundred dollars more, Papa. Ain't right. I need the rest I got to buy him meal for slop and all such things."

"A hundred dollars more for what?"

"For Perfecta's boyfriend."

Killie Willie shook his head. He couldn't make anything out of what she was telling him.

"I sent home to Frog Level," Ollie Gus said, "for another pig. And Montgomery says here that I ain't sent enough money yet."

"Why in the world did you do that?"

"Don't know," she said. "Except Perfecta needs her a boyfriend. All women needs at least one boyfriend. Once in a while. I guess."

Killie Willie scratched his head. It seemed that each time he felt he had an idea of who his little girl really was, she did something completely out of character. First this friend of hers whom he had never met, and now sending home for a pig without consulting him. He scratched his head. "How much did you send him?" he asked.

"Two hundred—cash."

"You did not!" Where could she have gotten that much money, he wanted to ask. Why would she lie to him so brazenly about such a thing, he wanted to know. His own daughter, the one he had always felt confident would do only those things which she understood to be right, why would she lie directly in his face?

"Yes, sir. Did," she said.

"You don't have two hundred dollars."

"Got five hundred left," she said. "Uncle Montgomery wants a hundred more. That would only leave me four hundred to raise the pig into a boar. Ain't much, ain't enough. I don't know what to do, Papa."

Could he believe what she said? Five hundred dollars?

He had to believe it. She took the envelope of bills and placed it in his hands. "You do it, Papa, you send the money. I don't want nothing more to do with it. Hate damn responsibility."

"Where did you get this?" he asked.

She pointed at all the pictures on the floor.

He nodded. And left her room.

That morning before he left for work, he had Cora New write Montgomery another letter and included fifty more dollars of Ollie Gus' money. It was posted, and he became a bit excited over the prospect of adding another pig to his sty in the rubble pile.

Billo was the first to show up. He didn't have a gun like Vaughn Brodie had ordered. He didn't know where to get one. He was the kid on the outs, after all. All he could do was hang around and hope that somebody would show up with an extra gun or two.

It was around nine-thirty when Nate the Wino showed up. He was drunk out of his skull and didn't have any idea of what was going on. He staggered to the concrete fence, leaned over the side, and upchucked all he had inside him into the mud. It took Billo a full ten minutes to get the sot off the fence and headed toward the tenements. But no sooner had Nate staggered off than he became twisted around and straggled back to the sty, where he stretched out on the ground and went to sleep.

That was where Nate the Wino spent the night. And even though he had been there, Nate had no idea what happened that night at the pigsty.

Right at ten, Jimmy, Gregalee, and the rest of the kids came swaggering across the rubble toward the pigsty. There were five of them in all, each with some sort of gun. Jimmy's was the most impressive: a sawed-off 12-gauge shotgun, a mean-looking weapon that sent shivers through Billo's hide. Gregalee had a .22 automatic. There was a Saturday Night Special and a Magnum. The last kid carried a BB gun that had been doctored to fire a homemade shell that was filled with hand-honed shot.

Billo greeted them all. But they ignored him, talking instead among themselves. Jimmy kicked Nate aside and sat on the concrete fence. He laid out his ammo, two boxes of 12-gauge shotgun shells. Then he stacked up three boxes of .38 cartridges and pulled a pearl-handled Colt from inside his shirt. Everybody gathered around and admired the pistol, which looked as if it belonged in a Western movie. Where'd you get it? You can shoot that thing? You stole it? Everybody wanted to know. Jimmy just laughed and shrugged his shoulders. Got it at the getting place, he said. Of course I can shoot it, done so a hundred times, he said. Yeah, I took it, he said and laughed.

The others followed Jimmy's example and laid out their ammo. The only other one doubly armed was Gregalee. He pulled a blade from his belt. It looked strangely fat for a sticker. "That's for if they get in too close," he said. "Gonna skewer me some rat meat."

Billo edged as close to Jimmy as he could get, admiring the Colt, longing to reach for it and lay claim to what Jimmy wouldn't need, not if he kept his shotgun busy. "Nice little piece," he said.

Jimmy ignored him. Which was easy for Jimmy to do.

"Ain't got a gun myself," Billo said. But nobody paid him any attention.

The kids talked among themselves, quiet and sincere. They were facing a true adventure, that was sure. Two of them had flashlights which they kept shining into the sty.

Perfecta cowered in her lean-to. She hated the kids after what they had done to her. She kept as far away from them as she could.

"Where the hell's this junkie fellow you was telling us about?" Gregalee said. Jimmy just shrugged.

Vaughn Brodie came from nowhere. He was suddenly just there. He gave Gregalee a shove that threw the kid up against the sty with enough force to knock the breath from him. Nobody else moved. Vaughn Brodie stood there, a smile on his face. He was high, everybody could tell that, but he was also completely alive. A spark came out of him, something that seemed to say that here was the leader of this shenanigan, here was the boss-man.

"Everybody got them a piece?" Vaughn Brodie said. All the kids but Billo nodded.

"I ain't," Billo said.

"You know how to shoot?"

"Shoot, man," Billo said. And Vaughn Brodie gave him a small German Luger that looked like it had seen its better days forty years before.

"Anybody else?" Vaughn Brodie said. Nobody said a word. Nate snored. "Then somebody gimme a hand with this."

All the kids jumped, all but Jimmy, to help Vaughn Brodie move one of the concrete slabs so that he could enter the sty without crawling over the side. Vaughn Brodie then made his way to Perfecta and slipped a homemade halter over her head and pulled it tight, making sure not to choke her or cause her fright.

Perfecta seemed to know that Vaughn Brodie wasn't

out to do her harm. She made no move to avoid him and as he slipped the rope about her neck she didn't flinch. She just grunted.

Then Vaughn Brodie led Perfecta out of her sty. It was her first time outside the place. The ground was firm and the rubble was tough for her to stand on. He led her to the set of bedsprings where he tied the loose end of the rope. He left her there some twenty feet away from the sty, far away from what he had hopes for being a good ol time.

Vaughn Brodie dragged a tow sack to the sty. "Spread this stuff in there," he said to the kids.

"What's it?" Gregalee said.

"Bait," Vaughn Brodie said as he pulled a semi-automatic weapon from the tow sack. The kids gasped. They had all seen such rifles before, sure, but not out in the open, not where they fully expected the thing to be fired.

"You crazy, man," Jimmy said. Vaughn Brodie had almost forgotten him.

"Yep," he said, "guess I am." As he loaded the weapon with round after round, the kids spread the contents of the sack—cheese, lettuce, rotting fruit, and tomatoes—about the middle of the sty.

"Where'd you get this stuff?" one of the kids asked.

"Stole it," Vaughn Brodie said. He checked his weapon. It felt just right.

"That's wicked," Billo said, reaching out for the semi.

"Keep off!" Vaughn Brodie said.

Jimmy watched Vaughn Brodie with admiration. It was like he was suddenly seeing this junkie for the first time, and what he saw he liked. Anybody willing to sport such a weapon out in public had to have something for guts. At the same time, it made his sawed-off 12-gauge, a weapon he had been proud of, seem awfully feeble.

"Okay, punks," Vaughn Brodie said, "you gonna do

what I say?" Everybody but Jimmy said yes. Vaughn Brodie looked hard at Jimmy and threw a shell into the chamber of his weapon.

"Sure," Jimmy said. "Why not?"

"Good. Now nobody does nothing—and I mean *nothing*—until I give the word. You got that?" Everybody, even Jimmy, said yes. "We wait. You hear them rats coming over the concrete, you wait. You hear them rats fighting over the goodies in there, you wait. You don't move, you don't breathe. What you do is wait. We want every one of them suckers in our sights before we does nothing. Anybody got flashlights?" Two of them were turned on. "Cut the damn things off. And keep them off till I give the word." Vaughn Brodie was feeling the surge of power in him. He was having himself a ball. "When I shuts up, you punks, ain't nobody to say a word. Nobody's to do nothing and I mean *nothing* till I says so." He took a moment for his orders to sink in before he said, "If you ain't loaded, get loaded. I'm shutting up."

Nobody said a word. Even Perfecta held her peace.

An hour passed. Then another. It was past Billo's bedtime and he kept yawning. But nobody paid him any attention.

One of the kids dozed off and fell into Jimmy, who poked him in the belly and woke him. By twelve-thirty, Gregalee was ready to pack it in and head home. But he didn't say a word. He was afraid to. Vaughn Brodie smoked a joint and didn't pass it around. He enjoyed the night. The stars were out and he liked to imagine himself floating through space like those Hollywood actors in a movie he'd seen a few weeks back.

Then they heard the first squeak inside the pigpen. It was so faint that at first all the kids doubted their ears. But it was followed by another and then several at once. The sounds of the rats sent any sleepiness in the kids flying. They were all wide-awake. And they hung in the dark waiting for the rest of the rats to come, waiting for the word from their leader, waiting for the blast that was sure to come.

The sty was pitch black. There was no moon. The only sounds they heard were the squeaks. There was no rustle. There was no fighting. Vaughn Brodie waited. There had to be more than what was in the sty then. He waited for what seemed to him to be a full half hour. He could hear a few rats chewing at the bait. Once he heard a brief tussle between two or three rats. And of course there were the squeaks. But by any standard there was nothing in the sty to raise suspicions. What was missing was the pig. "Damn it," he said under his breath.

The kids took that as the word. On came the flashlights. Up went the guns. Vaughn Brodie was forming the word "wait" when what he saw silenced him. The sty was a sea of rats. They were milling quietly in the mud, eating the bait, pushing each other, but being quiet as mice as they did so.

Vaughn Brodie heard somebody scream NOW!!! He didn't know it was himself until late the next afternoon. And the silence of the night was blown away as seven guns and Vaughn Brodie's semiautomatic opened up.

Opened up! Screamed awake!! The dark was done in by the flashes from the gun barrels. The noise of round after round being fired into the mass of rat flesh was like that of a jungle battle in Nam. The semiautomatic was the true star, though. It spat lead like a rivet gun in double overtime. And the rats in the sty were torn apart. They tried to scamper and a few did, but the blanket of fire was too intense. The bullets tore through the rats and ripped into the concrete slabs. The kids were whooping like Indians. Some had to stop to reload after a bit, but the semi kept on going. Maybe some of the rats got clear of the pigsty, but not many. The semi saw to that as it poured its rapid fire into already dead bodies and wounded bodies and bodies that were dead but didn't know it.

The shoot-out was finished in less than two minutes. There were no rats left to shoot. What stopped Vaughn Brodie was his empty chamber. And even that didn't do the trick. The chamber clicked at least ten times before he relaxed his trigger finger. The whooping from the kids was followed by a cheer and then quiet. They didn't want it to be, but the fun was over.

Vaughn Brodie was the first into the sty. There were hundreds of dead rats buried in the mud. When he found one alive, he ripped it open with Bertha. Gregalee was beside him, having the time of his life. Vaughn Brodie picked each rat up by its tail and tossed it over the concrete fence. "Put em in the tote sack," he said.

They did.

It was a messy business getting dead rats out of a pigsty.

"How many you suppose we got?" one of the kids asked.

"Thousands," Billo said.

"Millions," another said.

They sacked the rats up. Two of the kids lugged the first sack three blocks over to a dumpster. The second sack was dragged to the street, where it was left for the garbage collectors to find if they were interested. The third sack was left out in the middle of the rubble pile.

Vaughn Brodie and Gregalee and Jimmy cleaned the sty as best they could in the dark.

"How many you think got away?" Jimmy said.

"Some," Vaughn Brodie said.

"Reckon they'll come back?"

"Might."

"Suppose we should come back again tomorrow night?"

"Nope." Vaughn Brodie led Perfecta back into her sty.

"Want me to come around in the morning," Jimmy said, "and help clean up the rest of this mess?"

"No need," Vaughn Brodie said.

"Wouldn't mind."

"Appreciate it."

"You got it."

Vaughn Brodie was tired. It had been a long day and the effects of the shooting and the dope were wearing off. He wanted to be with Fay Leigh, in bed, sleeping. He didn't want to have to deal with these punks anymore. He had done his due for his papa and his papa's pet. He just wanted to be with Fay Leigh, curled next to her under a sheet, sleeping, sleeping.

"Hey, junkie!" Jimmy called as Vaughn Brodie wandered back across the rubble pile. "This was great."

"Yeah," Vaughn Brodie said.

"Damn great!!"

Nate the Wino slept through it all. Billo for the first time felt that someday he might become part of the gang that ignored him. And Jimmy—well, Jimmy did not go home. He hung around the pigsty by himself. He was too high to go home.

He noticed the dark, stick-looking thing lying against a piece of rubble. He picked it up. It was Vaughn Brodie's semiautomatic. The weapon was light. It felt good in his hands. The chamber was empty but that could easily be fixed. He looked around. Nobody watched. The rest of the world was asleep. He slipped the piece under his baggy shirt and made his way home. He felt like a big man as he sidled through the streets of Buttermilk Bottoms that night.

Killie Willie heard the shooting. But in the Bottoms gunfire was as common as tying a shoelace. The next morning Billo told him everything. At first Killie Willie was filled with anger over what his son had done. The sty was a mess. Vaughn Brodie's semiautomatic had done a job on the concrete fencing. Most of the lean-to had to be replaced with new lumber. And Killie Willie cleared away a bucket or two of spent lead and shells. Billo talked on and on as Killie Willie removed the shells and pieces of dead rat from the sty.

In a strange way Killie Willie was proud of his son too. It struck him that for the first time in his life Vaughn Brodie had done something constructive. He had rid the sty of its plague of rats. The whole neighborhood was proud of him. Nobody said anything about it, but the rat population in that part of the Bottoms was reduced significantly, and it made living around there a little bit more pleasant than before.

It was Saturday. Killie Willie was due a day off from his work at the savings and loan, so he took it. He worked all morning rebuilding the lean-to, listening to Billo's constant chatter, hearing the tale of the Great Shoot-out over and over.

Vaughn Brodie stopped by the sty on his way to Junkie's Corner. His eyes were bloodshot and his nose ran. His nightlife was taking a toll on him. "Need any help, Papa?" he said under his breath.

Killie Willie stopped what he was doing. He wasn't sure that he had heard his son right. "Huh?" He looked at his boy and blinked.

"Ah, nothing," Vaughn Brodie said and went on his way.

Killie Willie scratched his chin, ran his hand through his hair, and returned to his work. Perfecta tried to help by rooting in the mud around the lean-to, making discoveries of rotting vegetables left from the baiting of the night before. It seemed to Killie Willie that his pig knew that the pesky rats had been shooed away.

At noon, Ollie Gus came down the fire escape with a bucket of slop, perfectly stirred and smelling a bit of nutmeg. Perfecta greeted her with a grunt of recognition.

"Hello, pretty baby," Ollie Gus said and started talking to the hog in a high-pitched nasal voice that would have been better suited for a three-month-old child. Ollie Gus didn't notice her papa, who was behind the lean-to, or Nate the Wino, who had trailed along behind her. So she poured the slop into the trough and talked her baby talk. What she said amounted to, "You pretty baby . . . you getting a boyfriend soon . . ." Fill that with all the ohhhs and ahhhhhhs and other cooing sounds and that is the gist of her conversation with the pig. "Papa's taking care of it all just for you," she said. "He's gonna make sure that you're the best damn sow in the whole wide world."

"Folks are going to put the Matt clan away," Nate the Wino said. Ollie Gus nearly jumped out of her skin. She had no idea anyone was around, and being caught talking to her pig made her feel ashamed and scared. She whirled around, swinging the slop bucket at Nate's head. He stepped back and chuckled. The chuckle sent a sharp pain through his head. "Yep," he said, "the whole Matt clan's as batty as a flock of birdbrains, out here talking baby talk to a stupid pig."

"Ain't stupid," Ollie Gus took exception. "Got more sense than three of yous."

"Some folks say only crazy people talk to pigs," Nate said. He grinned his toothless grin and ran his tongue through the hole. It had worked for him before, so why not give the gesture a second try? Just because she had rebuffed him once was no indication that she would do the same again. He rubbed himself as he looked Ollie Gus up and down. "You getting this here a boyfriend, huh?"

"Course!" she yelled at him to make sure he caught her meaning. He merely grinned at her and rubbed himself. "You ain't wanted around here," she said.

"You need a boyfriend yourself, little piggy," he said to her. He leaned toward her in a way that made her flesh crawl.

"You get away from here!" she screamed.

"Every little piggy needs a boar every once in a while."
He leered at her, making squeaking sounds with his lips.

"I done had me a man once," she said, quietly and with
fond memories.

"What you and me done ain't what I'd call having you
a man."

"Ain't talking about you," she said. She studied her pig.
She knew what she knew and felt what she felt. She didn't
need a man like Nate the Wino, not after the gentleness
and comfort of her precious Wilbert Sease. She looked at
Nate and felt that she would puke all over him.

"You know you want me, little piggy."

"You get away from here!" Ollie Gus screamed. "You
get so far away from here—"

With that Ollie Gus hurled a chunk of concrete at
Nate's head. She missed, but he yelped with pretended
pain. Perfecta grunted and Ollie Gus yelled.

"I ain't hurting nobody," Nate said. "You got no right
chunking things at me. I ain't hurt you."

"I'm calling the cops."

"What's the cops gonna say about this here pig you
got?" Nate said. "They got laws, you know. They got laws
against throwing things at folks who ain't meaning nobody harm. So you leave me alone, hussy."

They stood there, sizing one another up. "You ain't
natural," she said.

"Come on. Give old Nate a kiss."

That stopped her. He stank, sure. But he was a man, a
man who was willing to kiss her and make her feel good
all over. When he grabbed her by the shoulders and tried
to pull her to him, she was almost overcome with the ro-
mantic notion that Nate could be as pleasing an experi-
ence as Wilbert had been. In fact, she had doubts that
she would ever see her Wilbert again. She had no way to
find him. She hardly remembered how he looked. Nate
ran his tongue over his lips as he neared the kiss that he
was certain of having from Ollie Gus finally.

Then the pig squealed.

That shook Ollie Gus out of her near trance. She swung her foot with a vengeance, catching Nate on the shinbone.

"You messing with me, hussy!" he yelped. All the yelling was giving his head as many throbs as her foot gave his leg. He stumbled and tripped over the old set of rusted bedsprings. He fought the springs as he tried to get up, and Ollie Gus hurled another chunk of rubble at his head.

"Get, you damn pervert!" Ollie Gus yelled.

And he ran as best he could across the rubble pile, limping and cursing under his breath. Nate rushed past Billo, who was making his way toward the pigsty. "Stupid bitch," he heard Nate mutter as they passed.

"What did ol Nate do?" Billo said to Ollie Gus.

She cared little for Nate the Wino and even less for Billo, so she screamed at him, "You too, get!!"

"What you yelling at me for? What did ol Nate do, pee on the pig again?"

"What you mean, again!" Ollie Gus said. "THAT SUM-BITCH PEED ON MY PIG?!!" She could have killed.

"Couple of times."

"And you didn't stop him?"

"Why should I do that?" Billo said. "I watched him do it."

"You watched?" Ollie Gus was getting overwrought. "You pervert! Ol Nate, he's a pervert! And you, you a pervert!! Ever last one of you all is nothing but SUM-BITCH PERVERTS!!!"

Billo thought she was going to throw something at him, so he ducked.

Instead she said, almost too calmly, "Billo, you see that sumbitch round here again, you heave a brick at him. You do that? You do that if he pees on my pig again?"

"Sure," Billo said. "For a dollar."

"Pervert!!!" Ollie Gus screamed, throwing a brick at Billo as he scooted out of sight. "Hate damn perverts!"

Killie Willie stepped from behind the lean-to. He was grinning from ear to ear. He was brimming with pride for his very special and only daughter. "You tell em, Gussy," he said.

Ollie Gus shook with shock and disgust and anger. How could her own papa whom she loved so much spy on her and let her make such a fool . . . She fainted dead away.

The lean-to was repaired. The concrete fencing was fixed. All the spent shot that Killie Willie could find was picked out of the mud. And Perfecta lounged in her favorite spot, the far corner of the sty. The world of the back lot was at peace, and Killie Willie sat on the ground outside the pen and relaxed. It was hot. The sun put a kind of glaze on top of the mud. The day was a nice one, a good one to be alive.

Then Nate came back across the rubble pile. He was breathing hard when he found Killie Willie. "They're a-coming," he said in between gasps.

"Who's coming?" Killie Willie asked. "What're you talking about?"

"The pigs" was all Nate could get out. His old legs hadn't been made for running over rubble. After a bit, he got enough breath to say, "We got to hide the hog."

"Hide Perfecta?" Killie Willie thought Nate was having the D.T.'s or something. He didn't know what was going on. "From what?"

"Ain't got time," Nate said. And with that he climbed into the pigsty.

"Hey, wait a minute—" But Nate was already pulling at Perfecta, trying to lug her to the lean-to. Perfecta weighed more than he did, though, and she wasn't about to give up her spot in the early afternoon sun.

"You gotta help me, Killie Willie," Nate said.

For some reason, Killie Willie did. He crawled into the sty and gave Nate a hand and pulled the hog to the lean-to. Perfecta gave in to them and went into the hut without much coaxing. And Nate collapsed against the wood of the lean-to. He was spent, or so it seemed, but he was up and busy again in less than a minute.

"What's going on?" said Killie Willie.

Nate crawled out of the sty and began pulling at the set of old bedsprings. "Gimme a hand," he said. Killie Willie didn't know what to think, but he gave him a hand. For some reason, Nate wanted to put the set of springs in the sty. So Killie Willie helped him. They threw the springs into the mud right in front of the lean-to. "Tow sacks," Nate said. "Hurry."

Killie Willie had no idea what was going on, but he did what Nate said. He couldn't explain it. It just seemed the thing to do at the time. He threw a bundle of tow sacks into the sty and Nate spread them over the springs. What he devised almost looked comfortable to Killie Willie. It made him feel tired. But it was Nate who stretched out on the springs.

"They on their way," Nate said. He feigned going to sleep.

Nate was right. They were on their way. In a few minutes, Killie Willie heard them coming across the rubble pile. The pigs.

"What am I supposed to do?" Killie Willie asked.

"Just leave it to me," Nate answered. "You don't know nothing, okay?"

"Okay." Killie Willie stiffened like he was facing the Inquisition.

"For God's sake, relax! Thank the Lord I ain't too sober." And Nate took a drag from the bottle he had in his hip pocket.

The two policemen made their way across the rubble to the pigsty. How could Killie Willie relax? After all, there were the laws he had heard so much about.

"Well, would you look at this?" the tall policeman said.

His name was Bobby; he had grown up in the neighborhood, Killie Willie knew—that was why he could venture
into such an area with just his partner by his side. He
had seen it all, he said, but what he saw made his mouth
flop wide open.

"I'll be damned," the shorter and stockier policeman
said. Killie Willie had seen the two policemen before, but
this was the first time he had come so close to them, and
he didn't know what to say. So he said nothing.

"Howdy," said Nate. "How's your old lady's crabs,
Bobby?"

"Put a stopper in it, man," Bobby said.

The policemen walked around the outside of the sty,
giving it a good look-over. It was the shorter one who
spoke first: "You ever seen anything like this before?"

"Nope," Bobby said. "What's it supposed to be?"

Killie Willie didn't say a thing.

"Answer the man, buddy!"

"Take it easy, Cowboy, don't want to scare these folks,
now do we?" Bobby edged up to Killie Willie and got too
close. "What's your name?"

Killie Willie gulped. He tried to smile. He wanted to
grin so bad he could feel it, but his face muscles were
frozen. So he just shrugged.

"What's a-matter with him?" Cowboy said. "Can't he
talk?"

"Sure," Nate said. "Me and Killie Willie's great buddies. Ain't that right, Killie Willie?"

Killie Willie nodded.

"Shit, man," Cowboy said. "You hard up for buddies,
you claim this stinking wino as a friend."

"I had me a friend like Nate once," Bobby said. "He
damn near burned our house down one day and me inside it."

"I had a friend like Nate once too," Cowboy said, "and
I blew the sumbitch's head off one day."

"You kill him?" Nate asked.

"Nah. You can't kill anybody by shooting that head off," Cowboy said. "And he knew he deserved it. He was messing with my sister."

"Which sister's that?" Nate said. "The one I had last night or the one from last week?"

Bobby laughed at Cowboy's expense, but Killie Willie just stood there. Then he laughed too, until he realized from the glare he got from Cowboy that he should stay as quiet as a field mouse.

"Okay, Nate," Cowboy said, "come on out of there."

"What for? I ain't done nothing."

Bobby tossed a chunk of concrete into the sty. The piece splatted in the mud and sank out of sight. "What is this place anyway?"

"My house," Nate said, stretching out on the springs.

"You live here?" Cowboy said. He turned to Killie Willie and said, "He live here?"

"Sure do," Nate said, yawning, and Killie Willie nodded.

"What's that for?" Bobby said, pointing to the lean-to.

"For when it rains. Just crawl right inside and stay as warm and dry as a ladybug."

"How about that?" And Bobby pointed to the trough.

Nate waited a bit, trying to think up something quickly that the two would believe. But his head wasn't working like it should. He drew a blank.

"That's for the rats," said Killie Willie.

"Yeah, for the rats."

"What's that supposed to mean?" Bobby said.

"You want me to tell em, Nate?" Killie Willie said.

"Might as well."

Nate was just as interested in what Killie Willie was going to say as the two policemen. Whatever it was that Killie Willie said about the rats was going to be a lie, and Nate was convinced that Killie Willie didn't know how to do that sort of thing. So when Killie Willie cleared his throat and ran his hand through his hair, Nate leaned forward. He figured this was going to be good.

"Nate draws rats," Killie Willie said. And that was all.

After a bit Bobby said, "So?"

"Well, he can't help it," Killie Willie said.

"Just my nature," Nate said.

"What's that got to do with that thing?" Cowboy said. He reached over the concrete fencing and lifted the trough out of the sty. "Looks like this thing's been chewed on. Is that some kind of mesh in the bottom, Bobby?" The two men inspected the trough.

"Course it's mesh," Killie Willie said. "Poison mesh."

Cowboy dropped the trough.

"You're lying, man," Bobby said.

"Killie Willie don't lie," Nate said.

"The rats bothered Nate, so we put out this here food with rat poison in it."

"Did it work?" Cowboy asked. He was having some rat problems in his apartment, so he was interested.

"Sure did," Killie Willie said. "Made those old rats fat and sassy. They grew to be as big as alley cats. Ain't that right, Nate?"

"Bigger." Nate held up his hands and indicated a rat at least two feet long.

"Shit," Bobby said. "Let's tear this place apart and run these ol coots in. What say, Cowboy?"

"Sounds okay by me."

"On what charge?" Nate said. Killie Willie's stomach went tight when he thought of these two men tearing the lean-to to bits and finding Perfecta hidden away. Fact was, he was surprised the pig was staying out of sight. The bedsprings in front of the hut were something but not enough to keep a hog her size from doing whatever came to her mind. So Killie Willie was glad that Nate had the presence of mind to question the officers. But at the same time he wanted to get them away before it was too late. He just didn't know how to do it.

"Charge?" Bobby said. "Who says we need a charge? Come on, Cowboy."

As they moved to the first concrete slab and began struggling with the heavy bugger, Killie Willie said, "Guess you fellas heard about the shoot-out last night."

"Course we heard about it," Cowboy said. "Why else you think we're here?"

"Don't you want to know what it was all about?"

"We already heard—something about some bums from way cross town who came around looking for Nate and missed him. What did you do to those fellas, Nate?"

Nate just grinned. He was having a good old time out there in the middle of that pigsty.

"Well, you heard wrong," Killie Willie said. "We had us a rat kill out here last night." Cowboy and Bobby looked at each other. "Must of bagged us two hundred of the critters, maybe more."

"What for?"

"Cause the only thing a rat's good for is target practice. Ain't that right, Nate?" Killie Willie said. Nate nodded. "This place—well, just look at it. Perfect for trapping a rat. Take a whiff of that smell. Look at all those tracks in the mud." They did. Perfecta's tracks were all over the place. "Big rats make big tracks," Killie Willie said.

"Them rats must of been wearing cowboy boots," Bobby said, looking at the cloven prints in the mud.

"There were some kangaroo rats too," Killie Willie said. He was soaring now. His imagination was being tested and he was up to the task. "A kangaroo rat has a hoofed foot like a deer. Ain't you ever seen a kangaroo rat?"

Cowboy didn't want to admit ignorance, so he said, "Well, sure. We got them all over out in Illinois."

"Right," Killie Willie said. "We got us kangaroo rats in this neighborhood that's as big as collie dogs." Nate was agape at Killie Willie's brazen lie, but the two cops seemed to believe him for some reason. "You should see them buggers," Killie Willie said.

"So you came out here and shot up this back lot, huh?" Cowboy said. "Wish I'd of known about it."

"Well, we gonna have us another shoot-out in about a month," Killie Willie said. "You want, we'll let you know and make sure you're here before we set into them."

"Hey," Cowboy said, "sounds good to me."

"You see, we needs this kind of place, Nate's house, to draw the rats in from all over the neighborhood. Then we puts out all kinds of food stuffs over the ground and wait. The rats show up and then we light into them." Killie Willie was shocked at himself. Lying was coming easier to him than he had expected. "Course, we're careful not to let our shooting stray much. We keep the guns low so the ammo goes into the ground or into the concrete. Ain't a bad way to keep the rats under control, and it sure helps Nate out, don't it, Nate?"

"Guess so."

"So you tear Nate's house apart, and you're doing the rats a favor. We can't bait the trap if the trap ain't here." Killie Willie was sweating. He didn't know if these fellows were fool enough to believe him, but it was worth the try.

"Well?" Bobby said.

"Guess we can leave it up, huh, Bobby?" Cowboy said.

"Well, this is city property," Bobby said. Killie Willie took note of that. He hadn't known who owned the back lot.

"Ain't doing no harm, though," Cowboy said. He was already looking forward to the next shoot-out. "Come on. We got better things to do."

"You guys . . ." Bobby wanted to say something, anything that would put the fear of the law into the two men, but he couldn't think of a thing. "Don't catch cold out here, Nate," he said. And the two started back across the rubble pile just as Perfecta poked her nose out of the lean-to and grunted. The cops stopped.

"You hear something?" Cowboy said.

"Just a kangaroo rat," Bobby said, and they disappeared over the rubble in the direction of the street.

Killie Willie sank against the pigsty. Perfecta came out of her hiding place and began rooting at the bedsprings. Nate crawled out of the sty and sat down next to Killie Willie. The two stayed that way for a bit before Killie Willie finally said, "Thanks, Nate."

Nate chuckled. He had had a ball during the confrontation. "You some liar, Killie Willie Matt."

"Yeah, guess I am," he said. He got up and started off toward the tenement.

"Where you going?"

"To pray," Killie Willie said. "Got to ask the good Lord to forgive this old sinner." And he wandered off, a tired but relieved man.

Word spread. Ollie Gus had a crate down at the station. And Killie Willie had left early that morning to go down and pick it up.

There was a carnival atmosphere in the back lot. Folks gathered in the afternoon sun, hanging around Perfecta's sty, waiting.

Michael Pogo was there. He had closed his grocery store at noon and lugged two bushel baskets of rotting vegetables to the sty. That meant that Martha Bird Blotchley was there too. She wasn't sure if she was still on Killie Willie's blacklist or not, but with Michael Pogo hanging around she couldn't restrain herself. Part of the carnival was watching Martha Bird make a total idiot of herself over the man. It was almost embarrassing how she fussed over Michael Pogo's every move.

Cora New was there. She had seen the crowd gathering and had come down the fire escape to make sure that nothing evil was done to Killie Willie's pet. Besides, she liked people. With her work, she didn't get much chance for socializing, so this was a boon to her afternoon.

Ollie Gus was there in the sty, brushing her pet. She whispered sweet nothings into Perfecta's ear as she rubbed and scratched. Since Ollie Gus was there, so was Nate. He hung around the outside, wanting nothing better than to crawl over the concrete and brush Ollie Gus the way she was brushing the pig. He kept rubbing himself. He rubbed himself so much that Vaughn Brodie, who was there with a joint in his mouth, said, "Jesus, you're disgusting, wino."

And Nate said, "Ain't I, though?"

Billo was there too. But nobody paid him any mind.

Jimmy, Gregalee, Mo, and the rest hung around. They didn't want to draw attention to themselves, so they kept their mouths shut and their eyes open. Eyes open because there were maybe three or four, depending on when they looked, whores hanging around too. Jimmy sneered at the whores every chance he got. There was something about the female body that depressed him, and to handle the feeling he made fun of it all. He preferred the good sweaty smell of men and boys about him. And he made no bones about his preference. That's why he tended to hang around Vaughn Brodie after the Great Shoot-out. Vaughn Brodie had proven himself to Jimmy. Now Jimmy wanted the chance to prove himself to Vaughn Brodie. But all he did was make Vaughn Brodie uneasy, though neither one of them was in any hurry to put a finger on the reason why.

Nate passed his bottle around. It was a scummy thing that had a mean-looking crust on the edges of the top. That didn't keep a couple of the kids from testing what Nate had to offer. But Michael Pogo scolded him for setting a bad example for the kids of the neighborhood. Nate just laughed and kept his bottle going round. Nobody could accuse him of being a tightwad.

Michael Pogo munched on an overripe pear. Martha Bird was nervous. When she had seen Michael Pogo making his way across the rubble pile, she had put on her prettiest frock and made herself up to look like the beautiful women she had seen in magazines, and she was afraid that she might have overdone it a little. Anyway, Michael Pogo ignored her as best he could, as best as anybody can ignore a person who is hanging on every word you say or every bite you take from an overripe pear. Finally, he offered her a pear and that made her happy for a bit.

One of the whores, cackling like the wicked witch from Oz, leaned over the concrete fence and gave Ollie Gus a solid whack on the rear end. Ollie Gus straightened up and screamed, "Pervert!!!" That made the whore laugh even harder.

"I like fat young things," the whore said through all her laughter.

"Then get in here with Perfecta," Ollie Gus said. "Hate damn whores."

"Yeah, get in there with Perfecta," Billo said. "Like to see that."

For the first time, the whore noticed Billo. He had been around the whole time, but she hadn't seen him. She sauntered over to him and whispered, "Got five bucks?"

"What for?"

"Three would be enough."

"Christ!" he yelled. "I'm just a damn kid!"

"I've made it with younger than you, baby," the whore said and screamed with laughter. Old Billo hung his head. He was less than a man, and Jimmy and Gregalee and the others lit into him with all they had. But for some reason Billo didn't leave. Any other kid wouldn't have shown his face in the neighborhood for a month of Sundays, but not Billo. To him negative attention was better than no attention at all. The whore wouldn't leave him alone. She fondled him the rest of that afternoon.

It was then that Keister Wertz waddled across the rubble pile. He was so out of place there with his three-piece suit and his smell of Old Spice. A hush settled over the crowd. It was left to Cora New to make the newcomer feel welcome.

"How are you today, Mr. Wertz?"

"Just fine. Killie Willie ain't back yet?"

"On his way."

"Cain't wait, can you, Cora New?"

"Could wait for the rest of my life."

Perfecta sniffed the air. An old friend was around. She sniffed her way to the side of the sty and grunted her welcome to Keister Wertz. "Hi there, old lady," he said.

Perfecta's welcome did the trick. Keister Wertz was accepted by all into the gala of the festival. Nate, Billo, the whore, Martha Bird, and Ollie Gus all said hello to the newcomer, and before long it was Jimmy and the other kids and Vaughn Brodie who were on the outs, because all the rest had a whole truckload of things they wanted to ask Keister Wertz.

Fay Leigh slipped her hand into Vaughn Brodie's. He jerked away. "Jesus, scared me," he said. "Where did you come from?"

"Mother's womb," she said and took his hand in hers. "Your papa back yet?"

"No."

"Come on," she whispered and led him toward the fire escape. "Nobody's home—they all out here. Come on," she said.

"I ain't got the money for it today, Fay Leigh." It was an excuse. He had the money. He didn't want to deal with her, not that day. Besides, he hadn't had anything at all to get him loose. He was tight and antsy. Still, she tugged at him.

"For old times' sake," she whispered. "Come on. What's the matter? Don't you love me anymore?"

"Course."

"Then come on."

Cora New could only watch as her son climbed the fire escape steps following that woman, Fay Leigh. She wanted, oh, how she wanted to tell him, "This ain't good for you, boy, this is the baddest thing in the world for you," but she couldn't. She could only watch and wish that somehow things would change, knowing full well that they wouldn't.

One of the whores was playing around with Keister Wertz, much to his comfort and discomfort, when Killie Willie made his way across the rubble pile.

Quiet hung over the place. Killie Willie had the biggest damn grin in the world tacked to his face as he made his path over the piles of junk. Nobody seemed to breathe. Nobody dared move. Killie Willie greeted all with a nod and an even broader grin. He shook Keister Wertz by the hand and kissed Cora New squarely on the mouth. A whoop went up from the whores and Martha Bird in her joy hugged Michael Pogo so hard he felt attacked.

Everybody wanted to know, Did he have it? Did it come? Was it healthy? How big was it? And on and on. Killie Willie raised his hand for quiet. A hush fell over the back lot. All questions were answered when from beneath Killie Willie's black and tattered coat came the sign: the squeal of a tortured new pig.

A cheer went up as the squeal grew in intensity. The cheer was loud and happy, and it lasted so long that the pigeons roosting on top of the tenement buildings rose high in the air and circled about.

Killie Willie drew a large poke sack from inside his coat. It squirmed with the kicks of something completely alive. He lowered the sack into the pigpen, pulled the tie, and dumped a dumbfounded Carolina bristled back Yorkshire piglet into the mud.

At first the pig was disoriented. It lay in the mud, its eyes darting about at all the new sights, at all the new and happy faces, at Perfecta standing over her trough like a sphinx.

"Is it a he?" Keister Wertz asked.

Killie Willie chuckled. "Yep," he said.

The new pig shook himself so hard that he slid with a splat back into the mud. If a pig could smile, he was smiling as he came out of the grime. He was free, and to prove it he raced about the sty, ramming into the concrete fencing and knocking himself backward. That didn't stop him. He was off again, racing around and around the edges of the sty. There was no way out.

"Ain't he cute?" one of the whores said. "Cutest little keister I've ever seen."

Keister Wertz grimaced.

"Perfecta's got herself a boyfriend!" Ollie Gus yelled.

And Nate the Wino pinched her on her rear end. Either she didn't feel it or she didn't mind. She didn't say anything about it.

Cora New clung tightly to Killie Willie. She along with most others there was full of joy and peace. And Keister Wertz felt like a proud papa as the little pig raced ridiculously around the sty.

It was Billo who spoke the first negative word. "Wrong color," he said.

Nobody had paid any notice at first, but Billo was right: the Yorkshire, solid white, was the wrong color for Perfecta, a Hampshire, black with a white collar about her neck. So everybody turned to Killie Willie.

"Don't make any difference," he said. "A pig's a pig."

"Don't seem right to me," said Martha Bird.

"Course it's right," said Killie Willie. "Right as rain."

"Perfecta's gonna eat that little old thing for lunch," Nate said. "Poor critter don't stand a chance."

And Ollie Gus let out a high-pitched scream and leapt into the sty to protect her prize.

"What you gonna name it, Killie Willie?" someone asked.

"Well . . ." And all considered for a moment.

It was Billo who spoke up next. "Kermit," he said.

All turned in his direction.

"Yeah. Best name in the world. Kermit. The perfect Kermit for our Miss Piggy."

Thus Kermit had a name. From that time on, he was a welcome part of the rubble pile sty. And Killie Willie Matt and his only daughter, Ollie Gus, were the happiest pig farmers in all of Buttermilk Bottoms.

Kermit was welcomed by all save one: Perfecta. The hog stuck her ears up when Kermit landed in her sty. She stood in her corner, bristles stiffening on her back, her nose flared, her teeth bared. Everybody thought she was grinning at the idea of having a boyfriend, but Killie

Willie knew his pig better than that. He recognized a snarl when he saw one. Perfecta snorted a warning when Kermit came too near, especially when he nosed around her food trough.

It smelled of food. So Kermit flipped the trough bottom-up. That was when he was blind-sided by an irate, ill-tempered, and overly pampered half-grown gilt. Kermit was sent sprawling as Perfecta stood with teeth clenched, straddling her personal property, the V-shaped trough.

Kermit wasn't one to be kept down, though. He was up again, nosing about the sty, looking for something to fill his empty belly. The whores cheered Perfecta on. One of them yelled, "Now that there's my kinda female!"

"Shoot," said Ollie Gus. "Guess we know who's boss in this house."

In less than a minute, Kermit was coated with mud. He seemed damn happy to be in the Bottoms. If only he could find himself something to eat.

"Little fella's hungry," said Michael Pogo. He threw handful after handful of rotting vegetables into the sty. At first Perfecta kept the little pig off the food as best she could. Then there were too many bits and pieces strewn about the sty. Kermit gobbled the food as fast as he could. That pleased Michael Pogo and that pleased Martha Bird. Michael Pogo had himself a new friend to fatten up.

"I smell me some barbecued ribs," Nate the Wino said, licking his lips. And Ollie Gus kicked him like crazy halfway across the rubble pile.

"We got us a real live pig farm now, Killie Willie," Keister Wertz said. He was eager for his pick of the litter. It wasn't every day that a man living in the city could sense the joy that comes only from the fact of harvest.

The two friends shook hands again, and Keister Wertz bid good-bye to all. It was time he was on his way home to kids and wife with the firm hope that someday soon a real live shoat would be his gift to family and friends. He was a happy man.

The folks started off. The whores were behind time for their posts. Nate had his rounds to make, looking for whatever he could find in the neighborhood garbage cans. Cora New had supper to fix. And Michael Pogo couldn't keep his grocery closed during the most important shopping hours of the late afternoon.

"Nice gilt," Martha Bird said to Killie Willie.

"Boar pig, ma'am, boar pig!" With that Martha Bird stormed off. "Stupid woman," Killie Willie said under his breath.

"Like damn Kermit," Ollie Gus said. Killie Willie smiled. After all, he was hers, she had bought him. It was fitten that she should like him, that she should like something in this world.

"He's yours to tend to, baby," he said.

"You expect Perfecta's gonna take to him?"

"Might," he said, not at all worried. "Just might. Why don't you help your mama with supper? I'm kinda hungry myself."

She came out of the sty, covered with sticky mud. She stopped, thought about it, then gave her papa a big hug. Killie Willie didn't know what to say as she climbed the fire escape behind her mama.

Killie Willie set about building a second V-shaped trough, placing it as far from Perfecta's as the sty would let him. Then he mixed up two buckets of slop. Kermit lit into his with relish. His new pig was going to be just fine, Killie Willie knew.

But Perfecta left her slop alone. She just stood there, watching Kermit as he pigged out on the stuff. Killie Willie could tell that Perfecta did not care for this sudden invasion of her world by one of her own kind. She hadn't seemed to mind it when he and Ollie Gus and even Vaughn Brodie and Nate the Wino had entered her sty. But Kermit, he was a different matter altogether. He was a threat.

Martha Bird was watching from her third-story window. She stuck her head out and yelled, "Kermit's just like my ex, Killie Willie! Chicken at heart but all pig!" And she guffawed so loud that Killie Willie figured everybody in the entire world heard her jeer. He didn't find what she had to say funny at all.

When Kermit finished his slop, he edged toward Perfecta's uneaten food. That was just too brazen for Perfecta—it was insult heaped on top of injury. She let out a squeal that was so indignant that even Killie Willie was a bit scared. Kermit lit out for the far corner, as far from Perfecta as he could get. There in the safety of his corner, he forgot all about the huge sow and wallowed in the mud, getting the freight smell out of his bristles. And he continued his rooting, always keeping his distance from Perfecta.

Killie Willie nodded. Things were going to be just fine. Things were looking good in his part of the world, no question about it.

Two days later, Perfecta was still guarding her V-shaped trough. Kermit had explored every inch of the sty a dozen times over, every inch but that right around Perfecta and her precious trough.

Killie Willie waited with the patience of a Frog Level pig farmer, hoping that Perfecta would relax her guard and accept Kermit into her world. But it was beginning to appear that poor Kermit was going to be a pig version of Billo, that is, the one always on the outs.

And maybe that was why Billo had taken to hanging around the sty more than ever. He was there every time that Killie Willie or Ollie Gus was there. He hung around even when nobody was about. Maybe Billo had sympathy for Kermit. Or maybe he felt close to the new pig because it was he, Billo, who had given him, Kermit, his name.

Seeing Kermit not being accepted bothered Billo more than anybody else. He wanted to blame Perfecta, but something inside him told him that it wasn't her fault. It was just the way her society was set up. Kermit was on the outs because he had to be on the outs. That was just the way of things, and Billo wasn't one to question such notions.

"What you gonna do?" Billo asked Killie Willie one morning.

"Bout what?"

"Bout Kermit. Bout him and Perfecta not getting along."

"Well," Killie Willie said, slow and thoughtful, "don't rightly know. Seems to me she's taking to him well enough."

"Shoot, man," Billo said. "That old sow can't stand the sight of that new pig of yours."

"Yep, maybe you're right."

"Course I'm right. Look at that. They don't even look alike."

"He'll grow," Killie Willie said.

"That ain't what I'm talking about!" Billo was getting a bit hot about it. He was seeing a problem and Killie Willie was ignoring it.

"What you got in mind, Billo?"

"Well, hell," Billo said, "I don't know. You ask me, I think Kermit needs a place of his own."

"You mean, like another sty?" Killie Willie was enjoying himself.

"That'd help, sure," Billo said.

"Where would you put it?"

"How the hell should I know? I ain't no contractor." Billo could see that the idea was taking shape in Killie Willie's head. At least the man was thinking about it. And if he thought about it, Kermit would get himself a place of his own. To Billo, that was important.

"Well," Killie Willie said, scratching his chin and running his hand through his hair, "guess we could build him a separate sty and put it over here."

"Yeah," Billo said, "guess you could."

"Chink out an opening between the two, give them a chance to visit," Killie Willie said. He was already seeing the new sty in his head. "What say, Billo?"

"Hope you get it done soon," Billo said and wandered off over the rubble pile.

That was exactly what Killie Willie did: he got it done soon. He cleared away more of the rubble pile and struggled with three large concrete slabs until he had a new and much smaller pigsty butting up against the wall of the first.

When it was finished, he was ashamed to call what he'd made a sty, but it was the best he could do with the materials at hand. He put up a couple of boards and a piece of tin in a corner of the new sty and called it Kermit's Shebang. It really didn't even rate as a shebang, but when there was a rush—and Killie Willie was rushed for a reason he didn't understand himself—almost anything would do.

That afternoon Killie Willie crawled into the new sty with a claw hammer and a wood chisel and began pecking away at the concrete wall that was common to both sties. It was a hot early September afternoon, and beads of sweat rolled down his face and back and chest like the waters in the Edisto River. It felt good to sweat. It felt good to work at something that was worth believing in. Only thing was, the concrete was so hard and so well set up with sand and mortar and cement that pecking at it with a claw hammer was like taking on Caesar's Head with an ice pick.

"Looks to me like you could use better tools," Vaughn Brodie said. Vaughn Brodie had that way about him. He could just all of a sudden be there. Killie Willie hadn't heard him coming. That part of Vaughn Brodie shook Killie Willie just a bit.

"Well," Killie Willie said, "reckon I might. But these is all I have."

"Be back," Vaughn Brodie said. He was gone just as suddenly as he had come.

"That boy," Killie Willie said and went back to his pecking. What Vaughn Brodie needed, Killie Willie knew, was a little bit of Carolina home. That was what kept Killie Willie going—the memories of what it had been like back home in Frog Level, those warm September days down on the river with a line in the water, hoping that the next hit would be a blue cat as big as his leg. He wished he was there now, line in, stringer of bluegill and yellow-ear, a lazy breeze making everything just right. That was what Vaughn Brodie needed. He needed to be a boy back in Carolina, not a damn punk in Buttermilk Bottoms.

Killie Willie stopped. The thought bounced around in his head. If he hadn't moved his family to the Bottoms, what then? What would have become of Vaughn Brodie then? What about Ollie Gus? Would she have taken to drawing back home in Frog Level? Or learned to like something there as she had in the Bottoms? And Cora New. Good, honest Cora New. Salt of the earth, Killie Willie knew. There was no better woman in the world, he knew that. She hardly ever complained. She seemed not to let things bother her. She was Killie Willie's foundation. She was what kept him going, Cora New Magi, the finest woman ever to come out of Frog Level, the finest woman to come out of all Carolina.

Killie Willie sat on the ground. He had made a couple of dents in the concrete, that was all. "Oh, Lordy," he said out loud, quiet and plain. "Oh, Lordy," he said again and again.

"Hot, ain't it?" said Cora New. She was standing outside the new sty with a pitcher of water in her hand. "Thought you might need a bit of refresher."

Killie Willie allowed that he did. He drank two full glasses of water and poured a third over his head. It splashed off the hard earth just like off concrete. "You old fool," she said and started on her way back to the fire escape. He called her back.

They stood with the concrete between them, looking at each other. Killie Willie didn't say anything, so Cora New said, "What you want, Killie Willie?"

He reached for her. She squealed a little and pulled away from him. "Why, you old fool, we out here in front of God and everybody!"

"Don't you like it?" Killie Willie said.

"Course. You know that." Cora New tried to readjust her dignity. "Just that there's a time and place for everything. And this ain't it for that."

"You just too pretty, Cora New," he said. "Couldn't help myself."

"Get on with you," she said. "You too full of yourself today, ain't you?"

She left him to his work. And it went a little better as the pecking started to take effect on the concrete slab. At the rate he was going, it would be a week before he'd have the new sty ready for Kermit. He just hoped Perfecta didn't kill the poor thing before he was through.

Suddenly Vaughn Brodie was back. "You use some help?"

"Ain't one to turn it away," Killie Willie said.

So Vaughn Brodie crawled over the concrete and into the new sty. He brought with him a sledgehammer and a couple of huge wedges just right for going through hardened concrete. "Stand back," he said. And Killie Willie did.

The concrete started flying. Vaughn Brodie was strong and the sweat ran off him just like off his papa. Killie Willie watched with pride. It made him feel good to be there with his son and watch him work like a man. And a good man too. Vaughn Brodie was working like the best of men, swinging the heavy hammer into the concrete.

"You doing good," Killie Willie said. "You want me to spell you?"

Vaughn Brodie was hitting his rhythm. It felt good to be on the other side of physical labor for a change. So much doping had fouled his blood, he knew. Too much easy living had dulled his muscle tone. He liked himself as a laborer. He was accomplishing something, and it was good. Over and over the hammer found its mark and the concrete flew. After a bit Vaughn Brodie turned his work into song. He sang of back home.

He stopped to wipe the sweat from his eyes. Killie Willie asked, "Where'd you get the tools?"

"Stole them," said Vaughn Brodie.

Before the hour was out, Kermit was introduced to his own personal sty. He didn't like it a bit.

"How many more pigs you gonna get?" Cora New asked that night as she and Killie Willie lay side by side in bed.

"Guess that's up to the ones I got," he said.

They lay there talking in the dark of night and liking the warmth of each other. It was warm, it was good. It was almost like being back home as far as they could tell. Except for the stream of noise outside in the streets. Hard as they might try, they couldn't put those sounds of the Bottoms out of their heads.

"You suppose Perfecta'll ever accept him?" Cora New said. She had mixed feelings about that. She didn't mind Perfecta all that much. She had gotten used to all the time that Perfecta took up. She had also gotten over her feelings of playing second fiddle to a hog. But now with Kermit on the block and with the distinct possibility of Perfecta dropping a litter sometime soon, well, Cora New just didn't know what her feelings were supposed to be. "You think she'll ever figure out what we got Kermit for?"

"Soon as he grows a bit," Killie Willie said, "and Perfecta goes into heat."

"Yeah," Cora New said. "The time's gotta be right."

Killie Willie reached under the sheet that covered Cora New's body. He searched until he found her warm thigh. He pinched it lightly. "How about you?" he said. "Is the time right?"

"Shoot," Cora New said. "You ain't had eyes for me all summer long."

"Got eyes for you now." He edged closer to her.

"You won't be thinking of your pigs?"

"I'll be thinking," Killie Willie said, "bout palmetto trees and azaleas." He snuggled up to her and buried his head in her hair. She smelled of soap.

"I'll be thinking bout peach blooms," she said as she pulled Killie Willie on top of her.

"And wild strawberries," he said. "You remember that patch of wild strawberries?"

"Course," Cora New said. Their whispering was becoming almost a purr. "And I'll be thinking about camellias. Dearly love camellias."

"And magnolias."

"And magnolias. And sweet peas."

"And moon pies!!!" yelled Ollie Gus from the other room.

Vaughn Brodie was the night owl. He seldom slept at night, and when he did it was with Fay Leigh, which meant that he didn't sleep much. But he wasn't seeing that much of Fay Leigh these days. He had grown tired of sharing her with the rest of the world. He wanted somebody in his life who thought of him as special. He wanted somebody for himself like his mama was for his papa. And he told Fay Leigh as much.

"You're special to me," Fay Leigh said when he told her the way he was feeling.

"Special enough to marry you?"

"Marry? Shit." And she laughed at him as if he had told a joke.

"You know. That old-fashioned way that people who love one another have of spending time together."

"I'm not old-fashioned."

"Well, I am." He shocked himself with what he was saying. "Some," he said.

"Why would you want to marry? I mean, we got all that married folks have, probably more. We got time together, we got good times—"

"But we ain't got the one thing that matters. Our own self-respect."

"I'm not lacking in self-respect," she whispered, trying to bring him closer.

"No? Well, I am."

He dressed and left, and he didn't see Fay Leigh for at least a week. He began running the thought through his head: what would it have been like if he had stayed home in Frog Level? There had been a girl, too young but she was getting older, real cute, sort of plump but that was her baby fat, it would go away. What was her name? He strained to remember. She was the prettiest little thing in all of Frog Level. He had admired her from his distance even though she was only fourteen. But she would grow and come of age, and he had told himself that when she did he would make his move. Then he moved to the Bottoms.

"Wonzetta," he said aloud. That was her, Wonzetta Poe. A beautiful name, he thought, as beautiful as the girl who sported it. He remembered his last full day in Frog Level. He had made sure he was where Wonzetta would be so he could see her one last time. And he had planted himself just outside the school grounds and waited. She hadn't come by. He had a difficult time remembering her. It was almost as if she didn't exist, almost as if he had made her up. He wondered, did she even know that he, Vaughn Brodie Matt, existed? Or was he a figment of someone's imagination too? He wondered if . . . if maybe he should . . . would she know him if he should . . . ? He couldn't afford to think of Frog Level that way. Frog Level was a different world. He had left it far behind. There was no need to consider returning to it. Not even for a dream person like Wonzetta Poe.

Vaughn Brodie had few friends. He was a loner. In fact, he was a loner by his own choosing. He didn't want any friends. The kinds of folks who lived in the Bottoms weren't the kinds he wanted to be close to. He had no trust in them. If they came on with friendliness, it was because they wanted something from him. And if they wanted something, as far as Vaughn Brodie was concerned it would only cost him money.

That's why it bugged him having Jimmy the punk tailing him everywhere he went.

Vaughn Brodie had no use for Jimmy. He didn't like the kid, even though Jimmy liked Vaughn Brodie as much as anybody he had ever met. There was something about the way that Vaughn Brodie controlled people and got things done. Jimmy admired that. He admired Vaughn Brodie's coolness. Nothing bothered Vaughn Brodie, nothing at all. So Jimmy tailed Vaughn Brodie wherever he went, and Gregalee and the others followed along behind—that is, until Jimmy yelled at Gregalee in his most determined tone, "Get lost, Roonie, you a pest!" And Gregalee got lost along with the rest of the kids.

It was late that night, after Vaughn Brodie had spent much of the afternoon pounding away at the concrete pigsty, that he decided he had had enough. He was wandering down to Junkie's Corner with Jimmy trailing along behind. He took a strange route, so much so that Jimmy wondered if Vaughn Brodie was lost. Without the kid noticing it, Vaughn Brodie was leading him deeper and deeper into the back streets of the Bottoms, an area where Jimmy feared to go without the rest of the kids.

There were junkies and winos and pimps and whores and scum all over the streets. Nobody bothered Vaughn Brodie because he had convinced them that he belonged. But it seemed that everybody was grabbing at Jimmy. He was ripe meat. Nobody connected him with Vaughn Brodie, the noted loner of the Bottoms. Besides, Vaughn Brodie acted as if he had never seen Jimmy before.

Jimmy knew he was a goner when two whores, one on each side of him, began giving him a hard time and a pimp came along and grabbed him from behind by the back of his shirt and pulled him into a dark alley with the two whores following. Oh, they knew how to manage a kid like him. It was fast and simple. Jimmy knew how it worked, and since he had broken the rule by wandering too far abroad after dark, it was as if he had what was coming to him coming to him. There was nothing he could do about it. The whores pinned his arms and lifted him off the ground, pushing him back on top of a crate. The pimp ran his hands all over Jimmy's body and came out with his blade, a couple of quarters, and not much else.

"Damn kid's broke," the pimp whispered. "You guys can have him." And he took Jimmy's blade and ripped open his pants for the whores, leaving him there. That is, he tried to leave.

As he turned, something caught him on the side of the head. Jimmy couldn't see. He had his hands full with the two whores. But it sounded like a fence post landing across the pimp's face. The pimp let out a strange-sounding groan and crumpled to his knees.

"Get the hell out of here," a voice said to the pimp, who was crawling as fast as he could across the dark alley. "Gonna cut your balls off and stuff them down your throat," the voice said with emphasis.

The whores disappeared. And Jimmy didn't note where the pimp got off to. He was too concerned with getting himself back together, trying to make himself decent again, when Vaughn Brodie reached out and touched him on the shoulder.

Jimmy yelped at the touch.

"You okay?" Vaughn Brodie asked.

"God . . ." That was all Jimmy could say. "God . . ."

"What you think you doing in this part of town anyway, punk? Ain't you got no sense?"

"God . . ."

"Come on, let's get out of here."

They walked back toward their part of the Bottoms. They didn't appear to be together even though they walked along side by side. Vaughn Brodie didn't speak. It took Jimmy a long time before he finally said, "You set me up, didn't you?"

"Yep."

"What did you do that for?"

"Teach you something," Vaughn Brodie said.

"Like what?"

"You don't know, you ain't learned nothing. Damn, you're stupid."

Jimmy walked along for a minute, thinking about it. He was having a hard time keeping up with Vaughn Brodie, the rip in his pants making his stride difficult to manage with dignity. Finally he stopped in the street and yelled, "Why don't you like me, junkie?!"

Vaughn Brodie stopped too. The street was buzzing with life, but he stood there in the middle of the sidewalk staring at the punk kid. "Who says I don't like you?"

"You do, fool."

"I do?" Vaughn Brodie studied it for a second or two. "I don't recall hearing me say anything like that."

"The way you act—"

"How you want me to act?"

"I don't know," said Jimmy. "I mean . . . oh, the hell with it." They walked along for a block before he said, "I like you."

"How come?"

"Cause you a cool dude."

"I'm a damn junkie who's near to being hooked on his own stuff. You call that cool?"

"Yeah, man."

"You're sick."

One of Vaughn Brodie's rivals from Junkie's Corner caught sight of him from the other side of the street. He gave a hoot and yelled out, "Yooooo, junkie! Soooooooey!" And burst out laughing.

Jimmy rushed into the street and was halfway across it when the second "Soooooooey!" rang out. The sound seemed to echo all over the Bottoms. "Soooooooey!!"

"Shut up!" Jimmy yelled. "Shut the fuck up!!"

The rival sauntered into the street, took a look at Jimmy's split pants, and cavorted. The street rang with laughter.

"Leave him be," Jimmy said.

"Who the hell are you?" the rival demanded.

"His friend," said Jimmy, trying to pull himself up taller than he was. Vaughn Brodie stood by with his arms folded. It didn't bother him. He had been taunted with the pig call day in, day out since Perfecta arrived on the block.

"You his friend, huh?" the guy said. "That mean you have sex with his damn pig too?" The laughter trilled up and down the crowded street.

But his laugh was cut short as Jimmy landed his right fist squarely on the fellow's nose. He felt the cartilage flatten under the blow. And that shocked him. Jimmy didn't know he could punch so hard. But he didn't stop. The guy staggered backward as Jimmy followed, landing blow after blow about the guy's head. The rival flailed away, trying to ward the kid off, but he couldn't get him off. It took Vaughn Brodie, pulling Jimmy away from behind. He was still swinging with all his might as Vaughn Brodie dragged him across the street. He was screaming such things as "I'll kill the sumbitch! Let me kill the sumbitch!"

"Hey, Jimbo," Vaughn Brodie said over and over until his friend calmed down. "Let's go home, Jimbo, come on now."

"He can't say those things about you."

"Why not?"

"Ah, shit on it."

Vaughn Brodie put an arm around Jimmy's shoulders. They walked home at a slower pace.

"We had us some night, ain't we?" Jimmy said.

"Guess so."

"Vaughn Brodie?"

"Still here."

"I think I broke my hand."

Vaughn Brodie was too keyed up to sleep that night. Instead he stepped out back to the pigsties. He wanted to say hello to his pals, the pigs. It was hot. He knew it would be dawn before he witnessed any rest.

"Sooey," he whispered. He was answered by a soft grunt. He didn't know which pig it came from. He didn't care. He was thinking about that "soooooooey" out in the street. He remembered that at first the taunts bugged him, made him hate, made him want to fight the way Jimmy had fought. But now it didn't matter. And that was what bugged him. Was he becoming immune to the Bottoms? Was the Bottoms getting to him? Changing him? Making him like those who had lived there forever? The thoughts he was having were hateful to him. But at the time he knew of no alternative. The Bottoms was his home.

Jimmy the punk found Vaughn Brodie the next day down at Junkie's Corner.

"Well," he said, "what do you think?" He modeled his new pants, shirt, shoes, et al.

"For God's sake!" gasped Vaughn Brodie. Jimmy was dressed in the exact same fashion as Vaughn Brodie. It was almost like looking in a mirror. Even Jimmy's hair was frizzed in the same way. Even the bandanna about the neck, even the way the shoelaces were tied, even the necklace and the wristband and the buttons on the shirt. "What you trying to prove, punk?"

"Tell me, what you think?"

"I think you're some sort of stupid punk kid, that's what I think."

"You don't like it?"

"Looks like shit, man."

"You the one what looks like shit, man."

"Jesus Christ," said Vaughn Brodie and stormed off, leaving Jimmy befuddled and not at all pleased.

"What the hell's the matter with you, junkie? Don't you like how you look?"

"Go to hell!" Vaughn Brodie called.

"You the one, man!! You the one!!!" Jimmy screamed at the retreating Vaughn Brodie. "You nothing but shit, man!" And he rammed his fist into the lamppost. If he hadn't broken it the night before, it was broken then, and Jimmy doubled up in pain.

He wandered off toward his place, holding his hand like it was a broken vase. He wasn't good enough, that was it. Just not good enough. What was there left for him? He didn't know. What could be left?

Late that afternoon when the streets were filled with folks milling about, Jimmy came from his place with an unusual bulge under his jacket. Something looking like a strange stick poked out the top near his chin. And he made his way down the street toward Michael Pogo's grocery store.

He lolled about for a bit, waiting. His nerves were frayed. His broken hand was loosely wrapped in a piece of white gauze. He was itchy. His face was drawn with pain. After a time of fussing about outside the store, he entered.

The shop was mostly empty. There was a sweet smell of earth around the fresh vegetables. There was a putrid odor near the pears as the fruit was turning soft. Michael Pogo stood near his register behind the counter, greeting all with a simple nod of his head.

Jimmy found an apple to his liking. He chose it with his good hand and rubbed it loosely on his pants, giving the red skin a brilliant shine. He approached Michael Pogo, held out the apple, and asked, "How much?"

"Quarter," said Michael Pogo.

Jimmy's nerves were causing his voice to shake. He didn't want to shake. He wanted this to be the doing of a man. He straightened himself and said as steadily as he could, "I'll take it. Long with the cash you got in your register."

"You what?" Michael Pogo said, his eyes nearly popping out of his head.

"I said—" And from beneath his jacket Jimmy pulled the semiautomatic rifle that Vaughn Brodie had left behind at the pigsty. "I said—I'll take what cash you got in your register."

Jimmy didn't see Michael Pogo's finger under the counter as he pressed the buzzer that connected him with the station house two blocks away. What he saw was fear on Michael Pogo's face and surprise and dread and the desire for what was happening not to be happening at all.

"You want my money?" Michael Pogo said.

"You heard me."

"Nobody robs me. Nobody needs to rob me. You want food, I'll give you food. You want credit, I'll carry you."

"Empty the cash in a grocery bag," Jimmy whispered. "Now."

"Son—"

"NOW!!!"

Michael Pogo opened his register and emptied its contents into a brown paper sack. Jimmy was pointing the wickedest-looking weapon he had ever seen at his belly button. It was all that Michael Pogo could do to keep from passing out behind his counter. Afterward, he thought that his passing out might have been a good thing to do, if he had only known.

Jimmy grabbed the bag with his broken hand. He had to clutch it against his chest with his forearm. He backed his way to the door.

"Please. Jimmy, please, don't do this," Michael Pogo said over and over. But Jimmy did it. He turned and rushed into the street.

He was armed. He was dangerous. He was in the act of breaking the law. So the law opened fire. They had received Michael Pogo's distress call and had responded immediately. Two cars were waiting in the street. Four Magnums opened up at once. Twelve slugs entered Jimmy's body and threw him like a sack of wet mash against the brick wall of the store. He bounced loosely to the ground as the cash from the paper sack floated around him in a shower and the heavy semiautomatic clanged to the sidewalk, a harmless piece of empty junk. It all happened with such rapidity and such finality that all Michael Pogo could do was kneel behind his counter . . . and pray.

Jimmy's death filled every mouth that afternoon and night and for days afterward. Jimmy was just a punk kid, they said. Just a misled little junkie, they said. A rightful justice for his kind, they said. Nothing lost, they said. Vaughn Brodie heard of it from Ollie Gus, who had seen it all. And Ollie Gus hated it, hated everything about it. They didn't give Jimmy a chance, she said. Just shot him like he was a fox in the chicken coop, she said. Paid no heed to what he was about or who he was or anything like that, she said. She hated everything about the Bottoms, she said. And so did Vaughn Brodie. More than ever, he hated the Bottoms. More than he could possibly say, he hated everything about the Bottoms.

"Onliest thing that makes life worth living," Ollie Gus said to her brother, "is my pretty little pig. Kermit makes living have meaning."

Vaughn Brodie couldn't agree with that. He didn't know how he felt, really. Nothing, not even his stuff, not even his pills or his powders, nothing was worthwhile. Except his memories of Frog Level.

"Mama," he said that night to his mother as they stood together on the fire escape landing, "you ever miss Frog Level?"

"Don't let myself think much about it," said Cora New.

"You don't wish you was back down there every once in a while?"

"Can't think about such things, Vaughn Brodie. Can't let myself. When we chucked it all and moved up here, we put that life behind us, come what may."

"For me too? Or just for yourself?"

"What you got on your mind, son?"

"Not much. Sometimes . . ." He didn't know if he could put his thoughts into words. "Just don't seem like there's much use to living in a place like this. Seems that maybe Jimmy's the lucky one, him and all the others who break out of this place."

"I just can't think like that, Vaughn Brodie."

"Well, I can." He left down the fire escape, heading for Jimmy's place. He didn't know what he would find there. He didn't care. He knew, though, that he had to go.

Killie Willie was sleeping hard that night. He dreamed of six little piglets scampering about his sty. He dreamed of six more separate sties and of the back lot filled with the aroma of hogs. He dreamed of . . .

He popped awake. He had heard something. Or had it been in his dreams? His dreams were of pigs, and he thought he had heard a pig scream.

He listened. Nothing. Strange sounds were not unusual in the Bottoms. There was no need for concern.

He rolled over, hoping to find his dreams once again.

He heard it again. He sat up in bed. Yes, he heard it for certain this time. There was no doubt. It was Perfecta. She had bellowed her rage and terror. Just the sound of it filled Killie Willie with such fear that he sat frozen to his sheet. And again, she screamed again.

When he moved, it was with speed.

"What's the matter?" Cora New said as he slipped out of bed and into his clothes. Then she heard it. "Oh, God," said Cora New. "Hurry, Killie Willie, hurry—" She didn't have to urge him on.

"Papa," Ollie Gus said. She was standing in the bedroom doorway, naked as a freshly dressed chicken.

"Get your clothes on, girl," Killie Willie said as he pulled on his pants. "And run fetch Vaughn Brodie."

"I don't know where Vaughn Brodie is," Ollie Gus said.

"Well, find him!!" Killie Willie yelled.

He raced out of the tenement and down the fire escape and into the rubble pile. Again there was the scream. It was higher and more penetrating this time. It sent shivers up Killie Willie's spine, and it put an extra charge into his legs. He had worked hard the day before, but that didn't matter now. His prize was in pain and he had to do something about it.

His head was too fast for his feet and he tripped over the bedsprings that were in the rubble pile again. He fell across the metal and rammed a piece of a spring deep into his palm. But he didn't feel it. Fact was, he didn't know anything about his wound at the time. He ignored the blood that was pouring out of his hand and splashing on his pants and shirt. He had to get to Perfecta's sty. Something was messing with his pig.

He came over the top of the rubble and stumbled down the slope to the sty. It was too dark. He hadn't thought to take time and get a flashlight. Never crossed his mind. It took him a minute or two for his eyes to get accustomed to the dark.

Then he saw it: the glint of light off what had to be the metal of a blade. And the blade was in the hand of something unsteady and drunk. There in the sty was Nate the Wino, and in his hand was a tiny but wicked-looking switchblade that would have glinted more than it did if it wasn't coated with blood.

Nate was clucking with his tongue against his teeth, trying to lure Perfecta out of her corner. He had a half-eaten watermelon in his free hand, and he was trying to coax the pig away from the wall. He was slipping and sliding in the mud and Kermit was running round and round the sty.

Killie Willie took it all in. At first he was too shocked to do anything. Then he found his voice. "Nate!!" he shouted.

The suddenness of his name being called in the dark caught Nate right in his balance. His feet flew straight up over his head, and he landed squarely on his behind. Killie Willie could have sworn he heard a muffled crash like something glass being shattered. Nate's cry of pain had to be caused by more than a fall in the mud. He yelped and cursed and grabbed for his butt and did all he could to right himself. But his feet seemed leadened by the mud. And the more he flailed about, the more he got covered by the sticky stuff.

He made it to his knees, but Perfecta was ready for him. She charged and caught the drunk in his midsection and sent him skidding across the sty. By then Killie Willie was over the wall and deep in the mud himself. He grabbed Nate by the lapels of his coat and lifted him high and shook him like he was a schoolboy needing a sound scolding.

Nate still grabbed for his butt. "Look what you made me do!" he shouted as he pulled the top part of a broken bottle from his hip pocket. But the rest of the bottle stayed behind, some of it undoubtedly embedded in his tail. "Ninety percent Kentucky straight, Killie Willie, and you made me bust it!!" Nate was almost moved to tears over his loss.

"You drunk?" Killie Willie said, shaking the wino even harder.

"No," Nate said, trying to stifle a hic with the back of his hand. "I ain't never been drunk a day in my life," he said.

"What you think you doing here, Nate?!" Killie Willie was getting riled. He'd seen the knife. He'd seen something on it. It'd been too dark, though, to make out what it was. "What you doing here?!!"

"Just come to get me some spareribs," Nate said with a silly little chuckle.

Killie Willie couldn't believe his ears. Spareribs? In a pigsty? He dropped Nate with a thud. He moved with expert ease to where Perfecta stood groaning in her corner. She whimpered almost like a little child. Killie Willie had never heard a pig make such a sound before, and it bothered him.

"What's a-matter, baby?" he said, cooing like a mama to a naughty child.

He reached out to touch her, but she snapped at him—the first time she had ever snapped at Killie Willie. "Easy, now," he said, trying to soothe her. "Ain't nobody else gonna hurt you. You gonna be just fine."

Perfecta stood silent. Killie Willie would have thought she'd stopped breathing, except that he felt her hot breath on his hand as he reached out. But she didn't make a sound. The only sound in the sty was that of Nate as he struggled to dig the broken glass out of his hip pocket.

Killie Willie touched his pig. She felt cold to his touch, and her bristles were like those of a catfish fin. He ran his hand down along her side to her right flank, and there he felt the moisture that was thick and warm, almost hot.

Maybe a few seconds before, it had been hot. He held the wetness to his mouth and tasted blood.

"You goddamn sumbitch." Killie Willie didn't know if he said those words or not. He knew that he heard them, but it was like somebody outside himself was speaking in his ear and he couldn't help but hear. The words repeated themselves over and over inside his head. "You goddamn sumbitch! You goddamn sumBITCH!!!"

And Killie Willie forgot himself. He forgot that he was a Carolina pig farmer. He forgot that he didn't believe in violence. He forgot that he was himself, an old man with wrinkled skin and creaking joints. He remembered, though, that he was strong, and it was his strength that did what he did next. He threw himself so hard against Nate the Wino that both men flew against the concrete slab and knocked it cattywampus.

The blow knocked all the wind out of Nate, but Killie Willie's strength had only just begun to exert itself. He hit Nate again. This time the blow toppled the concrete backward and the two men fell over it and out of the sty.

"You killing me, Killie Willie!" Nate finally got out. Or he got something like that out. Killie Willie didn't know. He wasn't in any mood to listen. He was sitting on top of Nate with the wino's head between his hands. He was banging that head with every ounce of his strength against the concrete. He wanted the life to leave the body that was beneath him. He wanted to feel the collapse of strength that would come only when the body was dead. Killie Willie was the strongest man in the world and there was nothing Nate could do but scream for help. And he did, over and over.

There was a brief moment when Killie Willie thought he heard something like "oh, sweet Jesus" coming from the mouth of Nate. It was like Nate had given in to the fate of dying there in the back lot at the hands of a manic pig farmer. And all because the fellow had wanted a few barbecued spareribs. What was that to lose one's life for? Oh, Jesus Christ . . .

But he didn't die. It wasn't Killie Willie's fault. He was knocked sideways off Nate by a well-placed blow to the side of his head. And Vaughn Brodie stood over him. Vaughn Brodie was smiling. Killie Willie couldn't understand that. Why was he smiling?

"No need to kill the sumbitch," Vaughn Brodie said. "It ain't worth it, Papa."

Nate scrambled to his feet as best he could. And Killie Willie would have been back at him if Vaughn Brodie hadn't held him down.

"Let me up, Vaughn Brodie!" Killie Willie yelled. "I'll kill the sumbitch! I'll kill him!!"

"You ain't killing nobody, old man," Vaughn Brodie said, still smiling. That smile was about to drive Killie Willie right out of his head.

"You hurt me," Nate said, holding the back of his head. "Whatcha do that for, Killie Willie? I never hurt you. I'd never hurt you. We friends, Killie Willie."

"Get while you can," Vaughn Brodie said.

"Just wanted me some spareribs was all," Nate said.

"I'll kill the sumbitch!!" Killie Willie yelled.

"You nothing but cockshit, Killie Willie," Nate said from what he thought was a safe distance.

"You ain't away from here in one minute," Vaughn Brodie said, "I'm letting him go and might even help him bust your skull, Nate. You listening to me?"

"Let me up, Vaughn Brodie," Killie Willie said. "Let me kill him, okay?"

"Cool it, old man," Vaughn Brodie said.

"Nothing but cockshit," Nate said as he backed away. "And here's what ol Nate does to cockshit." He spat on the concrete with such force that he lost his footing again and fell flat on his face.

Vaughn Brodie walked over and picked Nate up like he was stuffed with chicken feathers. "Look, wino," Vaughn

Brodie said. "You got to three to make yourself invisible, cause then I'm letting my old man loose and him and me are gonna rip your arms out of your sockets. One . . ."

"But he busted my bottle—"

"Two . . ."

Nate scampered across the rubble pile as fast as his drunk legs would take him. He kept hollering back all kinds of obscenities, but Vaughn Brodie just laughed as he helped Killie Willie to his feet.

"You okay?" Vaughn Brodie said.

"Hand hurts," Killie Willie said. "What did you stop me for? I wanted to kill the sumbitch."

"Cause they got laws against murder, Papa."

"They got laws against folks cutting up on somebody else's pig?" Killie Willie said. "He was cutting up on Perfecta something bad, Vaughn Brodie."

Vaughn Brodie and Killie Willie went into the sty. That was easy now that the concrete slab had been knocked out of the way. Vaughn Brodie lit his Bic. It didn't help much, but it did help them find the pig.

Perfecta had gone to her knees in her corner. Her right hind leg was bleeding, and she was breathing heavily. The warm blood turned cold in the mud.

Killie Willie saw the blood and his legs went limp too. He sank down beside his sow and would have wept if he hadn't been a fully grown man.

Vaughn Brodie inspected the open wounds and said, "We gonna have to sew her up."

"Oh, God . . ." Killie Willie said.

"Ain't so bad, Papa," Vaughn Brodie said. "Pigs got thick hides. They got worlds of fat under that skin, and I don't think Nate got too deep."

"Oh, God . . ."

"Come on, Papa, you gotta help me." Vaughn Brodie thought for a bit. "You ever sew up a hog before, Papa?"

"No," he said. He was swaying slightly. Vaughn Brodie figured that the old man didn't have any idea where he was. All he was feeling right then was hurt, a hurt that couldn't be put aside.

"Well," Vaughn Brodie said, "I watched a fella do it once down on the Corner. Didn't look like there was all that much to it." He stood up. He'd need special tools, like a needle and some heavy-duty thread. "You be all right if I leave for a minute?"

"Yeah," Killie Willie said.

"Why don't you just talk to her, okay?" Vaughn Brodie said. "Be right back." He took off across the rubble pile. And neither Killie Willie nor Perfecta made a sound. It was like they were both waiting to see if the other one was going to live.

It could have been hours, but it was only a few minutes that Vaughn Brodie was gone. He came back with Cora New's sewing box as well as Cora New herself, carrying a flashlight, and Ollie Gus, who carried herself. That was a job in itself.

With Cora New holding the light and Killie Willie kneeling near her head and Ollie Gus pacing back and forth like an expectant papa, Vaughn Brodie sewed up Perfecta's wounds. They were deep and long and it took him quite a while, but he did it.

Perfecta didn't flinch as the needle moved in and out of her flesh. She must have known that they were doing all they could to save her. But it hurt Killie Willie to watch. Instead he kept his eyes on Perfecta's one good eye and tried to tell her with his inner voice that all was going to be just fine . . . just fine.

"Where's Kermit?" Ollie Gus asked, but nobody paid her any attention. "Kermit?" she called. "Kermit!"

When the sun came up the next morning, Killie Willie was still by Perfecta's side. Ollie Gus had demanded to stay with her papa, to look for her Kermit, to do something, anything, everything. But Cora New had put her foot down. No, and that means no, young lady, she said. Sun'll be up soon, she said. No need to look for anything so late at night, she said. Kermit will be fine, just fine, she said. Cora New had been right about one thing: the sun did come up soon. And Ollie Gus was out with the first light, searching the back lot for Kermit, that damn stupid idiot of a pig that didn't have any better sense than to go wandering off like he did. Damn stupid pig.

In the daylight, Perfecta's wounds didn't seem quite as bad as they had the night before. Three long gashes ran along her right hindquarter and there were several other ones not nearly so long or nearly so deep along the underside of her ribs. It was those last three that made Killie Willie's stomach turn. They were mean. It took a mean knife in a mean hand to make such cuts in a living animal's hide. Vaughn Brodie's stitching was ragged, making the wounds seem more sinister than they really were. Strings hung from Perfecta's hindquarter and ribs. And she gnawed at them out of irritation.

For the first time in his memory, Killie Willie knew what it meant to hate. He could forgive the kids for Perfecta's eye. But these cuts had been made by a grown man, a man Killie Willie had almost learned to trust because of the help he had given before. But then, too, he knew how alcohol could make a monster out of the meekest of men. Just as Nate couldn't help himself when it came to drinking, Killie Willie couldn't help himself for hating Nate for it.

Then there was the specter of infection. The Bottoms was too unhealthy for a pig, especially one with multiple knife wounds sewn up with a common household needle. Infection could so easily set in, and if it did there was nothing that Killie Willie or anybody could do. He thought of going back to Vernadetta Hope, but he didn't want to burden her with another rescue job. Perfecta had to be on her own with this problem. And if she died, well . . .

"I can't find Kermit," Ollie Gus said. She stood on one of the piles of rubble, her clenched fists resting on her hips. She looked like a giantess, the mother earth of the back lot. "Papa!" She wasn't sure that Killie Willie heard her or, if he did, that he even cared about her pig.

"What say, baby?"

"I can't find Kermit nowhere!!"

"Well, he's got to be about. Just keep looking."

"Papa!" she screamed. "You gotta help me find him."

"We'll find him," Killie Willie moaned. He was so tired. All he wanted to do was sleep. But he knew he had work to do, both at the savings and loan and in the Bottoms, trying to find his stray boar pig.

"Where? He ain't in the back lot!"

"How do you know?"

"Cause I done looked, damn it! Papa!!" And she wailed.

"It ain't all lost, baby, it ain't all lost." But he couldn't convince himself. How did he hope to ease his little girl's feelings?

"What if we don't find him?" she begged.

"We will, we will." His logic amazed him. "If we don't, then I guess we don't. But we will."

"I'll find him! Damn stupid ignorant hog!" And she was off again, searching.

"Lordy," Killie Willie said, more to the world than to himself. "Pigs were never this much trouble back home in Frog Level."

Before noon, Ollie Gus had half the neighborhood looking for the missing Kermit. Most of the folks didn't know how to go about looking for a lost pig, so they weren't that much help. Some wandered around whistling as if they were looking for a dog. Others clucked as if they expected Kermit to squat down and lay an egg. Still others actually moved about the streets mooing. Of course, that was more a joke than it was serious—at least Killie Willie hoped so. Still, it was all ridiculous as far as he was concerned. Folks in the Bottoms knew as much about pig farming as their television sets would allow, and he didn't envy them at all.

Billo rounded up a dozen or so kids to help. Even though none of them cared for Billo (who was still on the outs), they couldn't pass up the chance to be in on the Great Pig Hunt that was taking place in the Bottoms. Besides, the hunt kept their minds off the funeral that was coming up. They entered the pig hunt like they would enter a hundred-yard dash, with all the energy one could want but with no control. The kids were all over the block, exploring crevices and holes that they had always avoided before. Kermit's being lost gave them the chance to do some exploring that they had all been wanting to do.

Even Vaughn Brodie joined in the hunt, though not with all his heart. He was beginning to dislike the presence of pigs in the Bottoms. They were too much trouble. From start to finish, Perfecta had been a pain in Vaughn Brodie's butt. Still, he couldn't help but feel a little affection for the beast. He strolled to the sty to check on his stitching and found her lolling in the mud as if nothing had happened the night before. She bore her bruises like a valiant soldier, and he admired that. The stitches were holding up, and except for the few splotches of blood here and there in the mud, nobody would ever suspect that the sty had been the scene of a major crisis.

Vaughn Brodie leaned on the concrete slab that he and his papa had replaced. Perfecta looked up at him with her one good eye. To him, the poor animal was so pathetic. Yet he couldn't swear to it afterward, but it seemed as if the pig smiled at him. She knew him. She trusted him. She relied on him as her true protector. And he saw in her a good and devoted friend. There was no way that he could do anything about such a friendship as that. So he joined in the hunt for Kermit. He passed up a day at Junkie's Corner. He passed up a visit with Fay Leigh, something he no longer cared about anyway. He didn't know why he joined in the hunt. He couldn't help himself. He had too much of his papa in him, he supposed.

Martha Bird joined in the hunt because Michael Pogo did. Michael Pogo had closed his shop when he heard from Ollie Gus about the escaped pig. He did it with relish and seemed to enjoy himself greatly. But Martha Bird was the biggest waste of time on the block when it came to hunting missing pigs. All she did was bassackards according to Ollie Gus. She tried to keep up with Michael Pogo. All she did was hold others back. So finally she had to go off on her own, looking mainly in the middle of the streets.

Nate the Wino, semisober and with a splitting headache, joined in the hunt too. He had little recall of the night before and what he remembered he blamed on the demon in the bottle. He couldn't explain the huge knots on the back of his head or the slivers of glass that populated his butt or his shattered whiskey bottle. He complained that his head was the size of a Halloween pumpkin and that his rear end was as hot as the back burner of a wood stove. But still he helped look for Kermit. Once during the day he asked Killie Willie, "How did the bugger get loose?" And Killie Willie almost took a swing at him. Would have if Cora New hadn't grabbed him by the arm and answered, "Accident." That seemed to satisfy Nate for the time being.

Nate wasn't much help, though. He couldn't focus his eyes very well, and that kept him from going into the more inconvenient places that a pig might choose to hide in.

Every basement, every back alley, every rat-infested crevice, every floor of most tenements within a three-block area was searched time and again. Each time a person thought he had found Kermit, it turned out to be an alley cat or a stray dog or a kangaroo rat, at which Killie Willie just scoffed. There was no such animal, never was, never will be. Not in the Bottoms, as far as he knew.

By the time the sun came near the top of the tenements, Killie Willie was ready to call the Great Pig Hunt off. Kermit was not to be found. He had the notion in his head that Kermit didn't want to be found. Either that or maybe he wasn't in the neighborhood anymore. Maybe he had gotten free of the Bottoms and hightailed it south into the park or Lord knows where. He even considered letting Keister Wertz know of Kermit's disappearance, but he resisted that notion.

Hunt as everybody did, Kermit was not to be found. Ollie Gus was dumbfounded. How could a stupid animal like Kermit, so new to the Bottoms, disappear so completely and not leave a trace? It befuddled everybody.

By late afternoon the enthusiasm for the search had slipped away. Folks swore that they had searched every possible hole, every potential hideaway at least four times, and Kermit simply was not in the neighborhood anymore.

"If that pig's on the street," Michael Pogo said, and Martha Bird agreed, "there ain't no telling where he is. Futile," he said with Martha Bird's agreement, "nothing but futile, if you ask me."

"Amen to that, yes, sir," said Martha Bird Blotchley.

"Ought to call the cops," one of the whores suggested, but then she thought better of her suggestion when she considered what the police would do if they found a pig in the Bottoms.

"That pig's probably somebody's brunswick stew right now," another whore said, making Ollie Gus shudder.

"Nuff!" Ollie Gus yelled. "Hate damn brunswick stew!"

"It's over," said Killie Willie. He didn't know what else to say. "Guess everybody's done about all they can do. It's over."

"Well," said Ollie Gus, "that pig's mine. I paid for him, he's mine, and I ain't giving up. No, sir. Ain't. Ain't giving up. Who's going with me to look some more?"

Nobody moved except Billo, who slipped away unnoticed.

"Ain't nobody?!" screamed Ollie Gus.

"Guess we done lost us a pig," Killie Willie admitted. And the neighbors began making their way home.

"Quitters!" Ollie Gus yelled at the peak of her lungs. "I ain't never quit. Ain't gonna quit now!! Hate damn quitters, every last one of you!" And she darted off to search the back alleys and the basements and the empty tenements and the deserted back lots for the umpteenth time.

Vaughn Brodie wandered off toward Junkie's Corner. And Killie Willie, Cora New, and Nate the Wino entered their place in a mood that verged on the depressed.

"What you gonna do now?" Cora New asked.

"Tend to Perfecta best I can," Killie Willie answered. What else could he say?

Nate curled up on Ollie Gus' cot without being invited, and before anyone could complain he was sound asleep. Killie Willie sat on the escape landing by himself, thinking. In a bit he wandered out to Perfecta's sty. It was the only place he had where he felt he could be himself.

He sat on the concrete fencing, scratching Perfecta behind her ears. She grunted lightly with pleasure. At least he still had his Hampshire shoat. That's what he told Keister Wertz when he came by that evening. He told Keister everything, all about losing Kermit, and ended with "Well, still got Perfecta, praise the Lord."

Keister had come by because of all the work Killie Willie had been missing. It embarrassed Keister for a man like Killie Willie, a man whom he had recommended for the top janitorial job at the savings and loan, a man who he had assured those in charge of such things as personnel would be a safe and secure bet, to fall short of what was considered to be acceptable. "You don't come to work in the morning, they gonna fire you, Killie Willie, and that'll make me look bad. Don't want to make me look bad, do you?"

"Well," Killie Willie said, "well . . ." That was all.

Keister could see that Killie Willie was more concerned with other things. He was full of sympathy and regret and hope that Kermit would show up sooner or later. Killie Willie could tell that the man knew better. He was just being nice, and there was no need for anybody to be nice, not anymore. Killie Willie's pig farm, or what might have been a pig farm, was falling apart—he could see that, Keister Wertz could see that, and they both disliked what they saw.

"Guess I should of stayed down home in the first place," Killie Willie said as they leaned together against the concrete fencing. "This hog would have been better off down home. Look at her. Stitches hanging out. Only one eye. And this damn mud's too slick and sticky. Not like the mud back home in Frog Level. Makes me hate myself sometimes when I think that I deprived Perfecta of ever knowing the sweet mud of Carolina. Yep, we'd all of been much better off if we'd stayed home where we belong."

"That's self-pity if I ever heard it," said Keister Wertz. "There's no room in this world for an ego that's intent on self-pity."

"I know what you mean."

"Besides, Kermit will show up. Just give him time."

"Yeah, maybe so. Maybe so."

The two were quiet for a bit, then Keister chucked Killie Willie on the shoulder. "I'll tend to things down at the office. Don't worry about it, okay?"

"Appreciate it, sir."

"Your pig'll show up," Keister said and started off across the rubble toward his waiting cab. But Keister knew that Kermit was long gone, probably dead and half-eaten already. There wasn't much hope for a hog loose in the Bottoms. That was a fact of life. It was sad for Keister Wertz. He had counted on the pick of the litter. It was sad and, in a way, a little defeating. Killie Willie wasn't one to take setbacks with any kind of lingering negative thoughts, though. It wasn't his style. But Cora New never knew when his ability to resist life's problems might wear thin. She waited on the fire escape until Keister Wertz had left the sty before she approached her man. She sat beside him and gently caressed his shoulders in the spots she knew he liked having rubbed. Her fingers were experienced.

"Thanks for the other night," she said. "Felt awful good."

"Yeah, did," he said. He slipped his arm around her middle. "You doing all right?"

"Tired. You?"

"Yeah, tired."

"I heard what you told Mr. Wertz."

"Things sort of fall to pieces, don't they?" he said. And they sat still for a while, watching Perfecta nosing around in her sty. Her wounds were not going to fester, he could tell that much, and he was thankful. "I could of killed Nate last night," he said. "Would have, too, if Vaughn Brodie hadn't come along."

"Thank God for our children," Cora New said, meaning it.

"Yeah, guess so." Killie Willie felt that there was something he needed to say to her, some sort of apology for carting her and her brood so far from their rightful place in Frog Level, but he couldn't put words to what he wanted to say. "You know, Cora New, we been away from home long enough."

"We are home."

"Never be home here," he said. "You know that. The other night? How nice was it? Just you and me and Ollie

Gus listening in, yeah, that was like home almost. But it ain't often enough. Not near often enough."

"That's up to you."

"Anyway, as nice as the other night was, and as hard as I tried, I couldn't for the life of me remember what a palmetto tree looks like. All I could see in my head were those palm trees you see in pictures. And they ain't like palmettos, not a bit. You remember what a palmetto tree looks like?"

"I don't see how that has anything—"

"Answer the question, Cora New."

"No," Cora New said. "I know what you mean too. I don't remember the smell of camellias, either, and I used to go sniffing every spring. Come to think of it, I don't know if a camellia even has an odor to it. Strange, ain't it? We lived with those things all our life. But here it just don't seem important."

"We been away from home too long," Killie Willie said.

"We are home, Killie Willie. Home is where you are and the kids and our bed. That's what makes a home." After a bit, she added, "You just lonesome for it, that's all."

He didn't say anything to that. He just sat there looking down at the sow, who was sprawled out in the mud. "Maybe we just ain't looked in the right places," he said.

Cora New couldn't help but smile. Life hadn't gotten to him yet. He still had hope. That was Cora New's hope, that Killie Willie would never give in to accepting life's hard licks.

"You know any other places to look?" she said.

"Maybe." But he didn't convince himself, much less her.

"Why don't you just let the poor little thing go, Killie Willie? Just forget him." Cora New knew her man. All she had to do was suggest a thing and she knew he'd do the opposite.

"If you was a new shoat in a strange neighborhood," Killie Willie said, "and you got loose, where would you go? Why, you'd go looking for something to eat, and after that you'd start in looking for some of your own kind. You'd try to find some pigs."

That put a thought into her head. "You want I should call the police?" she said.

"Shoot!" Killie Willie said. "What for?"

"To report a missing pig."

"We don't want no cops nosing around here, Cora New," he said. "They got laws and they find this hog out here, no telling what they might do. Might even put me in jail or worse."

"Well, they might of picked Kermit up."

"If they did, they did. Nothing we can do about it." Killie Willie feared that some such thing could have happened. If the police had Kermit, there was nothing he could do about it. It'd be the same as Kermit getting run over by a transfer truck or being picked up by the pound. Kermit was gone if he ever got taken to the police house.

"Well, I'm gonna fix me some supper," Cora New said. "You coming?"

"Ain't hungry," he said.

"You gotta eat, Killie Willie. No need to starve yourself."

"Be in in a bit. Got to figure out where my pig's gone."

So she left him at the sty alone. He felt the urge to talk to his hog, and every once in a while he did mouth a few words to her, and Perfecta grunted as if she understood. Killie Willie and Perfecta were two of a kind. His palm hurt and so did her rear end. He felt useless, and as far as he knew Perfecta felt that way too. And when he sighed, so did she.

"I reckon Kermit just wasn't meant to be," Killie Willie said after a long, long time. "I reckon just one pig's gonna have to do."

Perfecta didn't seem to mind. She'd never cared for Kermit anyway.

Vaughn Brodie didn't find Fay Leigh. She found him. He wasn't even looking for her. She was simply there.

"Where you been, junkie?" she asked with a smile and a flirt on her face.

He was squatting in his favorite spot at Junkie's Corner. "Right here," he answered. She smelled of honeysuckle in May.

"No, you ain't."

"Well, had to look for my pig, I guess."

"You and your damn pigs. Seems you care more for your damn pigs than you do for me."

He thought about it. Maybe she was right. Maybe he did. But he didn't tell her that.

"Want an hour with me?"

"Want a life with you," he said, looking down at his shoe tops. He hadn't put the words together on purpose. They simply came out.

"What?"

"You heard me."

"You mean, you want to be my pimp?"

"Jesus," he said. "Don't you know—" He could tell that she didn't. "My mama looks after and tends to my papa. What he needs she gives him."

"Shit house," she said with a mean little giggle.

"Perfecta's got my papa. Papa's got my mama. Ollie Gus has them both." He stopped and thought about it for a moment before he said, "Who have I got?"

"I met your papa. He's real cute. But he's got a real straight ass, you know what I mean?"

"Yeah. Wish I was more like him."

"You sort of look like him. I really dig your old man. He's something special."

"You didn't answer me, Fay Leigh. I said I want to spend more than an hour with you—"

"Cost you."

"No. Not that way."

"That's the only way."

He shook his head. His thoughts ran to Wonzetta Poe, to how much she might have grown since he left home, to how much he had admired her from a distance, not having the guts to walk up to her and say hello; he had had too much to lose to do a thing like that, too much at stake. But with Fay Leigh it was all a matter of money and time, two things he knew he didn't have enough of. He looked her in the eyes. They were tired, he could see that, worn by the demands put on her by her pimp, by her way of making ends meet.

"I'm offering you a secure life," he said.

"Since when has a pusher led a secure life?" She stood up. She could tell that things were going nowhere with Vaughn Brodie. Sure, she liked him a lot, he had been nice as a steady, but she could sense that he was growing away from her and there was nothing she could do to stop it. "Gotta go."

"I love you, Fay Leigh," he whispered. The words tried to stick in his throat, but they burst out anyway.

"No, you don't. You lust me. You sex me, cutie pie. But you don't love me. That's a word I don't know. It's a word I won't ever know. Shit. That's the word I know best. I know no such thing as love."

"Fay Leigh!" he called out to her. She was already half a block away. He wanted to draw her back, give her what it was she was missing in life. He said, "I'm going home to Frog Level, Fay Leigh. Come with me."

"Shit," she said. And she was gone.

He felt so empty then. Like something very dear to him had been cut away. He felt so lonesome. And lonely. And alone. More than he had ever felt in his life.

He sold his best stuff that afternoon for half the price it was worth. There were other things he wanted to do with his life.

"Mama?" Vaughn Brodie leaned against the sink in the kitchen, looking through the window out back.

"What?" She was busy with the washing, trying to get Killie Willie something decent to wear to work the next morning.

"Do you remember a girl back home name of Wonzetta Poe?" he asked.

"Who?"

"Nothing," he said and wandered to his cot and stretched out. But he didn't sleep. He tried to remember instead.

Nate the Wino woke the Matt clan the next morning by tapping on the fire escape window. He wanted in. At first Cora New didn't know who he was. She had never seen Nate in his best sports shirt before—it was something he had picked up from a garbage can once and washed until it was actually clean. But more than that, his hair was combed back and his beard had been shaved at. And he had actually made an effort to clean his skin. The cleaning was a result of the first bath he had had in over six months. And still more than that, he was cold sober. But the thing that Cora New noted most about Nate was the blue bruise under his left eye. Killie Willie hadn't been out of her sight so she knew the bruise couldn't have been his doing. She didn't want to let Nate into her place again. Clean or not, combed and shaven notwithstanding, Nate was a difficult body to deal with. The night before it had taken five times' shaking to get him out of Ollie Gus' cot and out of her place. So Cora New was hesitant to let the wino back in.

He had a begging look in his eyes. He had a longing look on his lips. He had a sorrowfulness about him that Cora New couldn't resist. He was like a wounded animal. And Cora New wasn't one who could turn her back on somebody or something who needed her tender and loving care.

So she opened her window to him. She thought she

might have caught the glimpse of a tear in his eye. She smiled at him in spite of herself.

"Any word?" Nate asked. He was shaky, Cora New could tell. He'd been sober a couple of hours, it looked like, and his hands were already showing the signs.

"None," she said.

"I meant about your pig."

"That's what I'm talking about."

"I was hoping there was," Nate said. There was a bulge under his shirt that kept slipping this way and that, and he was having some trouble keeping whatever it was out of sight.

"Ain't none," Cora New said. She wanted him to be on his way, but it just wasn't in her rearing to be rude to a body no matter what he might have done.

"Well," Nate said, "here." And he took a slightly cracked, slightly faded, old-fashioned piggy bank from underneath his shirt and handed it to Cora New. "Got something in it," he said. He rattled it. Must have had a couple of pennies or maybe some broken glass inside.

"What's that for?" Cora New said, not taking the bank.

"For you. For Killie Willie," Nate said. "Couldn't find him a real pig, so here."

Cora New took the piggy bank. She was touched. She wanted to reach through her window and give old Nate a hug, but she restrained herself. Instead she offered him her hand. "Thank you, Nathaniel."

He backed off from that hand reaching out toward him. He wiped his hand firmly on his shirt front before he took Cora New's offer. When he did take it, he shook too hard and too long. He couldn't keep his hand still. He worked at it, but the longer he held Cora New's hand, the harder he wanted to cling to it, to make the gesture that Cora New had given him last a whole lifetime.

And a tear came out of Nate's eye. He swiped at it with

the cuff of his shirt. But he missed and the tear rolled down his cheek toward his mouth.

"Why, what's the matter with you?" Cora New said.

He wanted to say that nobody but his mama had ever called him anything but Nate, that the name Nathaniel was the most beautiful name in all the world, that Cora New was so much like his mama he couldn't stand it, that everything, his life, his meaning, everything was coming down on him like a load of lead. He wanted to let her go, to burst wide open, to let this lovely lady who had called him Nathaniel know that deep inside him there really was good, that he could be worth something, that if he tried . . .

But instead of any of that, he said, "Just wanted . . . just wanted to say . . ." If he said more, every tear in his head would leak out. He knew that. And he had to block them with everything he had. "Just wanted to." And he let her overshook hand drop.

"Thank you, Nathaniel," Cora New said a second time. She turned from him. She couldn't stand to see a grown man like Nate the Wino weep like a little child. Anyway, she figured he'd be all right. Everything always had a way of turning out all right in the end. Sure, Nathaniel would be just fine.

It struck Cora New that maybe, regardless of how wretched a body might seem, maybe there was something good inside him. She contemplated the goodness in Nate the Wino as she crossed the kitchen. Somebody else was wanting her attention. Someone was banging away at the hall door.

She opened the door, piggy bank in her hand. She almost dropped it. Standing in the hall, looking past her into her place, were Bobby and Cowboy.

"Your name Mrs. Matt?" Bobby asked.

Cora New couldn't get any words to come out of her mouth. A multitude of thoughts raced through her head. Vaughn Brodie: he had finally killed somebody! And the neighbors: what would they think, seeing the cops paying a visit to the Matt place so early in the morning? And herself: what could the police want with her, she hadn't done anything, nothing she was aware of. She was filled with disbelief as well: how could the law even know that the Matt family lived in that section of the Bottoms anyway? So she didn't say a word, just stood there.

"That's her," Billo said. He was behind the police, pointing. She cut her eyes toward him in a hard, effective way. He scooted down the hall and hid behind the stair railing, hoping that she hadn't seen him at all.

"Mrs. Matt," Bobby said. He was too tall. His uniform was too spotless, too well ironed for her hallway. She nodded. "Your husband, Killie Willie, is he in?"

At first Cora New wanted to answer with an outright lie. Instead she chose a small lie. "I don't know," she said.

"They found your pig, Miz Matt!" Billo shouted, so proud of himself for having found Kermit for her and Killie Willie and Ollie Gus.

"Get lost, Scooter," Cowboy said. "Nobody pushed your button."

"Mind if we come in?" Bobby asked.

"Well—" But they pushed past her into the heart of what Cora New held sacred: her home.

Ollie Gus came from her room wearing only her underpants and carrying her shoes. She didn't see the cops, not at first. "Mama, you seen my——" Her voice froze in her throat. "Oh, Jesus Christ!" she screamed. "It's Vaughn Brodie! They done got him!!"

"Shhhhh," Cora New hissed as she tried pushing her daughter back into her room. It was like moving a boulder. "Get you some clothes on, girl." She finally shut the bedroom door with Ollie Gus on the other side of it, screaming about Vaughn Brodie being taken away and never seeing him again and on and on. Cora New returned to the policemen and smiled. "Now, then."

"Good-looking little lady, huh, Bobby?" Cowboy said with a sneer.

"State your business and get out," said Cora New.

"We were wondering, ma'am," Bobby said, taking a snapshot from inside his uniform shirt, "if you recognize this particular animal."

Cora New took the Polaroid. She expected to see Kermit's body smeared all over the pavement of some back street. Instead there he was, just as proud as a bowling trophy, sitting on a desk. If a pig could smile, Kermit was beaming. He had found himself a new home.

She was just on the edge of identifying the pig when Nate the Wino came in through the window, tears still running down his face. "You're a good woman, Corie New," he said. "And I just wanted—" He stopped. There were cops all over the place. Big, mean-looking cops. "Just wanted to say," Nate uttered, "I'll see you in a week or two. Bye, ma'am."

And Nate was gone. He had never gone down a fire escape so fast in all his life.

Cora New heard something glass break in Ollie Gus' room. "Scuse me a minute, please." And she went into the bedroom, gently closing the door behind her. "What's wrong with you, girl?!" she whisper-screamed.

"What's them pigs doing here, Mama?" Ollie Gus was primed to smash another porcelain knickknack against the wall of her room.

"Gimme that," Cora New said, taking the porcelain piece out of her hand. "I think they've come to talk to your papa is all."

"Ain't Vaughn Brodie?"

"No, it ain't."

"Then they gonna lock up my papa instead?"

"No, honey, they ain't locking nobody up."

"For life?" Ollie Gus was working herself into a tizzy. "They gonna lock me up too, Mama?" She ran into the closet and slammed the door, locking it from the inside. "Don't let em take me, Mama, please!"

Cora New was constantly amazed at how her little girl's head worked. But now wasn't the time to try to straighten her out. So she returned to the policemen, who were wandering about the room fingering things, making pests of themselves.

She handed the Polaroid back to the officer. She smiled as best she could when she said, "Guess I do recognize him, sir."

"Is he yours?" Bobby said.

"Any reason why I should say he is?" she asked.

"We're just looking for verification, ma'am."

"Scuse me again." She went into the bedroom where Killie Willie was supposed to be asleep. Instead he was hiding behind the chest of drawers.

"What you doing, Killie Willie?" Cora New said.

"They gone?"

"No, course not. They want to talk to you."

"Ain't coming out," he said. And he clung to the back of the chest of drawers like it was the only friend he had left in all the world.

"I've never seen you like this before, Killie Willie," she said. "What's the matter with you?" And she tugged at his arm.

"Ain't," he said.

"They gonna come in here if you don't," she said. "They got a picture of Kermit, and it looks to me like he's just fine."

"They ain't gonna lock me up?"

"How should I know that?" She pulled him free of the chest. "Now, come on."

Cora New led the way.

Killie Willie stopped when he saw the uniforms and the pistols and the billy sticks.

"You Killie Willie Matt?"

Killie Willie pushed by them into the kitchen, where he stuck his head under the faucet. "Been sleeping," he said.

"Sorry to bother you so early, but we want to talk to you," Bobby said. "You remember us, don't you, Killie Willie?"

Killie Willie nodded. "I ain't done nothing."

"We just wanted to know if you were missing a pig, Mr. Matt," Bobby said. And he handed Killie Willie the photograph.

He took it. And he found himself staring at Kermit, the happiest-looking little boar pig he'd ever seen in his life. It felt good seeing his pig safe.

"Where you got him?" Killie Willie said.

"You recognize that animal then?" Cowboy said, sort of pushy.

"That's Kermit. He's been lost for—" But he stopped himself. He didn't know if it was too late or not. "I mean, it might be my pig, that is, if I had a pig, which I don't, do I, Cora New?"

She didn't say a word. It was a mortal sin to lie, and Killie Willie had just put his soul in jeopardy. She wasn't having a thing to do with suchlike.

"Now, come on, Killie Willie," Bobby said. "Don't hassle us. We know that's your shoat."

"Boar pig," Killie Willie said. "Male pig's called a boar pig, till he grows some."

"And you got yourself a nearly grown sow out back, right?"

"Well . . ."

"Is that right, Mr. Matt?"

"They got a law against having pets?" said Killie Willie.

"You want to show us this other pig of yours?" Bobby was being as nice as he could. He saw that Killie Willie and Cora New were frightened, and he was decent enough not to push them. But Cowboy was another matter.

"We ain't letting you pull nothing over on us again, man. You and your damn kangaroo rats. Ain't no such thing in the Bottoms as a kangaroo rat. We know all about you and your damn pig farm and how you think you can shit all over the city and get away with it—"

"Slow it down, Cowboy," Bobby said.

"Well," Killie Willie glanced at Cora New. She was sitting with her hands folded in her lap. Beside her on the kitchen table was the ceramic piggy bank. She gave him no support. It was done with, and she knew it. Her advice to him if he had asked for it would have been own up to it and get it over with as soon as possible.

Killie Willie would have given a million dollars to be home in Frog Level right then, but he didn't have a million dollars. All he had was the truth. So he said, "Come on, I'll show you."

And he led the two policemen down the fire escape and across the rubble pile to Perfecta and her sty.

"I'll be damned," Bobby said when he caught sight of Perfecta. "Looks to me like that pig's been run over by a Mack truck." And he chuckled under his breath. Cowboy laughed right out loud.

Perfecta seemed pleased to have company. She grunted and wheezed in her special way, hoping that somebody had brought her a bucket of slop or at least a basket of vegetables. Cowboy laughed even harder when Killie Willie spoke to her in tones that were usually reserved for human beings. He laughed so hard that tears came to his eyes and he had to move away from the sty to regain his composure.

"What's so all-fired funny?" Killie Willie wanted to know.

Cowboy couldn't answer. It made him laugh even harder.

Perfecta, Killie Willie admitted, was a strange-looking sight. She hadn't been brushed in two days and mud was caked all the way up to her ears. Her one good eye was like a black jewel in her head. And the stitches Vaughn Brodie had put in her rear end were falling out, hanging like broken sinews out of her hide. She looked like a rag doll, coming apart at the seams.

"How long has this hog been here like this?" Bobby asked.

Killie Willie couldn't recall. It seemed to him that Perfecta had been part of his life forever. In fact, he couldn't imagine his life without her being part of it.

"Why?" was Bobby's next question. "I mean, who would want to keep a pig in the middle of a godforsaken place like this? Jesus, it's inhumane."

Vaughn Brodie appeared on the fire escape landing. He heard Bobby's question and considered it a good one. He wondered about the answer himself. But Killie Willie offered none. He honestly didn't know.

"Didn't you know there are laws?" Cowboy said.

"What law's that?"

"Well, the law against cruelty to animals for one."

"I ain't been cruel to Perfecta."

"Perfecta!!" Cowboy yelled. "I can't stand it!" And he laughed and laughed. Vaughn Brodie felt like crawling in a hole and pulling the earth in on top of him. But what else could Killie Willie do? He really hadn't been cruel to Perfecta. He would never be cruel to an animal, especially to a pig.

"Never been cruel, huh?" Bobby said. "Look at that poor thing. Got but one good eye. And look at that mess of a rear end. Listen, man, if that ain't a cruel way to treat a pig—"

"She's doing just fine—"

"What the hell you want a pig for anyway?" Cowboy exclaimed. "You gonna butcher her?"

Killie Willie wished these folks would leave him alone. He had had enough of their taunting. He didn't want to have anything to do with any of them anymore. Just leave him be! He wasn't a fool, even though these fellows were trying to make him out one. Butcher Perfecta. Nobody in his right mind would ever consider such a thing as that. So that was what he said. "She ain't that kind of pig."

"That so? What kind of pig is she?"

Killie Willie started to lie. But he stopped. "She's my friend," he said.

"Oh, Christ!" Cowboy hooted, grabbing his side he laughed so hard. Even Bobby had to laugh at that. Vaughn Brodie felt like heaving a brick at Cowboy's head for the way he was treating his old man, and he probably would have if Cora New hadn't put a calming hand on his shoulder. So instead he called out at the top of his power from his spot on the fire escape: "Who says it's against the law to have a friend, goddamn it?!"

Cowboy went for his gun. He wasn't used to having folks yell at him when he was in the middle of a vacant lot in the Bottoms. It spooked him.

"We got laws against trespassing!" Bobby called out. "That pig's living on city property, and there are laws against vagrancy. And you folks are vagrant having anything to do with this back lot! You get my meaning? We ought to run the whole lot of you in. That what you want?"

"Ain't said a thing, man!" Vaughn Brodie called. "It's bad, man, real bad." And he disappeared into the tenement. He had had enough of his papa's pigs. He had had enough of his papa being the laughingstock of the whole neighborhood.

"Let's call it in, Cowboy," said Bobby.

Killie Willie took exception to that. "Call what in?"

"This hog. You can't expect us to leave her out here, can you? We'll have her out of here in no time."

"You ain't taking Perfecta," Killie Willie said, barely above a whisper.

"Oh, yeah? Well, just watch us," Cowboy said, and he sat on the edge of the sty, picking his teeth, while Bobby crossed the rubble pile to call in his report.

Killie Willie tried to ignore the hurt that was growing inside him. He did it by chatting. He asked Cowboy where he was from, about his family, about his work as a cop, about his pets. Finally he came back to the thing that was turning him inside out. "You can't take my pig," he said.

"Why not?"

"Cause that pig . . ." Killie Willie stopped as he looked into Perfecta's one good eye. "Cause Perfecta's the only thing that means anything. She's the only worthwhile thing there is in my life."

Cowboy felt a sense of pity for the fellow. It was a genuine feeling. And he wanted to say something that would have meaning. All he could think of was "Sorry, old man. But the law's the law."

Killie Willie nodded. What else could he do?

Billo was beside himself with excitement when the city truck drove into the vacant lot that afternoon. They were bringing Kermit back home, he thought, and everything was going to be fabulous once again.

All that day he had hung around the sty, sitting with Killie Willie long after the police had gone. But Killie Willie wouldn't talk to him. Wouldn't even nod or shake his head at any of Billo's questions. Billo felt lousy. Things were not the way he thought they should have been. Even the truck as it backed its way to the edge of the rubble pile brought no joy. Didn't Killie Willie and everybody else know that they were bringing Kermit home? Why was he the only one excited? And he asked the question aloud.

Then Billo noticed that the truck was empty except for a large wire cage and five city workers. Could he be wrong? Could they be planning on keeping Kermit down at the station house? They didn't have a sty down there, did they? Lord knows, he considered, sometimes it seemed like one. What were they doing with an empty cage he wanted to know. So he asked his friend.

"They've come for her," Killie Willie said.

Billo felt sick inside. Couldn't be true, he said. They just forgot Kermit, he said. They'll go back for him, no doubt about it, he said. But they didn't do any of it.

The five city workers lowered the cage off the truck and lugged it across the rubble pile to the sty. They lowered it into the sty and tried to coax Perfecta into it. Billo felt cheated. He had led the police to Killie Willie because he had felt sure they would bring Kermit home again and everything would be the same as before. Killie Willie sat like stone. He didn't seem to feel a thing.

At first Perfecta had no problems with the men and their cage. But when they started poking her and tugging at her ears, she got her back up. The men were in a hurry. The mud was too messy for them. As they made Perfecta ornery, they became more ornery themselves.

It became clear: Perfecta was not going into the cage. There was nothing the men could do to convince her otherwise. Perfecta had been raised with a will of her own, and no amount of tugging, baiting, and dragging could get her near the cage.

It took only a few minutes of her negative view of the cage to frustrate the five city workers. Billo watched. Killie Willie didn't. He knew before they started that they would have to do what they did. He turned his back and would have left the sty if he didn't feel that his pig needed him there, needed somebody around who held something for her besides distaste.

One of the men tried to corner her. But she raced between his legs, sending him sprawling in the mud amid curses and slanders against Killie Willie's parentage. A couple of the guys grabbed an ear each and a third took her tail and twisted it as tightly as he could. Her screams sent shivers through Killie Willie. But still he could not watch.

Up on the fire escape, Ollie Gus began singing her song of the Gullah so she would not have to hear the screams of her pet. She drew picture after picture of Perfecta eating. Those had been the happy times for her.

Another of the city workers approached Perfecta with a four-foot-long two-by-four. "No need for that," Billo said.

That was when Perfecta ripped free of her captors and scampered into her lean-to. But the frail construction was no match for the city workers. The lean-to came apart without any trouble at all. And the men threw the bits in every direction.

Perfecta bellowed. It was as if she was crying for help. But no help came. She was being violated, and she didn't understand. She bared her teeth and snarled, the bristles on her back standing on end as the men closed around her. The man with the two-by-four swung at her as hard as he could and caught her a glancing blow across her lower back. The blow bounced off as she ran. Only there was no place for her to run to.

"Help me!" Billo yelled to Killie Willie. He was struggling with the concrete fencing, hoping to pull it aside and give Perfecta more room to run. But it was too heavy for him. "Help me, man!" But Killie Willie stood with his back to what was going on.

"I got something that'll do her," one of the men said. He crossed to the truck and returned with a crowbar and a jack handle. He kept the crowbar and gave the jack handle to another. Perfecta was cowering in her corner, trying to keep her one good eye on her attackers. Then the men, armed with metal and wood, came on her.

"Ain't no need——" Billo yelled out. What he saw was the maddest thing that ever took place in the Bottoms. Even madder than the time he and the other kids had caught a live rat and—

On the one hand there were five grown men determined to get a half-grown hog into a wire cage before the sun went down. They had homes and wives and families they didn't want to keep waiting. On the other there was

Perfecta, equally determined not to do the thing they wanted. It was as if she understood that to enter the cage would be the end for her. The back lot was filled with shouts and curses and the sounds of well-placed and mean blows. The back lot was filled with bellows of rage and pain. It all mixed together like in a blender so that nothing sounded quite right. It sounded like a movie with the sound out of sync with the movement of people's mouths. It sounded like hell itself. It had to sound, because nobody watched. There were people in the surrounding windows, but nobody watched. Even Billo, when he saw what was happening, turned his back. He grabbed Killie Willie's hand and clung to it as tightly as he could.

The sounds that Killie Willie heard echoed through him like so many metal balls in an oil drum. If only they would shoot the damn pig! He'd pay for the shell. Just put the rifle up close to her head and pull the trigger. Put an end to the sounds, to the screams, to the metal on flesh, to the crushing of bone under too much swing. Just STOP IT!

Then it was over. A cheer went up as the door to the wire cage clapped shut. And he heard the sobs of Billo, standing by his side. He didn't want to look. He didn't have to. He knew the sight. He had seen it before back home in Frog Level. He didn't need to see his pig again.

But he couldn't help himself. He heard her wheeze slightly, as if she was trying to bid him good-bye. He saw her. She was caked with mud, every inch of her was coated, even her head. And from beneath the mud seeped the blood and ooze of his hog's vital fluids. She moved only slightly. Her remaining eye was no longer there, so she couldn't find Killie Willie. And there was nothing he could do. Something inside him sealed off. He could not think. He could not talk. He could not do anything but watch as the men dumped the cage into the back of the truck and slammed home the rear door. What he could do was release Billo's hand.

"Jesus Christ," Billo whispered through his tears. "Oh, Jesus Christ, Jesus Christ, Jesus Christ."

One of the men, the one who had managed the crowbar, handed Killie Willie a clipboard and pen. "Sign," he said, tapping the bottom of the board.

"Huh?"

"You got to give us clearance to do what we just did," the man said. "So sign."

Killie Willie dropped the board, turned, and moved to the wall, where he stood among the garbage cans like so much trash.

"Gimme it," one of the other men said. "I'll sign the damn thing." And he did.

The men loaded into the truck. The gears ground into place. And off they went down the street.

From nowhere came Ollie Gus. She had a brick in her hand. She heaved it after the truck and screamed, "You damn pigs!!! Hate you all, you damn pigs!!!"

Her brick missed its mark and shattered into a hundred pieces in the middle of the street.

Vaughn Brodie came from the tenement and stood by her side. She was sobbing, and her sobs shook her body from deep inside. After a moment, he slipped his hand into hers and the two of them eased down the street, trying to find comfort somewhere, probably in just being there together.

Killie Willie went to work the next morning just like always. So did Cora New.

Midmorning, Billo, Gregalee, and some of the others went out back and tore the pigsties apart. They worked hard and long. And when they were finished, there was no way that anybody could tell that there had ever been anything there except what they could see: a rubble pile, just like the hundred or so other rubble piles that populated Buttermilk Bottoms.

It was said all over the Bottoms that three days after Perfecta was trucked off by the city workers, the police of the local precinct had the best late summer barbecue they had ever had.

PART THREE

Montgomery Matt and his whole crew turned out at Buddy's late that afternoon to meet the bus. It was a happy day. Some of his kinfolks were finally coming back home to Frog Level.

The bus was late, so Montgomery treated the little ones to icicles from the vast array of goodies in Buddy's One Stop. All the kids had red lips and tongues when the bus pulled to a halt near the gas pumps.

Montgomery had no idea who was on the bus. The wire had said for him to meet the so-and-so bus this afternoon, that there would be somebody on it coming home from Buttermilk Bottoms.

The bus door swung open. Several people debused. And then there was Vaughn Brodie Matt, stepping lightly to the ground. The kids rushed to him, each trying to grab hold of something about Vaughn Brodie to hug. Montgomery met the man with a firm handshake and a pat on the back.

"Welcome home, Bubba," Montgomery said, all smiles. "God, you've grown."

"Some, I guess," said Vaughn Brodie.

"So where's that ornery brother of mine and Cora New?"

"They gonna tough it out a little longer, I guess."

Vaughn Brodie felt so at home he wanted to dance. He wouldn't admit to anything, but he was tickled pink to be home. He even gave in to the impulse to hug his uncle's neck. Montgomery blustered at the expression from Vaughn Brodie, but he didn't fight it off. Instead he patted Vaughn Brodie soundly on the back.

"So tell me," Montgomery said as Vaughn Brodie's luggage was dumped in the back of the pickup truck. "How's your papa's pig farm coming these days?"

Vaughn Brodie pulled an envelope from his hip pocket and dropped it in Montgomery's hand.

"What's this?"

"Down payment," Vaughn Brodie said. "Papa said to

tell you he wants the pick of your next litter. Just let him know when he can pick it up at the station."

"Well, I'll be hog-tied!!" And Montgomery slapped Vaughn Brodie soundly on the back one more time. "Killie Willie must really love his pigs," he said with a laugh, "must really and truly love his pigs."

"Guess so," Vaughn Brodie said, as he wondered how he was going to go about finding the girl he barely remembered. Her name was Wonzetta Poe.